In the Midnight Hour

Brenda Adcock

Yellow Rose Books
by Regal Crest

Texas

ISBN 978-1-61929-188-1

First Printing 2015

9 8 7 6 5 4 3 2 1

Cover design by AcornGraphics

Published by:

Regal Crest Enterprises, LLC
229 Sheridan Loop
Belton, Texas 76513

Find us on the World Wide Web at
http://www.regalcrest.biz

Published in the United States of America

Acknowledgments

To me this is the most difficult portion of any book. No matter how much I try, I almost always forget to mention someone who should be thanked for their role in making each work a reality. This particular story was very nearly never completed due to an unforeseen medical issue on my part. The first draft was completed the night before I was taken to the hospital. Although my future was somewhat uncertain, I must thank my partner and best friend, Cheryl, and our daughter, Amy Knodel, for finding what I needed and getting my manuscript to my beta readers as quickly as possible. I also have to thank Amy for remaining calm during the entire trying situation until my partner returned from out of state.

I owe my deepest gratitude to my beta readers, Anita G. and Devi P. Both were new beta readers, but provided useful and thought-provoking comments. I can't thank them enough for their patience until I was able to contact them personally again. Since then, they have continued to lift my spirits with their emails and have become truly good friends.

My thanks to my friend and editor, Patty Schramm. She has called from the Netherlands and, as always, sent comments regarding the manuscript, forcing me to think more deeply than I may have intended, but appreciated nonetheless. She and the other editors do anything they can to make every story the best it can be.

I've said it many times before, but I must recognize my publisher, Cathy Bryerose, for her unfailing support. I can only wish to be as good a friend as she has been. She was able to re-arrange her publishing schedule to allow this story to be released at a later date to accommodate my somewhat lengthy recovery while dealing with family emergencies of her own. There is nothing I can say to let her know how grateful I am.

Lastly, I want to thank my readers. I have heard from several over the last few months and appreciate their concern and good wishes. They make my efforts worthwhile and their friendship is indeed priceless. I plan to continue writing, although perhaps not as quickly as I have in the past. Typing with one finger on one hand is challenging, but possible. I owe that effort to those who believe in me and my ability to continue the writing I love so much. You keep reading and I'll keep writing!

Dedication

For Cheryl, who forgives me when I'm a total ass.
I have loved you, baby, with mind and body and always will.
You make me wish I were stronger for you.

Chapter One

MARSHA BARRETT GLANCED at the large clock hanging over the door of Studio One at KLEW-FM and exhaled a long, cleansing sigh. Another night in downtown Omaha had passed relatively quickly. Back to reality in another thirty minutes. The building was already beginning to fill with those who worked throughout the day. Her job was to keep the night owls, insomniacs, and all night studiers or lovers entertained. Calls had come in at a steady pace through the night, requesting a song for themselves or a loved one.

"Hey, babe," her soundman, Boomer Pomerantz, said over her headphones. "Almost time for your wind up."

She smiled through the large glass window into the sound booth. "Got a request?" she asked.

"Like my old lady is conscious at six in the morning," Boomer said with a laugh.

"I feel a little peppy this morning," Marsha mused. "Feel like a little air drummin'. You up for your world famous air guitar?"

"It's radio, babe."

"Yeah, but we've got a live audience," she replied when she saw the morning newscasters leaning against the wall of the corridor. "Crank up the volume into the station after I finish the intro."

"I need this job, Marsh."

"You'll just be following orders, like Adolf's boys," she said with a laugh.

"Going live mic in three...two...live," Boomer said.

Marsha brought her mouth closer to the microphone on her console and punched in a song number. "Another sultry, seductive night has flown by too quickly, Omaha. I would like to make a personal request. Maybe the final song will remain stuck in your head all day. If it does, you have Desdemona, the Queen of the Midnight Hour to thank. Yeow!" Lowering her voice to a sensuous level, she added, "Coming home to you soon, baby, eager to feel your arms around me for a little morning delight." She groaned as she punched a button on her console and pulled a pair of drumsticks from her backpack. She began drumming the beats of "Call Me" by Blondie. Music filled the corridors of KLEW as Marsha and Boomer performed their impromptu concert.

As the song neared its end, Marsha stood and closed her eyes while she drummed on the console, visualizing Blondie stretched out beneath the bed covers, waiting to greet her when she arrived home. She couldn't stop the smile that spread across her face. With one final flourish, Marsha dropped into her chair, threw her head back, and opened her eyes.

Her smile melted away when she lowered her head and saw Blondie observing her through the studio glass. She blinked hard. Now her imagination had gone way, way too far. Blondie leaned slightly to her right and spoke to Ken Dickinson, the station manager. He smiled and nodded at whatever Blondie said to him. Marsha went through the public service announcements and punched up the music that led into the next segment of morning programming. Then she unlocked the studio door to allow the entrance of Omaha's dynamic duo, Alicia Terry and Geoff "Dull as Dirt" Kendahl. While Marsha filled her backpack with miscellaneous junk she had used during the night, Alicia leaned in front of her and set a large Styrofoam cup on the console.

"Don't burn that talented tongue, baby cakes," Alicia breathed into Marsha's ear before planting a sloppy kiss on her cheek.

"Is that what I hope it is?" Marsha rubbed her ear where Alicia's breath had caused it to tickle and wiped her head on her shoulder to remove Alicia's saliva.

"Star Mart's finest for KLEW's finest," Alicia chuckled.

Marsha carefully pushed in the spout of the cup's lid and allowed the scent of French Vanilla cappuccino to fill her nostrils. She brought the cup to her mouth and felt the hot drink flow over her taste buds as she took her first sip.

"It's entirely possible that I might be willing to carry your baby." Marsha sighed in contentment.

"Give me a fucking break," Geoff mumbled.

"I heard that, Goffrey," Marsha said.

"It's Geoffrey, you idiot," he shot back.

"Then it should start with a fuckin' J. Did your mama read it in a book and think it was neato keen or something?"

"No, she thought Americans were better educated, I suppose."

"Knock it off," Alicia said. "You two sound like damn kindergartners, which by the way is a German word." She winked at Marsha and set an armload of newspapers from various Midwestern cities to the side of her console before settling in her chair and adjusting her headphones. She was impeccably dressed in an expensive, tailored business suit, as usual. Why a radio personality needed or even wanted to dress up that much was beyond Marsha's comprehension. Who the hell was going to see how well she was dressed?

The minute she walked out of the studio, Marsha felt the effects of another night without sleep attack her body. She'd read reports that people who worked nights lived, on an average, ten years less than day workers. It was depressing, but she didn't intend to spend the rest of her life working nights. She walked down the fluorescent-lit hallway, a woman on a mission to get her usual daily order of two warm cheese Danish from the corner store. Raising her cup, followed by a bow, to acknowledge the waves of the day crew, she could almost hear her bed calling to her and smiled as she mentally visualized Blondie beckoning to her from beneath the covers. She pulled her jacket on and made a half-hearted attempt to get her curly, unruly hair under control, knowing it was a losing battle. She was certain her headphones had left their usual trench across her skull. She stepped into the lobby of the station, prepared to make a hasty retreat into the bright sunshine outside. She really needed something to settle her nerves. Shaking a cigarette from the pack in her pocket, she shoved it between her lips. Boomer paused and flicked his Bic for her. She inhaled deeply, appreciating the jolt of the nicotine as it spread through her system. Blinking hard to adjust her sunlight-deprived eyes to the assault she dug her clip-on sunglasses out of her jacket pocket.

"Marsha! Boomer!" a loud voice called out from behind her. Cringing she turned to see Ken Dickinson standing at the door leading into the station's administrative offices. Escape was a mere ten feet away.

"Morning, Ken," she said with a sigh, her freshly lit cigarette protruding from the corner of her mouth.

"Glad I caught you both. Come to my office for a moment. I know you're ready to head off for some well-deserved sleep, but I want you to meet our new account executive. She's got great plans for expanding your show into some new market areas and wants to discuss them with you."

"Can't it wait until we're at least semi-conscious?" Marsha asked. "It can't be that urgent."

"No time like the present," Ken beamed. "Then you can sleep on it. Literally."

Marsha looked at the receptionist and gave her a weak smile before joining Ken, who obviously wasn't going to take no for an answer. The receptionist pulled an ashtray from beneath her desk and set it on the counter.

"You're not supposed to smoke in here, Marsha," the receptionist admonished.

"I'm not supposed to be so fuckin' adorable either." Marsha exhaled smoke and crushed out her cigarette.

"Need a breath mint?"

Marsha shook her head. "Hopefully this won't take long."

She followed Boomer unwillingly down the hall. Ken opened the door to his office and waited for Marsha to enter, her eyes glued to the floor, her usual body position when forced to meet new people. A tall, attractive, leggy blonde dressed in a tailored suit that gently caressed her body in all the right places, stood and smiled. What the hell was Blondie doing here? Why wasn't she waiting in bed for Marsha as usual? They would definitely have to discuss this later. Without missing a beat, the woman crossed the room and extended her hand. Marsha was sure her mouth was open and her jaw was lying somewhere near her feet as she gazed into eyes the color of a robin's egg. Without realizing her arm had moved, Marsha took the woman's hand and felt a soothing warmth flow through her body. She was certain she would faint. The blonde goddess placed her other hand lightly on Marsha's shoulder and leaned down. Marsha saw the concern in her eyes.

"Are you all right?" Blondie asked softly.

"I'm sure she's just tired," Ken answered. "It's been a long week. Marsha, this is Colleen Walters. Colleen," he said, gesturing toward Marsha, "This is Desdemona, Queen of the Night, hostess of *In the Midnight Hour,* and her soundman Boomer Pomerantz."

Marsha's shoulder and hand went cold as the woman released her hand to shake Boomer's. Colleen smiled at her, but Marsha was certain she was staring at the thin white scar that neatly bisected her upper lip. She ran her fingertips over her lip self-consciously, wishing she could rub it away.

"Have a seat you two before you keel over," Ken said as he plopped into the cracked, green leather chair behind his desk. Marsha dropped her beat-up backpack next to a chair and stared at the gorgeous apparition seated across from her.

"I listened to your show last night and know it has a large following, many of whom call in each night with a request or simply to talk in order to hear your voice," Colleen said as she leaned slightly forward in her chair. "It's quite...seductive."

"There are a lot of lonely people out there looking for someone to connect with," Marsha said quietly, watching the mesmerizing rise and fall of Colleen's tempting deep cleavage.

"They identify with you," Colleen agreed.

"Good thing it's radio, huh?" Marsha said in a self-deprecating tone. "It's an illusion without much substance. I'm only a figment of their imaginations. Hence the lack of publicity shots. I wouldn't want to shatter their illusions."

"Marsha refuses to schedule a photo shoot for advertising purposes. Nor does she make personal appearances, preferring to remain...a woman of mystery," Ken explained in a creepy-sounding voice. "Hence the lobby photo."

Colleen cleared her throat, the hint of a smile tracing across her lips. "Yes. Very attractive," Colleen said, referring to the large picture of a panting Bulldog with a serious overbite that hung above her name in the main lobby.

Marsha had found Ken's attitude toward her condescending since the day he was hired to manage KLEW-FM. Now even her visual fascination with Colleen Walters couldn't keep the edge out of her voice. "It's my favorite breed," she spit out, before smiling innocently and reverting smoothly to her on-air persona. "My voice is my trademark. Not my face." She glanced at Colleen. "I don't want to spoil the fantasy by having my face plastered on the sides of buses belching carbon dioxide. My listeners can visualize me any way they want. I'm sure you can understand why." She tapped her lip and mustered a lop-sided grin. "And I can remain environmentally sound and dishwasher safe."

"From the data I've compiled, a significant number of your audience seems to be homosexual," Colleen said. She looked into Marsha's eyes and added, "Does that concern you?"

"Why should it?" Marsha shrugged at the unexpected question. She'd had this conversation in the past and now she would have to step around the fact that the woman of her dreams was sitting less than three feet from her. She closed her eyes to concentrate before turning her attention to Colleen Walters again. "I don't make a point of advertising my sexual preference on the air. Nor do I divulge that I'm a rabid liberal and a loyal Democrat in a highly Republican state. It's simply no one's business. Boomer and I screen every call before we allow it on the air. We only deal with friendlies." She leaned back in her chair and rubbed her eyes. "I don't care if my listeners are fucking Tibetan monkeys as long as they're listening to me while they do it."

"Are you afraid you'd lose a fairly large segment of your audience if they knew who you really were?" Colleen asked.

"Who do *you* think I am? Would you really care if you just needed someone, anyone, even a total stranger, to listen to your problem or share your joy at finding that special someone, at least for one night?" Marsha asked, pushing her curly hair off her forehead with a sweep of her hand, "I'm not prepared to become a fucking martyr for any cause. What I do in my personal life is no one's damn business, including yours. I don't choose my audience. They choose me." Marsha closed her eyes and concentrated on recapturing her Desdemona mind-set. When she opened her eyes, she stared pointedly at Colleen's perfect face, letting her eyes caress the soft, feminine features and flashed a lop-sided grin. "Unless, of course, I could convince you to share an evening to remember with me."

Colleen smiled, but didn't look surprised or offended by Marsha's remark.

Boomer slapped his knee as he laughed to bring the obvious tension between Marsha and Colleen to an end. Ken leaned back in his chair and blew out a breath. "Meeeow. This is your mission, Agent Walters. Should you accept it and fail, this station will disavow any knowledge of your existence. This meeting will self-destruct in thirty seconds. Good luck," he said in his best *Mission: Impossible* voice. He turned his attention back to Marsha. "You off tonight, Dez?"

"Yeah. I've done seven straight." She glanced at Colleen. "No pun intended, Ms. Walters. Minuteman is back from vacation. Can I go home now?" Marsha stood and turned to leave. "It was pretty close to a pleasure to meet you. Welcome to scenic Omaha. Gateway to Council Bluffs." She slung her backpack onto her shoulder and escaped the room as quickly as she could, Boomer close behind.

"I knew we'd never get a photo of Marsha for advertising," Ken said as soon as the door to his office closed. "Can't really say I blame her or that it would help to sell the program in other markets."

"Why is that, Mr. Dickinson?" Colleen asked.

Ken's eyes widened slightly. "I don't mean to seem insensitive, Ms. Walters, but Marsha's not exactly billboard material."

"You mean, she's not...beautiful?"

"She's not even kinda sorta cute," Ken sighed. "But she's got a voice that can make men cream in their pants. The only thing that might work is to use someone else's picture and pass her off as the woman who would fit Marsha's voice."

"I don't think she'd go for that," Colleen said with a frown. "And neither would I."

"I have to admit that when the station agreed to her program we never dreamed it would be so successful. Now we couldn't fire her if we wanted to and she knows it."

"How big a deal do you think the lesbian issue is?"

"Negligible. There's probably not a man out there who'd believe that voice could be coming from a woman who prefers other women. Even if they did, they'd pay to watch," Ken said as he leered at Colleen. "Well, maybe not with Marsha, but I'm sure they all believe if they could get Desdemona in the sack, she'd see the light. Hallelujah! Amen!"

"Have there been any threats made?"

"One or two, but nothing Marsha thought was serious enough to contact the police about. She's pretty good at talking her way out of a potentially bad situation and, like she said, she and Boomer screen the calls carefully. They both know the voices of the regulars and she knows how to take care of herself."

"Do they record any threats?"

"Yeah. We keep them for a few months and then erase them. No repeaters. Mostly drunk college students, I think. She's not really worried about her own safety. Since she won't do a photo shoot no one knows what she looks like and wouldn't know who to attack."

"Thank you for the introduction, Mr. Dickinson," Colleen said as she stood. "I still have some unpacking to do."

"No problem. Let me know if you need anything."

Colleen left the manager's office and hurried to the front lobby, stopping at the receptionist's desk. "Has Marsha Barrett left?"

"Elvis left the building a few minutes ago. Probably waiting for her bus down at the corner."

"What do you know about her?"

"Hello and see ya later is about it," the receptionist said. "She never hangs around to socialize, except maybe with Boomer. They both started here about the same time and she seems to trust him for some reason. Probably because he can be as off-the-wall as she is. She doesn't attend station functions or promotions. Never talks about herself."

"I've worked with a few truly egotistical personalities before," Colleen said. "But never one who didn't want to be recognized."

"Where were you before you came to Omaha?" the receptionist asked.

"A station back east."

She looked at Colleen as if she'd lost her mind. "You *chose* to come to the Farm Belt?" She paused before adding, "On purpose?"

"KLEW is in a growing market area," Colleen said.

"Honey, it's in a *corn* growing area," the receptionist said with a hearty laugh. "Good luck, sister."

Chapter Two

MARSHA SAT DOWN heavily on the bench at her bus stop and leaned back. She stuck a finger under her glasses and rubbed her eye. She rested an elbow on the backpack next to her and looked around. Her hand trembled slightly and she balled her hand into a fist to stop the involuntary movement and jammed a cigarette between her lips and lit it. She hadn't expected to come face-to-face with the woman of her dreams and it had rattled her. The nicotine flooded her system immediately, leaving her momentarily light-headed before its calming effect kicked in. She closed her eyes and turned her face up into the early morning sunlight, frowning as she struggled to forget the feeling Colleen Walters had created. It had been a long time, but she didn't have any desire to relive the past.

All she had ever wanted was someone who would look at her with desire, someone who accepted her for who she was, as she was. God knew her parents never had. They regarded her as a freak and refused to touch her. Nearly starved to death before the authorities removed her from their home for failure to thrive, Marsha was placed in the care of a foster family willing to care for a child with medical needs—for the right price. The state paid for Marsha's medical care until she became an adult, but she would always carry the scars of early neglect. She ran a hand over her mouth, feeling the thin line that bisected her upper lip, leaving it noticeably misaligned. When she was younger she convinced herself it gave her a roguish look. Even now she almost liked her smile...almost. It would always be a little off.

"Could I interest you in a cup of coffee and a little breakfast?" a warm, feminine voice asked.

Marsha looked up, squinting against the sunlight shimmering off the windows of the buildings around them. Scanning the tall, slender beauty standing over her, Marsha let a smile play over her lips. "You could probably interest me in any number of things, honey, but I need to get home." Her voice was husky after taking another lung-filling drag on her cigarette.

"Got a hot date waiting?"

"Yeah," Marsha said as she raked her eyes over Colleen's body again. "I like it hot in the morning." Her lips quirked to one side as she watched a slight blush move up Colleen's neck.

"It's been known to happen," Colleen said after collecting herself.

"Not to me," Marsha mumbled, looking away.

"I'd really like to run a couple of ideas past you while they're fresh in my mind. I promise to have you in bed in less than an hour and that's as far as my begging is going to go."

"It'd be hard to pass up a...promise like that," Marsha said, wondering if Colleen even realized the double entendre of her statement and couldn't resist a laugh. "I never make attractive women beg," she added as she pushed her body wearily from the bench. "There's an IHOP around the next corner. As long as I'm being forced to stay awake I might as well eat."

"I can drive you home after breakfast, if you like," Colleen offered.

"There's a bus about every forty minutes or so."

Marsha held the door to the restaurant open for Colleen and as they were shown to a booth her hand reflexively found the small of her companion's back. She stirred cream and sugar into her coffee and placed her order before planting her fingers in the curly hair that fell over her forehead and ruffling it around.

"Is your hair naturally curly?" Colleen sipped her coffee.

"Yeah, but only enough to be annoying. I had it permed tighter once so it wouldn't flop around when I walked. Didn't really work out all that well though," she said as she grasped a curl and pulled it down before releasing it. "Before you feel the need to ask," she tapped a finger against her upper lip, "a birthday gift from my mother." Marsha swallowed a mouthful of coffee and studied Colleen's perfect, unblemished face, settling on her sparkling blue eyes. "So, why are we here?"

"I thought it would be a good idea if I got to know you better. I know you're tired, but I've found that's when people are most agreeable."

"And that works for you, huh?" Marsha asked and looked around at the other tables.

"Pretty much," Colleen said.

Marsha didn't think Colleen could do anything to look more beautiful, but she was wrong. Her smile made her eyes dance and small dimples appeared on either side of her lips. Marsha frowned. It just wasn't fair for anyone to have so many attractive attributes, especially at seven-thirty in the morning.

"Okay, so lay it on me, baby," Marsha exhaled. "What's your big plan for my program?"

Marsha watched Colleen's eyes change from dancing to sparkling as her pupils dilated slightly. Marsha pulled her glasses off and placed them on the table next to her before rubbing her eyes as Colleen began laying out her plan for expanding Marsha's listening area. Marsha didn't hear much of what Colleen was saying as her imagination began to soar. After all, it wasn't every damn day she found herself sitting across a small table from the woman whose twin occupied her dreams and bed seven out of seven nights. Of course, she couldn't be certain Colleen Walters was *really* the woman in her dreams, but she was a fucking fine imitation. Attractive, slender, friendly, dangerously feminine. Her make-up wasn't overdone and the blonde hair that fell around her soft features made Marsha itch at the prospect of touching it and letting it slip through her fingers.

"Where are you from?" Marsha blurted, interrupting whatever Colleen was telling her about demographic studies.

"A suburb of Philadelphia," Colleen said. "Why?"

"You have a nice voice."

"Thank you. My parents will be glad to know their money wasn't wasted on my voice lessons when I was a kid."

Marsha rested her elbow on the table and propped her chin on the heel of her hand. "I bet you were a real cute kid," she exhaled.

"Are you flirting with me, Ms. Barrett?" Colleen asked with a smile broad enough to deepen her dimples.

God, her lips are so kissable, Marsha thought as she involuntarily licked her lips. "Probably. When I'm overly tired it's like having a nice buzz on," she said. "You'll have to forgive my crass behavior, but this was your idea."

Their waitress set plates of food in front of them and made sure they didn't need anything else before moving on to her other customers. As the scent of food reached her nose, Marsha realized she was hungrier than she thought. Beat the hell out of cheese Danish from a convenience store and she shoveled food into her mouth while Colleen ate almost daintily in between snippets of conversation.

Marsha refilled her coffee cup and leaned back in her chair, rubbing her rounded belly in satisfaction. "Delicious," she sighed. "Thanks for insisting I eat. I was starving."

"Feeling less buzzed now?"

Marsha took another sip of her coffee. "Ready and rarin' to go," she said.

"Are you from Omaha?"

Marsha shook her head. "Suburb of Chicago. Born about fifty miles west in one of the glorious suburbs. You know, close enough to say you're from a big city, but far enough away not to be associated with the seamier side of life."

"Only child?"

Marsha paused before answering. "Yeah. After I popped out they didn't want to risk reproducing again."

"I'm guessing you're not close with your family then."

"You could say that."

"Is it because you're gay?"

"Nope. I doubt they even know or care." Marsha glanced at the clock hanging on the wall near the kitchen area and took a deep breath. "Look, it's been fun and I appreciate breakfast, but I really need to get some sleep."

"No problem. We'll find some time to chat before I leave on my mission to sell your program."

"I'll be back to work in a couple of days, but since I work nights I doubt we'll ever see one another. Feel free to stop by the studio the next time you're suffering from insomnia."

COLLEEN SIPPED HER coffee and watched Marsha stroll out the front door, her backpack slung over her shoulder. She was an interesting woman. Intelligent, sassy, funny, flirty, and gritty, with a deep-seated self-esteem problem she tried to cover up with her own brand of humor and false bravado. Colleen had stayed up half the previous night listening to *In the Midnight Hour* and discovered she had been lured in by the veiled promises of Marsha's seductive voice. Definitely an interesting woman. Colleen vowed to get to know the woman behind the voice better despite Marsha's apparent disinterest.

Chapter Three

AT THE END of a long day familiarizing herself with the business end of KLEW-FM, Colleen turned the key in the front door of her new condo located in a trendy section of Omaha, not far from the meandering Missouri River. She stepped inside and punched in the code to disable the condo's security system. She juggled an armload of advertiser revenue files she needed to go through before finding an empty spot to set them down. She groaned as her eyes took in the stacked boxes that held her personal belongings.

The drive from Philadelphia had been long and tiring. There'd been nothing to break the monotony. In late March there were still fields of golden winter wheat waiting to be harvested. In other areas, the rich brown soil was already being plowed in preparation for planting spring wheat or corn. To Colleen it seemed like a never-ending process. A late snow shower had dusted the region a few days earlier and, despite the sun shining overhead, patches of snow clung stubbornly in low areas.

The miles had flown by as Colleen's thoughts wandered over her decision to apply for a position at a mid-sized station in the middle of the country. She never thought she'd leave the metropolitan area of the northeast. Raised near Philadelphia, she had worked her way up to a large station in Washington, D.C. by her mid-twenties, earning a salary that proved she was considered a valuable asset in the radio business. While she had no desire to be a radio personality and preferred to remain behind the scenes as an advertising specialist, there was no question that she held a position that made many others in her field envious of her success. Then almost overnight, and without any warning signs of calamity, it was all gone, leaving her with nothing but fear, pain, and self-doubt.

Now here she stood in a comfortably large condo across the Missouri River from Council Bluffs, Iowa. She was surrounded by the boxes and furnishings that had arrived over the weekend in a large moving van and been deposited haphazardly by burley men in overalls and flannel shirts. She had slept on an air mattress on the floor of the master bedroom for three nights. Most of her business clothing had been packed into her mid-sized blue and silver Mazda sedan. She stepped out of her shoes. After removing her jacket, she turned on her Keurig coffeemaker and wandered around looking for the code she and her mother had put on each box to help her eventually locate what she wanted.

"Ah-ha!" she said when she found the code. She returned to the kitchen, prepared a cup of coffee and grabbed a paring knife from a drawer. She savored the coffee and took a deep breath as she carefully cut through the heavy-duty packing tape along the top of the box. She flipped the flaps open and almost performed a Snoopy dance while clapping her hands together. Her favorite worn and washed out light blue jeans were folded neatly on top of everything else. They had been washed so many times over the years that they felt as soft as a new chamois. She stripped out of her dress pants and stepped into the jeans. Tears came to her eyes as she saw her favorite winter shirt lying beneath the jeans. She found a soft long-sleeve pullover and slipped it on, then topped it with the old flannel shirt. She folded the sleeves of the flannel shirt up to her elbows and went into the master bedroom. She wouldn't be sleeping on the air mattress that night.

MARSHA STEPPED OFF the bus two blocks from her house and stuck her hands into the pockets of her jacket. Winter was officially over, but there was still a nip in the air. She smiled as she thought about climbing naked into her warm, soft bed and snuggling down under her quilted comforter to wait for Blondie to magically appear, as she always did. The new account executive at the station had startled her. She was a dead ringer for Blondie and was friendly enough, but Marsha thought she seemed out of place. She was too sophisticated for Omaha somehow. While Marsha had been entranced by the woman's blue eyes, there had been something hiding behind them she couldn't identify. Fear? Perhaps. It had been a fleeting glance probably caused by beginning a new job surrounded by new faces. She seemed to know what she was talking about, but Marsha wished she hadn't brought up the gay issue. That was something Marsha never discussed. She wasn't ashamed to say she was gay, but it had never been a conversation starter. What difference did it make if she preferred to keep company with the ladies? Of course that was assuming a lady wanted to keep company with her. She had been in Omaha four years and no one had even looked in her direction. But that had been the idea to begin with, hadn't it? Her last relationship was a disaster and ended with Marsha being thrown in jail for weeks until the charges were dropped. It wasn't long after that she disappeared only to reappear in a new city, a new state, a new life. A quick trip to the city cemetery had allowed her to transform herself into a new person. As she always had, she found a way to adapt.

Chapter Four

EARLY SATURDAY MORNING Marsha punched in what would be the last request of the night and absently picked up a few things from her console. She stuffed them into her backpack and let her head bounce to the beat of the song. When the last strains of the request ended, she flipped her mic on, brought her mouth close to its protective cover, and closed her eyes. "Another memorable night has passed too quickly and it's time to say a fond *adieu* until we get together again, night owls. Time to go home and dream those sweet dreams. This is Desdemona, coming to you from KLEW-FM. Sleep well." She slowly brought up the music that closed out her show and unlocked the studio door.

Boomer met her in the hall and slapped her on the back. "Good show, Dez," he said.

"Same old, same old," she said with a shrug. "I think we needed to have a little more listener interaction. I'll see if I can come up with a topic after I wake up and can think more clearly." She turned around and walked backward as they talked. "You have any ideas?"

He laughed. "They don't pay me to think, just turn knobs."

"That's a topic. Job tedium."

"Hell, I don't even know what that means," Boomer said.

"How many people out there do you think are bored with their jobs?"

"Everyone I know."

"How could they liven up things at the office? How could the boss make the workplace better?"

COLLEEN BACKED THROUGH the front doors of the station carrying a stack of file boxes. She nodded at the weekend receptionist and moved down the corridor leading to the administrative offices of the station. She had stayed up later than usual unpacking the night before and her eyes felt as if she had sand in them. She peeked to the left of the boxes in her arms to see how much farther she had to go.

"Shit!" a voice cried out and the top box was knocked out of her hands.

Colleen looked to the right in time to see Marsha and Boomer dive to catch the falling box and collide in the process. Boomer grabbed the box, but his elbow caught Marsha in the side of the head and knocked her down. On the way down Marsha struck the other side of her head against the wall.

"Son of a bitch!" Marsha yelled, grabbing her head between her hands. "Why don't you watch where the fuck you're going?"

Colleen set the remaining boxes on the floor and reached out to help Marsha up. Marsha jerked her arms away from Colleen and thrust an arm up toward Boomer. He set down the box he'd grabbed and pulled her up. She leaned against the wall and gently rubbed her head as she glared at Colleen.

"Do you always walk backwards down the hallway?" Colleen asked.

"Not usually. I was talking to Boomer." Marsha grunted. She shook her head and bent over to pick up her backpack. When she stood up again, her body swayed slightly. Colleen reached out to steady her.

"Come into my office until you feel steady enough to go wherever you're going," Colleen said.

Boomer picked up the box and nodded toward her office. "I'll take this in for you so you can see where you're goin'," he said.

Colleen maneuvered Marsha's body to her office door and held her against the wall while she fished her keys from her shoulder bag and unlocked it.

"I'm good," Marsha said, batting Colleen's hand away from her chest.

"Just set that box on the desk please," Colleen said.

Colleen guided Marsha to the couch. "Rest for a few minutes while I get the other boxes." Colleen left for a minute and then returned. Marsha was lying down with her head resting on the arm of the couch.

"She just fell over and went to sleep," Boomer said quietly.

"Will she be okay?" Colleen asked.

"Yeah," he answered with a dismissive wave of his hand. "What're you doin' here so early on a Saturday morning?"

"I unpacked some things last night and thought I'd bring them in. I wasn't expecting to run into anyone...literally." She looked down at a peacefully sleeping Marsha. "I think I'll just let her sleep for a while."

"Need some help?" Boomer asked, stifling a yawn.

"Thanks, but I can spend a little time rearranging my files without being disturbed. A lot of the last account executive's paperwork can be thrown away, I think."

"Well, enjoy the peace and quiet until tonight and don't let Dez sleep too long."

"I won't and thanks, Boomer."

"Not a problem," he waved as he left the office. "See ya later."

Colleen spent the next two hours going through paperwork in the file cabinets behind her desk, tossing most of the old material and replacing it with a few things of her own. She pulled out the bottom drawer and propped her sneaker clad feet on it as she examined a few things more closely.

She looked up and removed her reading glasses when she heard Marsha roll over on the couch. Colleen stood and removed the lids on her boxes, looking through them until she found a crocheted throw her mother had given her. It felt soft and comfortable as she rubbed her cheek against it. It was the perfect combination of earth tones for her office and reminded her of her mother. She spread it over Marsha's prone body before returning to her work.

"HOW'S YOUR HEAD?" Colleen asked softly.

"As hard as ever," Marsha replied with a grin. Her eyes fluttered open and she sucked in a deep breath and pressed her body further against the back of the couch. She swung her legs over the edge and sat up, rubbing her eyes with the heels of her hands. "You got any aspirin? I seem to have the headache from hell."

Colleen took two aspirin from a bottle in a desk drawer. She picked up a drink from her desk and handed it and the aspirin to Marsha.

"Ow!" Marsha hissed as she felt around her head and located a tender spot.

"Let me see," Colleen said as she stood and leaned over Marsha. "Let me see how badly I hurt you," she said.

"Again you mean," Marsha said as she sucked on the straw stuck in the drink.

"I'm sorry. It was an accident."

"Well, who the hell carries crap that prevents them from seeing where they're going?"

"Probably the same kind of person who walks backward down a hallway," Colleen snapped as she parted Marsha hair and examined the small lump on the side of her head. She leaned over farther to see if Marsha had hit her head any other place.

Marsha took a deep breath and saw a stone washed pair of worn jeans that stretched tightly over a slender thigh. A mild floral scent mingled with a hint of lavender filled her nose. Marsha swallowed hard and licked her lips.

"It's not bleeding," Colleen said. "I don't think you'll need surgery, but..." she started as she leaned closer, her abdomen pressing against Marsha's shoulder.

Realizing the closeness between them, Colleen pulled back and Marsha blinked rapidly at the hips before her. They were perfect. "N...nice jeans," she managed.

"Thanks. Hungry?" Colleen asked.

Still staring at Colleen's curvaceous hips, Marsha answered, "Starving." It had been a very long time since she'd smelled the scent of a woman, but it was still arousing.

Colleen spun around and walked to her desk. "I didn't know what you liked, so I didn't get you anything too adventurous," Colleen said as she leaned over her desk, breaking into Marsha's thoughts.

Marsha thought there must be something seriously wrong with her because she couldn't seem to drag her eyes away from Colleen's body.

Marsha licked her lips again at the sight of the firmly rounded ass that moved so effortlessly beneath those worn jeans. Colleen returned with a bag and Marsha swallowed when her eyes raised to meet the perfect mounds that peeked from beneath Colleen's flannel shirt. Colleen set the bag on the coffee table and dragged a chair over to sit across from Marsha. "I just ordered you a ham and Swiss on rye. Almost everyone likes that." She settled in the chair and picked up her sandwich. "You don't mind if I join you, do you?" she asked.

"You'd be screwed if I was Jewish," Marsha said as she unwrapped her sandwich. "What's yours?"

"Pastrami and Swiss on whole wheat," Colleen answered as she took a big bite and chewed happily.

"What time is it?"

"About one." When she saw the surprised look on Marsha's face, she added, "You might have slept longer, but I was getting a little worried since you hit your head. Plus I'm almost done here for today and didn't want to leave you snoring away on my couch."

"I don't snore," Marsha said around a mouthful of her sandwich.

"How do you know what you do when you sleep?" Colleen smiled and waggled her eyebrows. "Or did your girlfriend tell you?"

"Nobody told me. I just know, that's all."

Colleen finished her food and washed it down as she watched Marsha take another bite of her sandwich. She cleared her throat. "You know, I've shared my bed with one or two women since I came out and every one of them snored." She smiled. "Of course, it was usually after an...active evening."

Marsha looked at Colleen, a twinkle of mischief in her eyes. "You volunteering to make me snore? I love a challenge." Marsha smiled a crooked smile as she stood and started taking her clothes off.

"What are you doing?" Colleen yelped as her eyes widened.

Marsha threw her hands out, bent at the wrist, and said, "I'm ready, so bring it, baby." She patted her now full belly. "Now that I have a full stomach, I'm game."

When Marsha's hands reached for the zipper on her cargo pants, Colleen stood. "It wasn't a challenge. I've just never met anyone who didn't snore. Maybe you should ask your audience about it some night. I'm willing to bet they will all have to confess to snoring after an intimate evening."

Marsha stuck her hand out. "I'll take that bet. What will I win if I find another non-snorer?"

Colleen thought for a moment. "A home-cooked meal."

Marsha shrugged. "If that's the best you can offer, I guess it'll have to do. Who's cookin'?" Marsha asked warily.

"I will, but if I win you cook." She leaned over the coffee table and met Marsha's eyes as she grasped her hand. "Should I place my order now, sweet thing?"

Marsha laughed. "I guess I better get busy then because the only cookin' I do is through the drive-thru window."

"Sounds delicious," Colleen said, still holding Marsha's hand. "I'll be out of town for a few days. I trust you to let me know who won when I return. Deal?"

Marsha stood mesmerized by the cool blue eyes that delved into hers. She forced her eyes closed to break the hold. "You're on," she finally said with an almost shy smile.

Colleen jerked Marsha's arm playfully. "Gather your stuff and I'll drive you home. I was only planning to drop my boxes off, not spend the day."

"It's okay, I can catch the bus."

"I insist. As you've already pointed out, that knot on your head was my fault. Still tender?"

Marsha released Colleen's soft, warm hand and gently palpated the bump on her head. "I'll survive," she said. She made her living flirting with her callers, but hadn't spoken to many who returned her provocative comments as well as Colleen did.

Chapter Five

COLLEEN FLEW TO North Carolina to pitch Marsha's show early the following Monday morning. During the flight she thought about Marsha. She had practically fought her tooth-and-nail when Colleen insisted on taking her home. Admittedly, Marsha didn't live in the high rent district. In fact, it was only a step or two above a slum. Marsha hadn't invited her in and Colleen hadn't pressed the issue. She enjoyed talking to Marsha and discovered she was nothing like Desdemona in reality, even though she put up a pretty good front. Despite her cocky attitude and infectious flirting, Marsha Barrett was a somewhat shy and insecure woman. Colleen wanted to know her better. Perhaps if she succeeded in selling *In the Midnight Hour* she would have a chance to work more closely with her. She decided her best strategy would be the mystery of the woman herself. There would be no pictures and certainly no mention of her sexual preference in the conservative *Bible* belt. There would simply be "The Voice." A station in Charlotte agreed to give the program a one-month trial. If their listeners responded positively, they agreed to pick it up on a two-year contract.

Exhausted after a long day of negotiations with the station manager of a mid-size station in Charlotte who believed he was the answer to every single woman's problem, Colleen left her hotel and wandered into a women's bar not far from the local station. It had been nearly three years since Colleen felt strong enough mentally to attempt making even a temporary connection with anyone. She vividly remembered her last night with her ex-lover. Rusty's words hadn't done enough damage so Rusty added emphasis via her fists. Only the sight of Colleen's blood mingled with her tears seemed to satisfy her lover's fury. Their relationship had been a disaster waiting to happen from the day they met. During the five years they were together, Rusty had disintegrated from a caring, attentive lover to an insecure, sadistic woman intent on controlling everything in her life, including Colleen.

Since her recovery Colleen had worked diligently with a therapist to rebuild her life and regain her confidence, devoting little time to her personal wants and needs. Her once open and easygoing trust of others had been destroyed. Months of therapy had allowed her to reclaim a part of her life while her confidence still struggled to heal. She no longer trusted other women as easily as she once had. The physical damage to her body had healed, while her psychological injuries remained raw and unseen.

The club was typically dark and, while not yet teeming with bodies, offered a variety of women to mingle with. The next morning she would rent a car and drive to Savannah, Georgia before flying back to Omaha.

She ordered a drink and carried it to a vacant booth midway between the bar and the dance floor. The DJ booth was elevated above the floor. A decent mix of music blared through the speakers.

Colleen was dressed casually in jeans and a soft, lightweight sweater. She tapped her foot to the beat of the music and watched as a young woman with short, dark hair danced her way toward her booth. Without saying a word, the woman held out her hand. Colleen smiled and took the proffered hand. While the woman was androgynous-looking with rather plain features, confidence oozed from her body. They danced around each other on the dance floor, their bodies occasionally touching, causing a burst of smiles and giggles.

The woman was a good dancer and knew it. Her technique was provocative, the movement of her hips promising something Colleen had once been unable to resist, a night filled with wanton lust and burning passion. A night where the only thing that mattered was a cool touch on her hot skin. The way the woman looked at her reminded her of the anticipation she had once felt, of a time when she had wanted to give her body to another. She ached to regain that feeling again.

When the dance ended, the brunette followed Colleen back to her table and slid in smoothly beside her. She didn't miss a beat before drawing Colleen into a heated kiss that swiftly led to hands seeking the feel of skin. Colleen returned the kiss, but wouldn't allow herself to become lost in it. When they parted, the brunette motioned with her head toward the front door, followed by a slow shake of Colleen's head. The woman shrugged and leaned in for another quick kiss before standing and dancing off to find another potential companion for the night.

Colleen chuckled to herself and finished her drink. It would have been simple to lose herself in the woman's touch. Once upon a time, in another life, she wouldn't have thought twice before following the boyish looking brunette. Although the brunette had been an excellent, and experienced, kisser, she hadn't offered the kind of evening Colleen was looking for.

Since her last night with Rusty, Colleen had been reluctant to give any part of herself to anyone. Her mini make-out session at the club reminded her how much she missed the intimate touch of another woman. She flagged down a cab and returned to her hotel to finish packing. On a whim she picked up her cell and punched in a long distance number.

"You're in the midnight hour, sweetness." Marsha's low, husky velvet voice poured over the phone. "What can Dez do to make you happy in the wee hours of a long, lonely night?"

Marsha's sultry voice sent a shiver down Colleen's spine.

"Cheer me up, babe," Colleen requested, dropping her voice an octave.

"What should I call you, darlin'?"

"Trigger," Colleen said after a pause, using the childhood nickname her brothers had given her.

"Are you out there all alone tonight, Trigger?"

"I had an offer, but turned it down."

"Oooh, the picky type, huh?"

"I know what I want," Colleen cooed softly.

IN THE STUDIO in Omaha, Boomer gave Marsha a thumb's up and fanned his face with his hand. Marsha laughed and returned to her microphone, lowering her voice slightly. "Tell me what you want, baby. I promise to only squeeze, and never jerk, your trigger," she said with a groan in her voice.

"Can you give me a 'Constant Craving', hot stuff?" Trigger flirted.

Marsha grabbed her console to avoid sliding out of her chair. "Comin' right at you, Trigger. Enjoy, baby." Marsha keyed the request and discovered her breathing had become slightly labored.

"Woo-hoo, you two were burning up the airwaves," Boomer said through the headphones.

"Talk's cheap. You know that, man, but she sure sounded h-o-t with a capital H," Marsha said as she punched the next blinking button. "Talk to me, honey."

MARSHA'S SHOW WASN'T being broadcast in Charlotte yet, but Colleen listened to her requested song on her iPod and hummed along as she put the last of her clothes into her suitcase and stripped for a shower.

As the warm water ran through her hair she used her hands to push the wet hair back from her face and closed her eyes. She let her hands drift over her breasts and skim along her abdomen, feeling it clench under her fingers. She bit her lower lip as her fingers slid between her thighs and toward her heated center. She spread her legs slightly and braced her free hand against the shower wall, allowing her other to glide slowly in and out of her body until the feeling was more than she could stand. Her body's release left her vaguely satisfied and somewhat embarrassed. She hadn't felt the need to self-satisfy since she'd been a teenager, but it had been more than three years since she'd allowed anyone to touch her. The memory of Rusty's touch, driving her to the point of ecstasy, had lost its pleasure as Colleen turned her face into the stream of water, letting it mix with bitter tears.

Chapter Six

THREE NIGHTS LATER, Marsha queued up the last request and waited for the phone to buzz again. The songs lined up to play would last about fifteen or twenty minutes. She leaned back in her chair and ran her fingers through her unruly hair, pushing her glasses up to rest on her forehead while she rubbed her eyes with the tips of her fingers. A tap on the studio door got her attention and she opened her eyes, surprised to see Colleen.

"What can I do for you?" Marsha opened the door.

Colleen smiled and Marsha found her dimples distracting. "Probably any number of things," Colleen said, using the same line Marsha had used on her earlier. "You told me to drop by some night when I had insomnia, so here I am."

Marsha shifted her weight a little, uncertain how to reply.

"Actually I got back in town a few hours ago and didn't want to wait until tomorrow to tell you the show's been picked up in Charlotte and Savannah on a trial basis," Colleen announced.

Marsha pointed to a chair across from her console. Marsha sat and rearranged her headphones to determine how much longer the current song had to go. "Cool. When will it start?"

"Beginning of the month probably," Colleen leaned back in the tall, soft, leather chair. "Then they'll check their demographics and make a long term decision."

"Again with the demographics," Marsha muttered. She couldn't stop her eyes from following Colleen's body as it swiveled in the tall seat. She cleared her throat and fiddled with a dial on her console. "You've been a busy woman."

"Just doing my job. Actually you pretty much sell the show yourself, or at least your voice does." A smile crossed Colleen's lips when she saw Marsha's eyes cruising her body. "See anything you like," she teased.

"One or two things," Marsha said, her face flushing at being caught. She shrugged. "I'm human."

"You underestimate yourself. There's something appealing about you, even though I can't quite put my finger on it yet."

"I've got a cute little birthmark on my ass you could put your finger on any time you want," Marsha said, waggling her eyebrows.

"Really?" Colleen laughed.

"Yeah. Looks a little like Ohio. Or at least that's what I think. Could be Indiana, I guess," Marsha said.

"Indiana's got my vote," Boomer piped in.

"Oh, shut up, Boomer," Marsha said. "You didn't even know I had a damn birthmark until five seconds ago."

"I got five on The Hoosier State," he said. "Do I hear ten?"

Colleen laughed at the duo's antics. "Ten!" she said.

"Gettin' too rich for my blood," Boomer sighed. "Maybe next time."

"Looks like I win," Colleen said. She quirked an eyebrow up and leaned her body over the console in front of her, displaying a tempting cleavage that left Marsha's mouth dry. Her mouth opened slightly as her tongue moved slowly across her teeth and her eyes toured Marsha's blushing face. "So drop 'em, stud, and let's see whatcha got," she challenged in a low, seductive voice.

"In your dreams," Marsha pooh-poohed her. No one had ever called her 'stud' before. She liked the image it conjured up and smiled, wondering how far she could push the mini flirting session.

"Aw, pretty please, Marshy-mallow," Boomer pouted, breaking into her thoughts.

"I can see it now, strip radio!" Marsha said.

"Only if we can get an audience that includes Helen Keller, Ray Charles, and Stevie Wonder," Boomer howled.

"Don't forget Roy Orbison," Marsha added.

"Or Ronnie Milsap," Colleen said. "Oh, and Jose Feliciano."

"Damn! You're good woman," Boomer laughed.

Moving her eyes back to Marsha, Colleen said, "I've been told that."

"You seem to know your music, Blondie," Marsha said with an appreciative smile.

"Oops, a call's coming in," Boomer announced. "Time to serious up, people."

"I got it," Marsha said as she wiped the tears of laughter from her face. "This is Dez. Make my night, baby," she answered.

"Play 'Another One Bites the Dust'," a woman's voice drawled softly.

"Oh, a playa," Marsha said, glancing at Colleen. "How many notches you got on your bedpost, sweetie?"

"Not enough."

"What should I call you and is there anyone special I should send this one out to as a warning?"

"Call me...Red and there's no one special...at the moment. I'm new in town."

Colleen frowned and rubbed her eyes.

"Here's hoping you find the one you're looking for soon, honey," Marsha said softly as she started the request.

"Sooner than she realizes," the woman said, ending the call with throaty laughter.

"Go get 'em, girl," Marsha said before disconnecting and moving on to the next request.

Colleen shook her head and flashed a smile. "Want to catch

breakfast when you're done here?" she asked. She looked through the studio window. "You, too, Boomer."

"I'd hate to cost you the price of breakfast, especially when you now owe me a home-cooked meal," Marsha said with a grin.

"You found someone who doesn't snore after sex?" Colleen asked with a surprised look on her face. "I don't believe it!"

"I have to admit I feel a little sorry about it though. It's actually Boomer's wife."

"That's cheating!" Colleen said.

Marsha punched a button on her console. "Hey, Boomer. Tell Colleen about that sexy wife of yours."

"What about her?" Boomer asked, looking confused. Then the light bulb in his brain came on. "Oh, you mean about the snoring thing."

"Yeah."

"She had an operation when she was a kid to remove her adenoids and tonsils. After that she never snored again."

Colleen squinted at Marsha. "How long have you known that?"

"Not long. I told Boomer about our bet and he told me about his wife." Marsha scanned Colleen's body again and smiled. "I always prefer a sure thing, but I do feel slightly guilty. I was striking out until then."

"Then it's a date the next night you're off," Colleen said. "What do you want me to cook?"

"It's *not* a date."

Colleen tried to gauge the look in Marsha's eyes, but wasn't fast enough. "Well, stop by my office after you sign off," she said as she stood to leave. "Breakfast will have to do for today."

"Me, too?" Boomer asked.

"Yes. You, too even though I consider you a traitor now."

Marsha watched Colleen slip out of the studio and wave at Boomer in the control room. A date. That was a joke, Marsha thought. Unless Colleen had a strange fetish for tall, skinny, myopic DJs, breakfast, or any other meal for that matter, definitely wouldn't be a date. It might happen in her dreams, but there were way too many mirrors in the world waiting anxiously to slap her back into reality. She hated mirrors. The woman she visualized in her mind had killer bedroom eyes like melting chocolate and soft hair that was never out of place. Women wanted to be with her and longed for more when she made love to them, gently and tenderly with an occasional loss of control driven by raw, hungry desire.

The stark reality of her life brought an end to her fantasy as she caught a glimpse of her reflection in the studio glass. She was none of the things her mind conjured up. Marsha squeezed her eyes shut as the sound of humiliating laughter crept into her mind. With only a word, Colleen could stomp on her as if she were a bug or the pathetic, needy loser she was.

She frowned and decided breakfast wasn't a great idea. Although Colleen more than held her own where flirting was concerned she would never be anything more than a work acquaintance. Surely she could manage to get past Colleen's office without being seen. She rationalized she would be doing Colleen a favor by not making her go through with the meal and being seen in public with a woman so obviously below her standards.

An hour later Marsha made a clean getaway, but chickened out on being a total cad. She left a note with Boomer explaining that she had developed a thundering headache and would take a rain check on breakfast. She was certain Boomer, who generally behaved like an overly exuberant Labrador retriever puppy could keep Colleen entertained. The fact was, the sexually-laden conversations with Colleen had begun playing havoc with Marsha's libido and she needed a long cold shower.

A KNOCK ON Colleen's office door preceded Boomer's entry. She smiled when she saw the young sound technician. "Ready?" she asked with a friendly smile.

"Benedict Arnold reporting for breakfast," he said, rubbing his hands together.

Colleen slipped her coat on and opened the bottom drawer of her desk to retrieve her purse. "Where's Marsha?" she asked.

"Split. Said she had a bitchin' headache. Left this for you though." He pulled a folded piece of paper from his back pocket and handed it to Colleen.

Colleen was disappointed after she read the brief note. She dropped it on her desk and prepared to spend at least an hour chatting with Boomer, who looked at her like she was his favorite dessert. "Shall we?" she asked, joining him at the office door.

Once they were seated at a booth and had placed their orders, Boomer looked around nervously and seemed uncertain about beginning a conversation with Colleen. She broke the ice by asking, "Have you been with the station long?"

"Two or three years. Marsha and I hit it off pretty quick and they made me her sound man."

"Where are you from?" Colleen asked.

"Virginia. Married a girl from Illinois a few years ago and she wanted to move closer to her home. This is about as close as I fuckin' wanted to get to in-laws." He blushed. "Sorry. I'm used to the way Marsha and I talk to each other. Sometimes I forget not everyone does that."

"I'm not offended, Boomer. I have four older brothers and managed to pick up a few choice words from them."

"Wow. Four brothers. Must have been a bitch datin' you," he said with a laugh as the waitress set a plate in front of him.

"It had its moments," Colleen said with a smile. "Tell me about Marsha."

"I don't know much. She doesn't talk about herself."

"Tell me what you know. Knowing her better will help me sell her show."

Boomer thought as he chewed a strip of bacon. "I know she's from someplace up north, near Chicago, I think. Came here about three or four years ago. Lives alone. Has a wicked sick sense of humor." He glanced at Colleen and shrugged. "Likes the ladies. That's about it. She is who she is. We're friendly, but don't pry into one another's lives. She's a pretty private person."

"Sometimes it's hard to tell whether I'm talking to Marsha or Desdemona."

Boomer scratched the side of his bearded cheek and leaned forward slightly. "Personally, I think Marsha is one of those people with a multiple personality disorder and Desdemona is the alter that protects her."

"From what?"

"Herself, maybe."

Colleen laughed. "Thank you, Dr. Freud. Psych major?"

Boomer nodded and laughed. "I think if Marsha had a choice she'd rather be Desdemona."

"Do you know how she got the scar on her lip?" Colleen asked.

"No clue. I learned the hard way it's an off-limits topic. She's self-conscious about it, but there's really no way to hide it."

"Anyone special in her life?"

"Well, she's got this friend who calls in from time to time, but I don't think she's more than a friend," Boomer said before stuffing a fork full of pancakes into his mouth. "How about you? Anyone waitin' for you to come home at night?"

Colleen shook her head slightly as she took a sip of her coffee. "No."

THE BUS RIDE across town lulled Marsha to sleep with its rocking motion over dips, bumps, and potholes. Her eyes jerked open when a hand shook her shoulder and she stared up into the familiar smiling face of Otis, the bus driver.

"This is your stop, Stretch," he said, his voice drawling, reminiscent of his hometown of New Orleans.

Marsha wiped a small line of drool from her lips and pulled herself up. "Thanks, man," she mumbled. She followed him up the aisle of the bus and waited for him to take his seat and open the door. It wasn't like her to actually fall asleep on the way home. She hoped she hadn't been snoring. The thought of that brought a brief smile to her lips. Half a block from her bus stop, she turned down the cracked sidewalk leading into her neighborhood.

"*Morgen,*" Marsha's neighbor called out.

She smiled as she spun around to face Jacobi Hershberger. She should have realized he would be up early. As the self-appointed neighborhood watchman, Jacobi came complete with notepad, pencil, and binoculars as he strolled onto his front porch and assumed his usual place in an old rocker.

Marsha strode across the street and up the three steps onto Jacobi's porch. "Everything peaceful last night, Mr. Hershberger?" Marsha asked as she accepted the cup of coffee Jacobi usually had waiting for her.

"Quiet like cemetery," he said in a heavily accented voice. "Jacobi sleep like baby."

At nearly forty, Marsha was the youngest person on her block. She estimated there were at least thirty-five or forty years difference between her age and that of her next youngest neighbor.

The old housing area Marsha shared with her elderly neighbors was one of the poorest and most forgotten in the city. Less than four blocks away, the towers of Brookside Manor loomed over everything. Originally built to provide low-income housing for some of the city's poorest residents, the four multi-story buildings served as a warren for prostitutes, drug dealers, gangs, and garden variety thugs. Most of the residents between eighteen and forty didn't work and lived off government benefits. The temptation for fast cash offered by selling drugs and pimping prostitutes was difficult to turn down, and few did.

Not long after Marsha moved to Omaha she found the old house she now called home. After checking the house for defects, Marsha decided it had what she considered "good bones." The realtor who handled the deal hadn't been able to get away from the neighborhood fast enough, fearing for the safety of his Lexus SUV. Despite its age and need for many repairs, the old house was still better than the apartment Marsha had been living in.

It took a considerable effort for anyone living in the two blocks to accept Marsha. No one understood why someone as young as Marsha would choose to live there. But Marsha persisted by talking to her neighbors when she saw them and volunteering to make repairs. After a few months her neighbors were at her front door regularly and she was promoted to unofficial neighborhood repairman. For the most part, Marsha enjoyed talking to her neighbors. They were the grandparents she never knew and for the first time in her life she had a sense of family.

Over the next eighteen months Marsha gradually negotiated an agreement with local gang leaders, drug dealers, and prostitutes to keep the two blocks neutral ground, off limits to illegal activities or graffiti. She made trips into the projects and after recovering from the minor attacks on her person each time, she found some kids who needed help. She paired each kid with one of her neighbors who agreed to serve as surrogate grandparents. Although it had taken some of her personal money and some fast talking for donations of plants, a lawn mower, and a weed eater, the yards in the old neighborhood were starting to look pretty damn good.

"Go rest now," Jacobi said when Marsha handed him her cup. He reached out and ran crooked fingers over the top of her head. "Haircut soon," he added with a nod. Jacobi Hershberger was a retired barber who now cut hair for his neighbors and some of the local kids. It was his small contribution to neighborhood improvement.

"Next time I have a few days off I'll scrape your porch," she said as she grabbed the railing to pull herself up. "Paint's peeling."

Jacobi dismissed her with a wave of his hand. "Take care of Gertie's first. Been longer."

Marsha trudged across the street and up the steps to her front door, unlocked it, and leaned against it as she reset the alarm system. She stripped out of her clothes leaving a trail as she walked into the bathroom. She turned on the water and relieved herself while she waited for it to get hot. The hot water felt wonderful as it ran down her body and she knew she'd sleep like the dead as soon as she hit the sheets.

She didn't remember finishing her shower or falling into bed. She wrapped her arms lovingly around her body pillow and brought it close as she would a lover, her fingers stroking the pillowcase. She sighed as Blondie wandered into her mind and nestled against her.

Marsha popped up quickly when 'Stars and Stripes Forever' played loudly on the nightstand. She grabbed the offensive phone and stared at the number displayed on the screen. Why the hell would the station be calling her now? She pushed the button on the side of the phone and silence fell blessedly over the room. She was beginning to feel Blondie invading her mind for the second time when the music sounded once more. Without getting up, she pulled the phone to her ear and answered.

"What the fuck do you want? If it's my first born anything, you're in for a helluva long wait," she said sharply into the phone. "I'm not into the egg meets sperm thing."

"I don't appreciate being stood up," an equally sharp voice retorted.

"I left a fuckin' note. We'll do it another day. Breakfast isn't exactly on the endangered list, you know?"

"I've been gone a few days and missed talking with you," Colleen said, her voice softening slightly.

"If you made a bet and it's your challenge to make the homely girl feel special, tell 'em you did. I'll cover your ass," Marsha snorted.

"What?"

"Give me a fuckin' break," Marsha mumbled as she turned the phone off and dropped it into its holder.

A TAP AT Colleen's office door caught her still staring at the phone in her hand. She couldn't believe Marsha hung up on her. "Come in," she said and placed the receiver back in its cradle.

"How's it going, gorgeous?" a smiling woman with medium-length caramel-colored hair said as she entered.

"Beverly! What brings you to Omaha? Mom send you to check up on me?" Colleen asked as she stood and moved around her desk to hug the woman she'd known since high school. They sat down and settled in for a chat.

"Nope. Just a little business, but since no one else was all that stoked about coming to Omaha, I volunteered. They didn't need to know that I was planning to combine a little personal visit with business. Besides I can write off the whole trip and have a generous expense account. Ready to party, girlfriend?"

"Uh, like you said, this is Omaha. I've heard a few people refer to it as Oma-ho-hum."

"So why'd you choose it? I'm sure you could have found something in a more up-scale city."

Colleen looked down at her hands. "It suits me for now."

"So how is your social life post-Rusty?" Beverly frowned as she looked at Colleen. She squeezed her hands into fists. "If I could've gotten to her, you'd never have to worry about her again. You know that, right?"

Colleen reached out and placed a hand over one of Beverly's fists. "Of course I do, but it was something I needed to do myself. I certainly didn't want my best friend in prison with her."

"I'm still a pretty fast runner," Beverly said with a grin. Then she opened her hands and relaxed. "So what's this town got to entertain their lesbian population? And you know they have one, mixed in somewhere with the rest of corn-fed everything."

"Honestly, Bev, I haven't been here long enough to look. I know there's a pretty nice club in Charlotte, in case you ever go there."

"Did you score?"

Colleen shook her head. "Chickened out. I'm not ready yet, Bev. I haven't even finished unpacking here. Why don't you come over tonight and I'll fix dinner?"

"Are you kidding? You cook about as well as I do. Plus I'm here on an expense account, remember? We'll find something to do. Who knows, I might even run into one of those wholesome types who can actually cook."

"Alice wouldn't like that. Besides, if I remember correctly, you never cared if they could cook," Colleen laughed. "Write down where you're staying and I'll pick you up around seven. Is that good?"

"Perfect. Maybe I can get in a power nap before you show up."

Beverly stood and Colleen walked her to the office door. She leaned down and gave her friend a kiss on the cheek and hugged her tightly. "I've missed talking to you, Bev. How long will you be here?"

"Two glorious days. I fly out Monday morning unless our client wants to quibble."

"Then we'll make them two fun-filled days since I'm off for the weekend."

"See you tonight then."

AFTER SEVERAL HOURS of uninterrupted sleep, Marsha felt much better. The only problem was that it was going on ten at night. It was her night off and she tossed and turned, trying to go back to sleep. Nothing worked. Frustrated, she grabbed her phone and punched in a speed dial number.

"Speak to me, baby. I promise you won't be sorry," the voice on the other end quipped.

"You'll make it worth my while, huh?" Marsha asked.

"Hey, Marsh! Where the hell you been, baby cakes? I haven't seen you prowling around after dark lately."

"I work nights, remember? What're you doin', Trish? Anything exciting I should know about?" Patricia Longoria had become Marsha's friend not long after she moved to Omaha. They'd met at a bar and whiled an evening away making up stories about the women who came in. Not that either one of them had scored, but it passed the time. Marsha had spoken to her on-air several times, and Trish had called in a few requests, but they hadn't seen one another in nearly a month. Marsha liked Trish's offbeat sense of humor and her eclectic fashion sense. Trish had a magnetic personality that seemed to make people gravitate to her. Marsha envied her friend.

"I'm perusing the pickings at the Queen's Court, my dear. Join me for a few drinks and then even we'll look good...at least to each other," Trish said with a giggle. "Whoa, hello, smoking hot mama," she breathed with a sigh.

"Find a new dream girl?" Marsha chuckled.

"Yeah, and the bitch actually smiled and waved at me. Be still, my thumping heart! You coming down to stare at the eye candy or what?"

"Thinking about it."

"That's your problem, Marsh. You think too damn much. You have to learn to accept what you get."

"Since I never get anything, I won't be disappointed. I'll be there in about an hour," Marsha said.

"The place will be jumping by eleven. You know no self-respecting queer's gonna make an appearance before then. Since I have absolutely no self-respect I'll save you a seat, providing I don't have to beat 'em off me with a stick."

A little after eleven, Marsha paid her cover charge at the front door of The Queen's Court and held out her hand to be stamped. She self-consciously straightened her slacks, making sure her shirt was neatly tucked in. It was the same outfit she usually wore if she decided to spend a little time at The Court. In fact, it was her best outfit. She hated tucking her shirts in, but liked the soft, well-worn feel of the long sleeved light blue work shirt. It glowed faintly under the black lights that dotted the interior of the club. Combined with her black, sharply creased jeans, it made her feel moderately attractive, at least to her eyes. She made her way to the front bar and ordered a beer before sauntering nonchalantly through the growing crowd, searching for Trish. Then she spotted a group of men and women gathered around someone and she couldn't suppress a grin. Trish was short, but attempted to over-compensate by wearing brightly colored, almost neon, clothing usually accompanied by huge loopy earrings that would make an African tribal princess proud. Her open, friendly smile and sharp wit never failed to attract a group of club patrons.

"Nice outfit," Marsha quipped as she joined the group, many of them familiar from previous visits.

"Hey Marsh," a tall, slim young man said as he threw his arm around her shoulders and leaned in for an air kiss. "We've been waiting for you."

"Hi. Ronnie," Marsha replied. "I bet."

"Save me a dance for later, okay?" Ronnie asked.

"Yeah," Marsha answered with a laugh as she looked at him. "Let me know when you're ready to get your toes stepped on."

"Didn't you wear that same outfit last time?" Trish asked as her eyes perused Marsha, making her feel slightly uncomfortable.

"It's comfortable," Marsha said, setting her beer on the table that obviously was Trish's. "So, what have I missed?"

"Not much," Trish answered as she and Marsha slid into the booth while the others drifted away to dance or cruise for a temporary partner.

Over her next three beers Marsha leaned back and observed the women in the crowd. Occasionally she would work up enough courage to ask a woman to dance. Many turned her down, but Trish encouraged her to keep asking. Marsha wasn't a great dancer, in her opinion, but Trish reminded her that the goal was to enjoy the feel of another woman in her arms.

Just as Marsha was preparing to call it a night, Trish slapped her on the arm. By then Marsha had broken out in a sweat and rolled her shirt sleeves up. The slap stung, but Trish wrapped her hand around Marsha's arm and squeezed.

"Ow!" Marsha hissed as she jerked her arm away and rubbed it.

"That hurt, Trish."

"I've just found the perfect little woman for you," Trish said, staring across the room. She brought her arm up and pointed.

Marsha slapped her hand down. "God, could you be any more obvious? It's rude to point, you know?"

"How could you have missed that one, Marsh? She's fuckin' adorable!"

"She looks about twelve," Marsha snorted.

Trish leaned closer. "Maybe, but her boobs tell me she's legal." She shoved Marsha. "Go on, you big chicken."

Marsha set her drink down and shyly made her way across the bar toward the young woman. As she got closer, she had to admit the woman looked older than she first thought. She glanced over her shoulder at Trish, who waved her on. The woman seemed a little out of place and Marsha couldn't imagine why no one was asking her to dance. She wore a short black cocktail dress and low pumps, she was shorter than Marsha. Her dark hair lay smoothly to just below her ears, the ends curved slightly toward her chin. She smiled shyly as Marsha shoved her hands into her jean pockets and stopped to lean against the wall next to her.

When the next song started, it was one of Marsha's favorites. She sucked in a deep breath and turned toward the woman. "Would you like to dance?" Marsha asked, expecting to be rejected.

"Thank you," the woman answered. "I would like to."

"I understand," Marsha said. Then she looked at the woman. "Really?"

"My name is Nora," the woman said, extending a hand.

"Marsha," she said taking the delicate hand. Marsha was so surprised that Nora had accepted an offer to dance that she couldn't come up with a snappy response. She held Nora's hand and led her onto the floor and paused a moment to pick up the beat of the music as Nora stepped into her arms.

"I'm not a very good dancer," Nora said with her arms resting on Marsha's shoulders.

"Then you're in good company because neither am I," Marsha said. She turned her head toward Nora's and inhaled the sweet scent of her shampoo.

"I'm new here," Nora said in a low voice. "It's taken me a month to get up the courage to come to a women's club. I've heard so much about them that I was a little afraid to come."

"Everyone here is pretty harmless. It wouldn't hurt anyone's feelings if you said no."

"To what?"

"Anything that makes you uncomfortable. You're beautiful," Marsha blurted.

"Thank you, I guess."

"I'm not hitting on you, Nora. You just looked lonely standing there all by yourself. Honestly, I was shocked when you said yes to this dance. Most people, like myself, are afraid to ask a beautiful woman to dance. Afraid of rejection, I suppose. That's just the way beautiful people are."

"Not always," Nora said, sounding insulted.

"No, not always, but from my experience, most of the time."

When the dance ended, Marsha escorted Nora back to where she'd found her. "Thank you, Nora. I hope you'll come back to the Court again sometime. Once the others get to know you, I'm sure your dance card will be full."

Nora leaned closer to Marsha and kissed her cheek. "Thanks, Marsha."

"Way to go, Marsh," Trish said when she returned to the dwindling group.

"Where'd everyone go?" Marsha asked.

"Dancing and milling around," Trish answered. She sat in her booth and took a deep breath. "Join me. I need to take a load off, literally."

Marsha ordered another beer and pulled a small notebook from her back pocket. She looked around and began writing her observations down, including her brush with the beautiful Nora. Observing women at The Court provided filler when there was a lull during her show. She'd watched women argue, make up, make out, luck out, get lucky, and generally trample through a vast assortment of emotions. It helped her identify with her audience of lonely listeners and made her a little sad that there were so many others like her. She hadn't always been this way, but it was the life that worked for her now. The Court seemed to have more than its fair share of women who had come in alone, hoping to make some kind of connection with another human being.

Marsha scooted back to rest her back against the wall at the end of the booth and took a long drink from her bottle as she watched two women on the dance floor who were oblivious to the bodies around them. They were totally lost in one another. *Didn't I meet you two in a lesbian novel a couple of months ago?* she thought with a smile. *Probably in every lesbian novel I've ever read,* she chuckled. A tall, slender, raven-haired beauty dressed in expensive form-fitting, stone-washed designer jeans and a cream-colored silk blouse, held a slightly shorter, equally slim and well-dressed blonde in her arms, pressing their bodies close in a way that virtually screamed "I want you."

Marsha wagered with herself that one or both women also had taunting blue eyes. What was it the books always said? Blue pools waiting to wash over the main character, or blue orbs in the moonlight casting new light into the soul of whoever, or some crap like that. Marsha snorted at her thoughts. She felt pathetic, sitting in a darkened booth and trying desperately to lead a vicarious personal life through her fantasies about total strangers.

"Take it easy on the beer," Trisha said. "It'll stunt your growth, you know."

Laughter bubbled out of Marsha and she smacked the table with her hand, rattling the empty bottles that occupied the space in front of her. "That's a good one, Trish. You want another one of whatever that slushy pink thing with the green umbrella is you're drinking?"

"No, thanks. If I happen to get lucky, I want to remember it in the morning for my memoirs. I'll let you know if you strike out as usual."

"I appreciate that. I'm splitting after this beer anyway. Then I can sleep it off before I have to spend another long night," she lowered her voice seductively, "*In the Midnight Hour.*"

While she was entertaining herself watching couples dance, Marsha caught a flash of straight light blonde hair that fluttered slightly as the woman walked. She shook her head and slid farther back into the shadows. She shouldn't have ordered that last beer. Unable to tear her eyes away, she watched as Colleen Walters and an attractive companion searched for an empty table. As the couple paused to order drinks, Colleen gazed around the club and when she smiled, Marsha clearly saw the dimples form near her mouth. Marsha was pretty certain Colleen Walters hadn't seen her.

Colleen rested her hand comfortably on her companion's shoulder and whispered something in her ear. They both laughed as they carried their drinks to a vacant table near the dance floor. Then the stunning woman with caramel-colored hair pulled Colleen toward the dance floor. Marsha felt her breath stop as Colleen wrapped an arm over her companion's shoulder and played with her hair as they moved into the crowd of women. The two were obviously close and Marsha felt the hair near her neck tingle as Colleen absently played with her dance partner's hair. She had once danced with another woman in the same way. Then it was all gone. Marsha didn't want to look away, but she did before her thoughts drove her crazy. She grabbed her pen and scribbled more notes into the small notebook.

"Dance?" a pleasant tenor voice asked from next to their booth.

Marsha glanced up to see a ruggedly handsome young woman whose military haircut seemed appropriate. The woman looked nervous as she stood next to their table. She wore a light blue and yellow plaid shirt over a yellow t-shirt that was tucked neatly into her faded blue jeans. She moved from foot to foot, her hands jammed into her front pockets while she waited for an answer.

Trish blinked and her mouth opened and closed in an attempt to say something. She reminded Marsha of a guppy at feeding time until Trish finally managed to speak. "Are...are you speaking to me?"

In all the time she and Trish had been taking up space in The Court, no one had ever asked either of them to dance. Marsha had to smile at what was very possibly the only contingency neither had anticipated.

The young woman with the military cut leaned closer. "I've been working up the courage to ask if you'd like to dance all evening," she repeated with a devastating lop-sided grin.

"Me?" Trish squeaked out.

"She'd love to," Marsha answered for her tongue-tied friend.

"How do you know?" the woman asked as she narrowed her eyes. "Are you a couple?"

"Just friends, but this is the first time she's been speechless in years," Marsha said. "I think she likes you."

"Who are you?"

"How rude of me," Marsha answered. "I'm Marsha and this temporarily mute woman is my best friend, Trish. If you hold your hand out, I'm sure she'll take it."

"I'm Mattie." She looked back at Trish and winked. "Come on, cutie. It's just a dance." She leaned closer to Trish. "I promise to be on my very best behavior." She leaned even closer and whispered huskily, "Even though I'd rather take you home and have my way with you."

Trish looked across the table at Marsha before her mouth broadened into a devilish grin. There was something almost feral about it. Trish gingerly took Mattie's hand and stood. "Please don't change anything on my account," she flirted. "Especially very bad behavior." She then wrapped an arm around Mattie's and set off for the dance floor.

Marsha watched as Mattie took Trish into her arms and brought their bodies so close together no light was visible between them. Mattie wasn't much of a dancer, preferring what Marsha called the lesbian sway. Since Mattie didn't have to concentrate on what her feet were doing, her hands were free to roam. The sheer bliss on Trish's face as she buried it against Mattie's chest made Marsha smile. For all the kidding they both did, she knew both of them missed feeling a woman in her arms. Marsha had experienced that kind of intimacy once, but knew she never would again.

Marsha didn't know how much time had passed until Mattie escorted Trish back to the table. "I have to go to work tonight, but can I see you tomorrow morning?" Mattie asked. "I get off at seven."

"In the *morning*? Is the sun even up that early?" Trish asked, looking astonished at the idea.

Mattie leaned down and dotted Trish's neck with kisses. "I can fix you breakfast," Mattie announced seductively. "And serve it to you in bed."

God! Marsha thought with a smile. The woman was like a puppy, eager to please. She must be related to Boomer. "Where do you work, Mattie?"

"I'm a firefighter."

Marsha glanced at Trish who looked positively enamored. Mattie leaned down and engulfed Trish's mouth in a devastating kiss before waving good-bye. A moment later she slid to a halt back at their table, panting slightly. "Address," she exhaled quickly.

Trish recuperated from her stunned appearance and grabbed Marsha's pen and a damp napkin, scribbling her address on it.

"Think she'll really show up?" Marsha asked after Mattie dashed off.

"Doubtful, but miracles have been known to occur," Trish answered with a shrug.

"She's cute."

"Yeah, for a twelve-year-old," Trish sighed. "I'm sorry I made fun of you earlier." She buried her face in her hands for a moment before sitting up dramatically and re-arranging herself. "God, I've been reduced to cradle robbing! How humiliating!"

"No, you haven't! Maybe she's older than she looks. Maybe she's thirteen."

Trish suddenly sucked in a deep breath and her eyes widened. Marsha swiveled her head to see what had gotten her friend's attention. Her eyes came to rest on a perfectly rounded pair of delicious-looking breasts peeking out of a low cut, bright red blouse, standing next to their booth. The cleavage in front of her looked strangely familiar and was deep enough to swipe her credit card through, causing Marsha to involuntarily lick her lips. She became fascinated by the steady in and out movement of the fabric as the woman breathed. She stared at the form in front of her in awe for a few moments before blinking hard. "Fuuuck me," she breathed.

"Was that a proposition?" a smooth, silky voice asked with amusement.

Marsha squeezed her eyes shut. A long-time admirer of well-formed, but not too large, breasts, she opened her eyes slowly, imagining the delights lying within the depths of the magnificent cleavage before her. "A lesbian's wet dream," Marsha answered, her voice reverent.

"Dance?" the voice asked softly. A well-manicured hand appeared and waited for Marsha to take it. She dropped her eyes to shapely hips and a clearly defined waist. Her eyes once again rose to linger on the perfect breasts. Daring to let her eyes travel farther north over the landscape of the statuesque body in front of her, Marsha swallowed hard at the sight of smiling full red lips and hazy, deep blue eyes, without taking in the features as a whole. This was definitely a femme's femme, she thought. The body in front of her was the dream of every butch, semi-butch, soft butch, or just plain old horny woman in the bar. Marsha was willing to accept any of those descriptions when she finally convinced her body to move. Before she could take the offered hand, however, the music ended.

"Damn," Trish sighed. "The song's over. That was a close one."

It had been a close call, one Marsha would probably dream about for the next year. She leaned back in her seat feeling strangely relieved after her brush with temptation. "There'll be another one," the voice said.

As soon as the music started, Marsha reached out to the offered hand again and held it a moment. She stood as tall as her body would allow and prayed she would magically transform into the woman who lived in her mind. She was certain Blondie would forgive this one transgression with reality. She knew that later she wouldn't remember much about dancing with the woman in the low-cut red blouse, but as slender arms pulled her closer, she didn't really give a shit. The woman was tall and thin, and Marsha couldn't prevent the lascivious grin on her face as her cheek rested comfortably against the woman's. For the first time, she knew where Heaven was located. It was literally right in front of her and had a heady, intoxicating fragrance. She wondered if she tasted as good as she smelled and licked her lips.

Chapter Seven

"ARE YOU SURE you don't need some help?" Beverly asked as she propped Marsha against the wall next to the door to Colleen's new condo.

"I'll be fine," Colleen said. She couldn't stop a smile as she looked at Marsha, who was attempting to keep her legs from folding beneath her. "Just help me get her to the couch so she can sleep it off."

Beverly pressed a hand against the center of Marsha's chest and shrugged as she looked at her. "Well, she's kinda cute in a strange way, but doesn't really look like your type." Marsha started listing precariously to her right and Beverly was forced to readjust her grip on the inebriated woman. As she straightened her back up, she said with a grunt, "Plus I can pretty much guarantee she won't be capable of doing much, if that's what you're thinking."

"Don't be ridiculous, Bev. We work together at the station. In fact, she's the hostess of our most listened to show, moving into regional syndication. It didn't feel right leaving her passed out in a booth and there was no way her friend was going to get her out of there."

"Really?" Bev bent her knees to get a better look at Marsha's face and tilted her head back.

"She has an amazing voice when she's not slurring." Colleen grunted as they guided Marsha into the condo and let her fall onto the large living room sofa. "Sorry, but if you could call a cab to take you back to your hotel, I'd appreciate it."

"No problem," Beverly said as Colleen began pulling Marsha's shoes off. She shoved a pillow under her head and drew a small lap quilt from the back of the sofa to cover her body. She brushed Marsha's hair back and slid her glasses off, smiling at the woman who had fallen soundly asleep in seconds, emitting an adorable squeak.

Beverly rejoined Colleen. "The cab will be here in a few minutes and I told them I'd be outside.

"I'm sorry about this, Bev."

"It's fine. I have to be up early in the morning for a meeting anyway." She laughed. "I can't wait to tell Rosemary that her daughter moved to Omaha to become a Good Samaritan for needy drunks."

"She will never believe that," Colleen said, shaking her head. "Up for dinner again tomorrow night?"

"You mean tonight?" Beverly asked, glancing at her wristwatch.

Colleen laughed before covering her mouth to prevent waking Marsha. Beverly looked over Colleen's shoulder. "Don't worry. An atomic explosion couldn't wake her now." She hugged Colleen. "Thanks for an interesting evening."

Beverly left shortly afterward. Colleen checked on a softly snoring Marsha before shutting the lights off and making her way into her bedroom. She wished she remembered where she'd put her hand-held tape recorder. Then she could prove that Marsha snored once and for all, but she was tired and could smell the cigarette smoke from the club on her body. She slipped out of her clothing, hanging her blouse and bra over the bedroom door knob and stepped into the shower to allow the hot water to cascade down her tired body. She crawled into bed nearly half an hour later and fell into a deep sleep.

MARSHA'S EYES FLUTTERED open into blurry slits and she groaned as she sat up and rubbed her face with both hands. She didn't remember taking the bus home or flopping onto her couch to fall asleep. Like most nights after an evening at the club, she was more than ready to stretch out in a more comfortable position and dream of Blondie. She stood and wandered toward the back of her house, bumping into a wall or two while awkwardly stripping her clothes off. She had to wash clothes on Saturday anyway and would pick them up then. She climbed beneath the covers naked and groaned at the feel of the softness of her mattress. She stretched and wiggled around a little to find the best position for sleep.

A hand on her hip surprised her and she mumbled, "Tonight's not a good night, Blondie. I'm really wasted, baby."

Blondie didn't answer and her hand slid slowly up Marsha's abdomen to rest between her breasts. In every dream, the only way to get rid of Blondie was to satisfy her. And Marsha knew she could do that, even if she was still half asleep and recovering from too many drinks. She turned toward the sleeping fantasy and began placing soft kisses along the side of Blondie's face, continuing along her jaw and onto her throat as she ran a hand into the long blonde hair.

Blondie jerked away slightly, but Marsha found her lips and settled into a deep kiss. Blondie's hand found the back of Marsha's neck and pulled her closer as her lips parted to invite Marsha's tongue inside. It was a more eager kiss than Marsha was accustomed to, but it had been a while since she had taken the time to really make love to Blondie. Obviously the fantasy woman had missed her.

"God, you're so damn hot, baby," Marsha managed in a raspy voice.

For an instant Marsha became lost in the softness of Blondie's lips as she responded eagerly to Marsha. She arched into Marsha as Marsha's hand slid under her shirt and caressed her breast. Then unexpectedly Blondie's hands grasped Marsha's shoulders. She twisted her head and pushed Marsha away roughly. A sharp stinging slap across her face finally awakened Marsha. Until then she had been enjoying the best fuckin' dream she'd ever had.

Chapter Eight

IN A FLURRY of movement, Colleen threw the bedcovers back and leaped out of bed, jerking the t-shirt she had worn to bed down to cover her exposed breasts. On the other side of the bed Marsha attempted to rub the sting from her cheek as she scrambled around the floor trying to locate her own clothing. She could hear Colleen breathing heavily through her mouth working to get herself under control.

"What the fuck were you doing?" Colleen gasped at the end of a deep breath.

Marsha finally managed to stick an arm in a sleeve she hoped belonged to her and wiggle into to a pair of panties lying near the shirt. "Well, what the fuck are you doing in my house?" she shouted as a reply.

"I'm not in your house! This is my apartment!" Colleen yelled back.

"How did I get here?"

"A friend helped me drag you back here after you passed out at the bar. Obviously not one of my better ideas," Colleen said. Her chest heaved when she leaned over and turned on a lamp on her nightstand. "Jesus!"

"Turn it off!" Marsha demanded.

"I can't see a damn thing without it," Colleen snapped.

"That's a good thing," Marsha snapped back. "Give me a minute and I'll be out of here."

Colleen glanced at the illuminated dial of the clock next to the light and picked it up. "It's four-thirty in the morning," she huffed. She set the clock down hard. "You can wander around in the dark like a fuckin' bat if you want to, but I'm going to fix a cup of coffee." On her way out of the room, Colleen flipped on the light and slammed the door closed. A second later she opened the door again and stuck her hand through the crack. "Pretty sure those are my panties," she added, snapping her fingers.

Marsha pulled the panties off and placed them in Colleen's hand. "Damn. That was a great dream," she muttered as she stood next to the bed dumbly looking around for the rest of her clothes and absently scratching her ass. She jumped when Colleen tapped at the bedroom door and cracked it open again, shoving a pile of clothing into the bedroom.

"Thanks." Marsha took the clothes.

"My pleasure," Colleen replied sarcastically.

A few minutes later, Marsha hesitantly opened the bedroom door and peeked into the front room. She craned her neck to look around and saw a now-dressed Colleen leaning against a kitchen counter holding a coffee mug with both hands. There was no way Marsha would be able to exit the posh-looking apartment without drawing Colleen's attention. Marsha was certain there would be a million questions to which she would have no answers. She blinked as she stared at the attractive woman and watched as she used an index finger to draw her blonde hair behind her ear. Marsha shook her head and glanced down, watching her hand curl into a fist. Her fingertips tingled as she remembered the velvety softness of Colleen's hair. She shook her hand out to make the feeling stop.

She couldn't remain in Colleen's bedroom all damn day and tried to think of what she could possibly say once they were face-to-face. She didn't remember how she'd gotten to the apartment in the first place. She rubbed her face briskly with both hands before opening the bedroom door. She sucked in a deep breath and walked out, showing more confidence than she felt. After all, she made a living talking. How hard could this be?

Colleen swallowed a sip from her cup. Marsha couldn't tell much about what she was thinking from her eyes. "Coffee?" Colleen asked coolly.

Marsha jerked her thumb over her shoulder and attempted a grin. "Thanks, but I'd better pass. I'm sure I've already worn out my welcome." She bit her bottom lip and spun around to leave. She stopped and looked back at Colleen. "Can you tell me which way the nearest bus stop is from here?"

Colleen finished her coffee and rinsed her mug out before turning back to face Marsha. "I have no idea where the bus stop is, but I think now would be a good time for you to cash in that breakfast rain check. I'm starving and don't think well when I'm hungry. I know a good all-night diner not far from here."

"Thanks, but no thanks. I need to get home and finish sleeping off last night's buzz."

Colleen shrugged. "Your choice." She walked into the bedroom and returned carrying her shoulder bag. She took her car keys from a bowl centered on the kitchen table. "Let's go. I know I was there once, but you'll have to give me directions again."

Colleen disengaged the alarm and opened the apartment door. She waited until Marsha was in the hall before leaning in and re-arming her security system. They silently rode the elevator down to the parking garage. Colleen pressed a button on her key fob and Marsha saw the brake lights flash on a blue and white Mazda sports car, accompanied by a chirping sound.

Marsha opened the passenger door and waited for Colleen to toss a bundle of papers into the rear of the car before getting in. She fastened her seat belt a second before Colleen threw the car into reverse and backed out of her assigned parking space. She braked as she piloted the vehicle around massive concrete pillars separating the garage levels and approached a metal barrier onto the street ahead.

Colleen stopped long enough to punch in her code and waited as the gate rose. She accelerated to the edge of the main street in front of her condo and glanced both ways before entering the mostly vacant street. She pressed a button on the driver's door and the windows lowered smoothly. The wind through the car blew Colleen's long blonde hair away from her face as she guided her car around the few others on the road at almost five in the morning.

"Drive to the station," Marsha said loud enough to be heard over the wind whipping through the car windows. "I can catch a bus there in about twenty minutes."

Colleen glanced at Marsha quickly and shook her head. "I'm starving."

"Drop me off at the bus stop, then go to IHOP," Marsha said.

"Actually, I'm getting a little tired of IHOP, aren't you?" Colleen signaled and turned sharply onto another street.

"I'm not hungry," Marsha said.

"Then you'll get to watch me eat," Colleen said with a smile. She slowed as she approached a well-lit diner and swung into a parking space in front of the already busy business. She unfastened her seat belt and ran a hand through her hair. When she opened the door she looked across the seat at Marsha. "Well, you coming?"

"I told you I wasn't hungry."

"Then get a cup of coffee. Maybe it'll make you less grumpy," Colleen teased.

"I'm not grumpy," Marsha muttered.

Colleen laughed. "I haven't seen a pout like that since my niece was told she couldn't kill her little brother." She stood and then leaned back down a moment later. "And by the way, you not only snore, you squeak as well." She closed her door before walking to the door of the diner and shoving it open.

Marsha leaned her head back against the car seat and closed her eyes. All she wanted was to go home, take a quick shower, and fall into bed, with the real Blondie this time. Her lips curled into a smile as she envisioned Blondie beckoning to her, but the smile disappeared when Blondie looked up at her and the face she saw was Colleen's. Marsha sat up and rubbed her face to erase the image. She threw the car door open and stepped out of the vehicle, straightening her clothes the best she could before entering the diner.

Colleen was drinking a cup of coffee and glancing through a newspaper an earlier patron had left behind. She looked over the top of the paper when Marsha stepped up to her table. "Change your mind?" she asked.

"Yeah. I was getting a crick in my neck from dozing," Marsha said.

An older woman approached the table and picked up the empty cup in front of Marsha. "Cream?" she asked, filling the cup.

"Please," Marsha said.

"Your breakfast will be up in a minute, honey," the waitress said to Colleen. She looked back at Marsha. "You want something, too?"

Marsha shook her head and took a sip of her coffee. Colleen's breakfast, which looked delicious, was served a few minutes later, along with a coffee refill for Marsha. Marsha sipped her coffee and watched Colleen chew the last of her breakfast. Colleen swallowed and washed the bite down with coffee before settling back in her chair and taking a deep, satisfied breath.

"Feel better?" Marsha asked.

"Much. Now what?"

"We should talk, I guess. You know, about last night, or this morning, I guess," Marsha answered with a shrug.

"Why? Nothing happened."

I might have been drunk, but that kiss sure as hell felt like something to me, Marsha thought with a frown.

"Nothing like last night has ever happened to me," Colleen finally admitted. "It's a little unsettling."

Marsha bristled. "Why? Because it was me you lip-locked with?"

"No. It's just that...well, honestly...," Colleen started.

"What?"

"I...uh...I haven't been intimate with anyone for a long time."

"You mean you haven't been intimate with anyone like me."

"Don't put words in my mouth, Marsha. That isn't what I meant at all." Colleen swallowed a gulp of her coffee. "There's nothing I can say that you won't take the wrong way, is there?"

Marsha shook her head. "Probably not."

"Last night was my first foray into the lesbian social world of Omaha."

"Not exactly what you thought it would be, huh?"

"It was like every other place women go to get together," Colleen said with a shrug.

Marsha leaned forward slightly and lowered her voice. "But you didn't expect to find yourself in bed with me."

Colleen smiled. "No. I didn't expect that. I thought it was a dream." She ran her tongue across the bottom of her upper teeth. "Of course, there was a time that would have been exactly what I was looking for. A meaningless fling to satisfy myself. I'm sure you've done it. We all have at one time or another."

Marsha stared at the top of the table. "I never have," she mumbled.

"What?" Colleen asked, leaning closer to hear what Marsha was saying.

"I said I've never done that before," Marsha hissed.

"You're lying! You sure seemed to know what you were doing."

"I wasn't making love to you. I was making love to my dream woman...a fantasy. It wasn't you."

"Am I your dream woman?"

"Of course not. That's ridiculous," Marsha chafed.

"What's her name" Colleen asked.

"Who?"

"This fantasy woman you mistook me for."

"Blondie," Marsha mumbled as she brought her cup to her mouth.

"Original. You should let Blondie know you cheated on her last night. Or at least that you tried to," Colleen said, crossing her arms over her chest.

"I did not!" Marsha insisted.

"What would you have done if I hadn't awakened you?"

"Well...I..." Marsha started.

"Would you have made love to her?" Colleen asked. When Marsha didn't answer, Colleen grabbed her wrist. "Would you?"

"I...I always do," Marsha admitted. "She never rejects me."

"In other words you would have made love to *me*." Colleen combed her fingers through her hair and expelled a breath. "Look, Marsha, I like you very much, but-."

"I get it! It was a mistake," Marsha interrupted. "I understand."

Colleen flagged down their waitress and handed her a credit card.

"Um...you're not going to tell anyone at the station about this, are you?" Marsha asked.

"Why?"

"Because I'd have to sue you if you did. Then it might get in the papers and people would know who I am. It'd be a big mess. Besides, no one would believe you."

"Then I guess we're both in luck, because I wasn't planning to discuss it with anyone." Colleen sighed and reached across the table to place her hand over Marsha's.

Marsha stared at her hand, but didn't move it.

"I wouldn't let you, or anyone else, use me to get off. I wasn't drunk, just tired. I should have slapped you when you touched me. But I didn't because I'm adult enough to admit I probably wanted it. I haven't been intimate with anyone for a long time. I enjoyed it. Probably even needed it. Now let's get out of here." She dropped a few bills on the table and signed her name to the receipt.

Marsha opened the diner door for Colleen and followed her outside. Colleen slipped sunglasses on and looked around. "They have good food here," she said. She inhaled deeply and released it slowly "I'll take you home, then I'll be out of your hair."

Marsha finally took a deep breath and glanced up and down the street. "You're actually Blondie's twin. If we hadn't had that accident or moment or whatever you want to call it last night, I wouldn't have a snowball's chance in hell of being with someone like you."

"You must think I'm terribly shallow," Colleen said as they walked toward her car.

"Most people are. Look at me! I'm plainer than dirt, skinny as a scarecrow, have out of control hair, wear glasses and can't even keep those straight on my damn face. I try to avoid mirrors because I prefer to see myself as I am in my mind. The only thing I have going for me is my voice, but if my so-called 'fans' ever saw what I really looked like, *In the Midnight Hour* would go down faster than the Titanic."

Colleen shook her head as she fastened her seat belt. "So you're looking for a woman who's skinny and plain looking. That would make you happy?"

"Yes...no. Never mind. You couldn't understand." Marsha said as she exhaled.

COLLEEN DROVE MARSHA home and insisted on following her into the house. She felt surprisingly comfortable in the small home, but was a little disappointed not to find any personal photographs that might help her understand why Marsha was the way she was. Marsha had done everything within her power to stay as far away from her as possible. She sat on the upholstered couch in the compact living room and said, "What would you like to do now?"

"Be alone."

Colleen stood. "Then I guess it's time for me to go. I have dinner plans with an old friend this evening."

"The same friend you were with last night?"

Colleen nodded, but didn't feel the need to say anything further.

"From what little I can remember about last night, she was beautiful. Would you have slapped her if you'd woke up with her in your bed?"

"I don't owe you an explanation," Colleen said.

"You're right, you don't. I'm sorry."

"Beverly and I have been friends since high school. I'll admit that when we were teenagers we played around a little. But we are much better at being friends than being lovers. Besides, her partner would come to Omaha and scratch my eyeballs out if she thought there was anything going on between us." Colleen smiled thinking about the demure, but fiery Alice.

"You could've just dropped me off, you know."

"That seemed a little rude to me. Besides I wanted to see the inside of your house. Maybe get a sense of the real you."

"Now you've seen it." Marsha swept her arm around. "Not much to write home about."

"It's cute. I like it," Colleen said.

MARSHA FOLLOWED COLLEEN onto the porch to escort her back to her car. She was relieved Colleen's sport car hadn't been stripped to the frame.

Halfway down the sidewalk, Marsha caught a blur out of the corner of her eye and intercepted a young boy, lifting him up and swinging his thin body around.

"What's up, Tariq?" she asked the giggling boy as she lowered him back to the ground.

"Gramma Gertie. She gots some new flowers to plant," the boy said.

"Really?" Marsha turned to look next door and waved at the old woman standing on the porch.

Tariq tugged on Marsha's t-shirt. "And she makin' brownies and lemonade," he added, jumping around, anxious to join the woman.

"Excuse me," Marsha said as she walked toward her neighbor. "Morning, Mrs. Funderburk," she called out. "Tariq said you have flowers to be planted. If you wait a few minutes I'll help you."

Gertie Funderburk came off the porch with the aid of her cane and met Marsha halfway. She placed a heavily blue-veined and liver-spotted hand on Marsha's arm. "I have enough for you too, dear. The nice man at the nursery was going to throw them away because he said they were dying. He gave them to me and had someone deliver them last night. Come see!"

Marsha rested a hand on Tariq's shoulder as they followed Gertie to the side of the house.

"I watered them and look how they've perked up," Gertie said.

Marsha stopped when she saw several pallets of plants spread out before her. She puffed her cheeks out and exhaled. "This will take most of the day, Mrs. Funderburk."

"It'll be beautimous," Tariq breathed out in awe.

Marsha took a set of keys from her pocket and handed them to the boy. "Open the garage and bring out the garden tools will ya, buddy. And see if you can round up some of the other kids to help."

"I'll make more brownies and lemonade," Gertie beamed as she turned toward the front of her house. She looked down the sidewalk at Colleen. "Invite your friend, honey. We'll have plenty."

Marsha returned to where Colleen was waiting. "I'm sorry, but something has come up. I'll see you at the station in a couple of days."

"What's going on?" Colleen asked.

Marsha looked back at Mrs. Funderburk. "According to Tariq, Miz Gertie's making brownies and lemonade in exchange for some gardening."

Colleen smiled. "Is your house still open?" she asked.

"Yeah, why?"

"The least I can do is help. I don't have any other plans, until tonight anyway."

Marsha started to leave then turned back around. "Um...would you mind scrambling up a couple of eggs for Tariq. I'm pretty sure he hasn't had anything to eat yet and will probably be in a sugar coma if he doesn't have anything else in his stomach besides brownies and lemonade."

Marsha separated the plants and was preparing to begin turning the soil in Gertie's front flower beds when a hand on her shoulder stopped her.

"Get Tariq, sweetie," Colleen said.

Marsha squinted up over her shoulder, but didn't acknowledge the special way she felt when Colleen called her sweetie. "Thanks," she said with a smile.

"You have a wonderful smile," Colleen said as she rested her arm around Marsha's shoulders as they walked. "You should use it more often. It's quite devilish."

Colleen poured Marsha a cup of coffee while they waited for Tariq to wolf down a plate full of bacon, scrambled eggs, and toast, accompanied by a glass of milk. "About last night..." Colleen started.

"It was a mistake." Marsha interrupted.

"Is that the way you see it?"

"That's the way it is," Marsha answered flatly. "That's the way it has to be. I can be your friend, but I can't ever be more than that. Non-negotiable."

Colleen frowned before shoving her chair away from the table and walking outside. A few minutes later five children followed her back into the house. Colleen smiled as each of them greeted Marsha with a kiss on the cheek and a hug. It wasn't long before the floor was littered with laughing children shoveling mounds of scrambled eggs into their mouths.

"You'll need more eggs, bacon, and bread," Colleen said as she re-took her seat across from Marsha.

"Thank you. I'm sure they appreciate a hot meal."

AS MARSHA FINALLY led the small troop of children outside, Colleen set plates and forks in the sink and began running water. She saw a young girl standing in the doorway to the kitchen, her arms holding more plates and glasses. Cornrows that fell nearly to her shoulders were decorated with colorful pony beads. When she smiled, Colleen noticed she was missing her two front teeth. The remaining white teeth stood out against her ebony skin.

"I kin he'p," the girl said.

"Thank you," Colleen said with a nod. "What's your name?"

"Jamila," the girl said.

"That's a pretty name. I'm Colleen."

"You Miz Marsha's friend?" Jamila lisped.

"Yes, I am. If I wash will you set the dishes in the drainer for me?"

Jamila nodded and spread a hand towel out on the counter next to the drainer. "For the glasses and cups," she said.

"Great idea," Colleen beamed.

After Jamila ran outside to dig in the dirt, Colleen spent a little time making Marsha's bed and picking up a few things to place in the laundry hamper before joining the work in progress. From the porch she observed children and elderly men and women digging, talking, and planting at nearly every house in the neighborhood. Occasionally the work was interrupted by a short water fight.

Colleen found a potato fork and started turning the dirt in the flower beds in front of Marsha's house. She was almost finished when she saw a gold older model Chevy Impala convertible low-rider moving slowly down the center of the street, its rear end bouncing up and down. The driver was an angry looking young black man. Three other men sat in the back seat and front passenger area. They all wore baseball caps with the bills turned to the side. Colleen was surprised when the vehicle U-turned at the end of the block and finally rolled to a stop behind her Mazda. As the men exited the vehicle, two approached her car and ran long fingers over the top. Their over-sized pants rode low on their hips, displaying silver gray undergarments, and seemed to pool around their ankles.

"Can I help you?" she asked pleasantly when they stopped in front of her.

"You don' live here," the young man in front stated. "Where's slim?" he asked, moving into Colleen's personal space and grinning to show off the gold star covering one of his large front teeth.

"*Marsha* is next door," Colleen answered, glaring into the man's eyes, but refusing to budge.

Marsha rounded the corner of the house pushing Tariq in the wheelbarrow. She stopped next to Colleen and released the handles. She lifted Tariq out and whispered something to him before patting him on the butt. Colleen tried not to smile when Marsha stepped protectively in front of her.

"Where's Kenyetta?" the man asked, his eyes still on Colleen. Although Marsha could look him in the eyes, he outweighed her by at least a hundred pounds. Colleen rested her hands on Marsha's shoulders. She felt muscles tighten beneath them.

"She's over at Hershberger's. Her mama need her?" Marsha squinted at the man.

He shook his head and snapped his fingers. The men behind him opened the trunk of the Impala and Colleen felt Marsha tense slightly for a moment. "Her mama sent lunch," the man said as the others lifted several aluminum containers from the trunk.

"Thank you, Ammon. Why don't you and your boys join us?" Marsha saw the men with him lick their thick lips hungrily.

"We got bidness." With another snap of his fingers the men shoved the containers toward Marsha and Colleen and quickly returned to the vehicle.

"Who is that?" Colleen asked.

"Local drug dealer and friends," Marsha answered. "He lives with Kenyetta and her mother. This week at least."

They carried the food into the house. Colleen placed as much as she could in the oven to stay warm while Marsha stacked containers of potato salad and deviled eggs into the refrigerator.

"Well," Marsha said as she stuck dirty hands in her back pockets. "If you like wings, potato salad, and deviled eggs, lunch seems to be a done deal."

"Have one of the kids bring some plants around and I'll get them in the ground for you," Colleen said as she reached out and wiped dirt from Marsha's cheek, letting her finger linger for a moment.

Marsha flinched and pulled away. "Sure thing."

About an hour later Marsha and a couple of the boys set up boards on sawhorses in Gertie's front yard and Colleen took the girls to get the food Kenyetta's mother had sent. It wasn't long before everyone had barbecue sauce smeared from ear to ear. Colleen watched Marsha interact with the only people she probably felt safe around, young kids with little future and senior citizens who'd basically already lived their lives.

AFTER EVERYONE ATE their fill of wings, potato salad, and argued over the last of the deviled eggs, Marsha turned on her front hose and held it for everyone to wash their hands and faces. She observed Colleen as she filled her hands with water and splashed it on her face. Her long blonde hair was piled haphazardly atop her head. Marsha smiled mischievously and slipped her thumb over the end of the hose, squirting a stream of water that ran into Colleen's shirt. She squealed as the cold water hit her skin. She grabbed the hose from Marsha, wrapping a hand around Marsha's arm before she could sprint away. They wrestled for a moment until Marsha was tackled by the children. They held her down, laughing, as Colleen stood over them with the hose bent in half in her hand.

"Don't do it," Marsha said through laughs. "You'll be sorry, woman."

"Promises, promises," Colleen smirked as she stuck the end of the hose into the neck of Marsha's shirt and released the bent hose, shooting the cold water down her chest.

With a nod from a still dripping Colleen, the children released Marsha, jumped up, and scattered, all to the laughter and delight of Marsha's older neighbors. Colleen's wet t-shirt clung to her upper body and it was all Marsha could do to tear her eyes away. Colleen wasn't wearing a bra and the chilled fabric outlined her hardened nipples and sent waves of sudden desire cascading along Marsha's spine.

Colleen winked when their eyes met and the tips of Marsha's ears began to feel as if they were on fire. Eventually a truce was called and the children began piling Marsha's tools into the wheelbarrow, putting them away for the day. Marsha's clothes were still wet by the time she hugged each child and sent them home before it got dark. She stood in her muddy front yard and looked at the work they had done that day.

"You should get those wet clothes off and take a hot shower," Colleen said, settling a warm hand on Marsha's shoulder.

"Yeah, you too," Marsha said. "You can borrow one of my t-shirts and head home. I can pretty much guarantee now that Ammon's boys have seen your car, it won't survive long after dark."

"I thought you said this was a neutral zone," Colleen said.

"Well, it's supposed to be, but the gangs around here aren't all that good at resisting temptation."

"What about your garage in back?"

"Full of garden stuff."

"It's a small car."

"You should leave before it gets any smaller. Only these two blocks are relatively safe."

"Are you trying to get rid of me, Barrett?"

"Nothing sneaks by you, does it?"

Marsha prepared a pot of coffee while Colleen showered and dressed. She kept an eye on Colleen's car. The days were becoming a little longer as early spring descended on Omaha and she welcomed the warmer temperatures. The sky looked clear, but within a month there would probably be periodic severe storms. She needed to check some of her neighbors' roofs to make sure they weren't missing any shingles.

"Your turn," Colleen announced as she entered the kitchen, wearing a clean heather gray KLEW t-shirt. Marsha smiled as she watched Colleen combing through her long blonde hair. She'd told Colleen she didn't remember much about the night before, but that had been a lie. She remembered the scent of Colleen's body as it filled her nostrils, the strength of her scent growing as her arousal began to awaken, the lightness of her touch, and the softness of her lips, especially the welcoming softness of her lips. She remembered the way her fingers slid easily through the silky hair. She didn't remember much after that. She didn't need to. That was enough. She shook her head to clear it.

"Oh, that smells amazing," Colleen said as she approached the fresh pot of coffee.

Marsha coughed after she swallowed. Colleen smelled amazing. "I'll take a shower after you leave," Marsha managed.

"Afraid I'll molest you in the shower?" Colleen teased over her shoulder.

Marsha cleared her throat and refused to look at her guest. "Have to let the hot water build up some."

Colleen took a long drink of her coffee. "I enjoyed today. Thanks for letting me help. The kids are a hoot."

"Yeah, they are." She argued with herself silently. Finally she bit the bullet and said, "I have a cook-out for them when school lets out for the summer. If you're still around, you might enjoy it."

"It's a pretty special thing you do for them."

"It's not much."

"If the station got behind it, you could really..."

"No!" Marsha said forcefully. "I won't use them that way. So everyone can give lip service to how terrible their lives are. They already know that, goddammit!"

Colleen held her hands up. "It was only a suggestion."

"Well, forget it. There are other ways to show them you care besides throwing money at their problem." Marsha set her cup down harder than she intended and rested her hands on the counter.

"At least let me donate my own money to help buy food." Colleen moved behind Marsha and placed her hands on her shoulders, massaging them lightly.

"Don't," Marsha said, shrugging Colleen's hands away. "Go home. Forget you were ever here. Please."

AS COLLEEN GOT in her car several minutes later, she glanced toward Marsha's house and saw the haunted looking woman staring back at her from the shadows of the front porch. She pulled away and signaled for a left-hand turn. Colleen drove onto the main artery into the city, running a hand through her still damp hair. Her mind drifted over the confusing past twelve hours. She had seen Marsha looking at her several times throughout the day, but hadn't been able to decipher what she'd seen in Marsha's eyes. Colleen smiled at a fleeting memory of Marsha kissing her while her hand sought contact with Colleen's skin. Colleen had to admit she had been aroused by the touch and wondered what might have happened if she'd reacted differently. After all, she responded to the kiss. During the day she had touched Marsha several times. Of course, they had been innocent touches. Or were they? Was she really hoping for a different reaction from Marsha? Colleen exhaled loudly. She had never been so confused about her feelings for another woman. But Marsha Barrett wasn't like any other woman she'd been attracted to. She was willing to admit she liked Marsha, but was she attracted to her?

THAT EVENING COLLEEN picked Beverly up at six-thirty and drove to a downtown restaurant that had a good reputation. Once they were seated at their table and placed a drink order, Bev looked across the candlelit table at her friend.

"How did your meeting go this morning?" Colleen asked.

"About the way I expected," Bev answered with a shrug. "Did your temporary houseguest make it home okay?"

"Yeah," Colleen smiled. "I drove her home pretty early and we spent the rest of the morning and most of the afternoon planting flowers around her neighborhood."

"Sounds very exciting," Bev said.

"It was different," Colleen said as their drinks were delivered. She tasted hers and nodded at the waiter. "Give us a few minutes, will you?"

"So are you interested or what?"

"What do you mean?"

"She's gay, isn't she?"

Colleen nodded. "Yes, but she's not interested in me."

"Did she give a reason for this non-interest?"

"I gather she thinks I'm too attractive."

"Really? I've never heard that one before."

"Neither have I, so I didn't have a response."

"But you like her, I'm guessing."

Colleen sighed and set her drink down. "I do. I'd like to spend more time getting to know her, but don't want to push her."

"Does she know how you feel?"

"I'm not sure." She frowned.

Bev downed the remainder of her drink and placed her glass back on the table. "But you haven't slept with her, have you?"

A blush spread over Colleen's face. "Not really," she muttered, then shrugged. "Sort of, in a way."

"That doesn't sound like you at all, Colleen."

"I know, I know. It just happened. I woke up and she was in bed with me. She claims it was a dream. It seemed like a dream to me too, for about half a minute. She kissed me and slid a hand under my shirt. I know I reacted when she touched me. I was aroused and wanted it so much. Then I woke up and slapped her." Colleen finished her drink in one long gulp.

"Then what?"

"Then nothing. I took her home and you already know the rest. Now I don't know what the hell to do, Bev."

Bev puffed her cheeks out and released a breath slowly. "Sounds like you need to have a mommy chat."

"I'm planning to fly home in a couple of weeks."

"Let me know how that turns out."

"I will. So how's your love life these days?"

"Definitely not as interesting as yours, but I can't complain. Alice is a very patient woman."

"Well, she does teach elementary school," Colleen kidded with a smile.

"Only during the day. When she comes home she still has to put up with my crap."

"She loves you, Bev. We put up with a lot when we're in love. Or...or believe we are."

"I'm pretty sure she'd never beat the shit out of me though."

"Like I said, you're a lucky woman. I appreciate having you and Alice as my friends."

Bev reached across the table and placed her hand over Colleen's and squeezed it lightly. "We always will be, sweetie. Does this woman, Marsha right? Does she know about Rusty?"

"No one here knows about Rusty and I've still got two more years before she's released. They're supposed to notify me before she gets out."

"Do you feel safe?"

"So far." She smiled. "Trust me, Rusty wouldn't be caught dead in a place as mundane as Omaha."

Chapter Nine

THE FOLLOWING SATURDAY was Marsha's weekend to work, but since she didn't have to go in until after eleven that night she found herself doing the same things she always did on a Saturday morning. She cleaned her house from ceiling to floor and went through her closet. She tried on every piece of clothing she owned, discarding some and throwing a few things she hadn't worn for a while into the laundry. She hated ironing, but unfortunately, the clothes she liked the most all required at least minimal ironing. She rearranged her clothes by color so she wouldn't have to look through everything to get dressed. She cleaned out her refrigerator and went through stacks of books, placing them in alphabetical order. She did the same with her CDs. She rationalized it would make her life more efficient. She even sucked it up and went to Jacobi's for a haircut. She gave the old man free rein and the much shorter hair would allow her more control of her curls.

Occasionally, Marsha thought about Colleen. She hadn't heard from her since the previous weekend. She was sure she wouldn't hear from her again. The harder she worked on cleaning her house, the more fragments of Colleen appeared. The hazy look in the depths of those amazing blue eyes when Colleen looked at her, the way her own body trembled when Colleen touched it. She wanted to tremble like that all the time, but knew it would never happen.

She hadn't heard from Trish either and that was a little unusual. She flopped down on her couch, popped open a soft drink, and punched a number into her phone. It was a weekend and Trish should be home. After several rings someone answered. "Hullo." The voice sounded sleepy.

"Trish?" Marsha asked.

"She took a load of laundry to the basement. She'll be back up in a minute. Who is this and I'll have her call you back in a few."

"Just tell her Marsha called. I haven't heard from her in a while and thought I'd check in to see if she was alright."

"Okay," the woman said, stifling a yawn. Marsha heard a door close in the background. She said, "It's Marsha, sweetie."

"Go back to bed, baby. I'll get you up for dinner," Trish's voice said, followed by what sounded like an obvious kiss. "Hey, Marsh, what's new?"

"Not much. Hadn't heard from you in a while and thought I'd see what you were up to. I didn't mean to wake your guest," Marsha answered. "I can call back later before I leave for work."

"No. Now is good. I'll have to get Mattie up in a couple of hours anyway. Poor thing was exhausted when she got here this morning.

Apparently a big fire somewhere last night. So what's new with you, cupcake? I want to hear every perverted detail."

"What are you talking about?"

"The blonde goddess you left the club with last weekend."

"Nothing to tell," Marsha said. "She took me home the next morning after I slept it off on her couch."

"I didn't think you were that drunk."

"Well, apparently I was. Don't remember a damn thing. Sounds like you found a friend though."

Trish sighed. "I'm sure she'll end up breaking my heart. Honestly, she's only a kid. Just sneaking up on thirty."

"But she makes you happy, right?"

"I won't shove her out the door unless I have to, that's for sure," Trish giggled. "She wants me to meet her folks. How fuckin' scary is that?"

"Then I guess she's out to her family. Where do they live?"

"Here! Practically been here since the city was founded. I'm worried though. One look at me and they'll know I'm on the far side of thirty. By about ten years."

"Shouldn't matter," Marsha said. "You're a good person Trish. They'll see that."

"Yeah, and they'll also see my basketball physique."

"You're not tall enough to play basketball."

"No, but I do a damn good impersonation of the basketball, round and bumpy."

"It'll be fine, Trish. Mattie doesn't seem to care."

"She told her mother I was cuddly," Trish said with a laugh. "Shit like that could ruin my reputation."

"So I suppose you won't be going to the club tonight then."

"Mattie wants to go and dance a little before she goes to work, but I don't know."

"If you do, have a drink for me. Have you got any plans for the last weekend in May?"

"I don't, but I'm not sure about Mattie. Why?"

"I'm off that weekend and am thinking about having the barbecue for the kids then. I have to start rounding up the food and stuff soon."

"I'll ask her about it when I get her up and let you know. Let me know what I can bring. You working tonight?"

"Yeah. I'll play something for you and Mattie. Got a request?"

"How about 'Someone to Watch Over Me'?"

"Okay. An oldie but goodie. I can do that. Look, I better fix something for later. Love you, Trish."

"Love you, too, Marsh. Talk to you soon."

Marsha strolled into her kitchen. Linguini with marinara sauce sounded good and would reheat well. Maybe she should make enough for Boomer too. As she chopped the ingredients for her middle of the night dinner, she wondered if Colleen would like it. She stirred the pot as the sauce simmered. Maybe she should do something for Colleen. She loved Trish, but could use another friend, especially now that Trish would be occupied with whatever was going on with Mattie. Maybe she would take a chance and invite Colleen over for dinner. Yeah, she could do that. Extend an olive branch to be friends.

She dialed the station's number and waited.

"KLEW-FM. How may I direct your call?" the receptionist answered.

"Colleen Walters, please." Marsha cleared her throat as she waited. Maybe this wasn't such a great idea after all. She was preparing to chicken out when someone answered the phone.

"Miss Walters' office," a young sounding, out-of-breath voice said quickly.

"Is Miss Walters in?"

"I'm sorry. She flew out of town this morning for a couple of days. Can I take a message?"

"No, that's okay. I'll contact her later. It's not an emergency."

"She should be back in her office Tuesday. You can try back then. Is this Desdemona? Your voice sounds familiar."

"Yeah. I just had a question about a contract she negotiated. No hurry."

"I'll leave her a message to contact you."

"Thanks," Marsha muttered before hanging up.

Chapter Ten

COLLEEN WAVED WHEN she saw her father waiting for her as she came through the door from the security area into the main lobby of the Philadelphia International Airport. She hadn't been home since her move to Omaha and knew her parents would have dozens of questions to ask about her new job. Even dressed casually, Quentin Walters was a sophisticated-looking man who exuded confidence. Colleen released the handle of her rolling carry-on and let her father sweep her into his arms. Of all the things she missed about home, this was at the top of her list. Although Quentin was shorter than Colleen by a few inches, he was a strong man. He adjusted his glasses when he let her go and smiled the broad, crooked smile he always seemed to have.

"Where's Mom?" Colleen asked.

"I didn't tell her you were flying in. I decided to surprise her," he chuckled. "She thinks I'm playing golf with the boys."

"How are they?"

"Intolerable, as usual. Too competitive."

"Gosh! I wonder where they got that from." Colleen laughed as they got into her dad's car.

"Okay. I know they inherited it from me, but competition is healthy."

"As long as you can accept the losses that go along with it."

"So why this sudden urge to drop in for a visit? I'm glad you did, but it is a little out of the blue."

"I returned from a business trip recently and found myself with a few days with absolutely nothing on my schedule. I used to come home more often."

"Washington is closer than Omaha. You could take the train and be here in a couple of hours."

"It seemed like I only came home when I had a problem though."

"Is your life calmer now?"

"Oh, yeah. I love my job. The travel is great. I spent a few days in North Carolina and Georgia pitching one of our shows that's going into regional syndication. In fact, while I'm here I might feel out the local market around Philly. It would give me a valid reason to make another trip home soon."

Quentin signaled and guided his car into the driveway of the large two-story Georgian home where Colleen grew up. "Your brothers and their clans are coming over for dinner. I already called your mother about that, so one more surprise guest shouldn't be a problem," Quentin said as he popped the trunk open and lifted Colleen's suitcase out. "Go surprise your mother, sweetheart. I'll bring in your bag."

Colleen opened the door from the garage and stepped into a large laundry room. She slipped her shoes off and dropped her purse on the dryer.

"Is that you, Quentin?" Rosemary Walters' voice called out from the kitchen.

Colleen cracked open the door into the kitchen and saw her mother at the sink, her back to the laundry room door. Quietly, Colleen tip-toed across the room and stood behind her mother. "No, it's not Quentin," she said.

Rosemary spun around and nearly lost her balance in the process. Colleen lived to see the smile on her mother's face and leaned down to hug her.

"What...what are you doing here?" Rosemary asked. "Are you all right?"

Colleen looked around the familiar kitchen with its custom designed lower counters and appliances. "Well, I used to live here and thought I'd drop in to see if it had changed," Colleen said.

Rosemary reached up with one hand and slung it around Colleen's neck, pulling her into another, tighter, hug. "I've missed you so much, my sweet girl," Rosemary whispered.

"Have you lost weight?" Colleen asked with a frown. "You're way too skinny, Mom. I'll have to come back more often to fatten you up. And to get in a little girl talk."

"Are you having a girl problem, Colleen? Beverly called after she visited with you, you know."

"Apparently she didn't waste any time snitching, but we'll talk more later. I'm staying a few days." Colleen leaned forward and looked at the pots on the stovetop. "Whatcha cookin'?" she asked with a mischievous grin.

"A standing rib roast. Your father told me he invited the boys and their families over for dinner."

"I did," Quentin puffed as he pulled Colleen's suitcase through the door. "What the hell you got in here? A dead body?"

"I'll get it, Dad," Colleen said. "Mom taught me to pack compactly."

"Well, there's compact and then there's overkill." Quentin abandoned the suitcase and walked over to his wife, leaning down to kiss her soundly.

"Not in front of the children, Quentin," Rosemary quipped.

"I can't help it, love. You're so beautiful I couldn't resist."

"You always were a sweet talker," Rosemary said as she patted his stomach. "Now get out of here and let me finish dinner."

"Let me change into something more comfortable and I'll help," Colleen offered.

"Not much left to do except let the roast finish cooking on low. What time will the boys be here?" Rosemary asked.

"In a couple of hours. Can I fix you a drink?" Quentin asked.

"Of course, I'll have my usual and whatever Colleen wants."

Colleen lugged her suitcase up the staircase to her second floor bedroom. She quickly hung up her clothes and slipped into a pair of Capri pants and a sleeveless cotton shirt before shoving her feet into a well-worn pair of sandals. She strode into the family room and accepted a drink from her father.

A moment later she heard the familiar sound of her mother coming toward them. Rosemary Walters leaned on her arm braces and swung her legs forward. Colleen could see, for the first time, that her mother was aging and her handicap seemed to be taking its toll on her. However, her face was still quite lovely, her once smooth skin now broken by smile wrinkles around her mouth and next to her eyes. Her hair was still a shiny dark brown and combed around her face in its perennial pixie-style.

Quentin waited until Rosemary was seated before setting her drink next to her and giving her another kiss. To see the affection between her parents warmed Colleen's heart. That was what she wanted someday. To have someone look at her the way her father looked at her mother, as if she was his whole world. Colleen sat on the couch next to her mother and slipped her feet out of her sandals to curl them under her. They killed some time catching up with what everyone was doing and gossiping about their neighbors.

"We don't really talk about it, but things between Rick and Amber are not going very well," Rosemary confided.

"What's the problem with Studly and the Prom Queen?" Colleen asked as she sipped her Jack and Coke. Within their family, Colleen and her siblings had always called one another by not necessarily flattering nicknames. Somehow it had all worked out and none of them were insulted. Rick was Rosemary's and Quentin's third born son. He had always been a jock in school and played college football. Now he was a football coach at a local high school. No one had been thrilled when he married a very young woman who had once been the prom queen at the high school where he coached. He swore up and down they hadn't known one another when she was a student, but Colleen had lingering doubts, as did the others in the family. Rick was pushing forty and his wife, Amber, had barely reached twenty-one when they married.

"She's too young for Rick," Rosemary said. "There's twenty years difference between them and there's no way she's going to catch up. She still wants to go out and party and can't understand why he doesn't. Thank God they don't have children."

"We won't talk about it tonight," Quentin said. "They'll have to be the ones to work it out. We used to argue, too."

"All couples argue, Quentin. It's perfectly normal when two people are together all the time. I'd be more worried if they never argued. We'll support them regardless of the outcome. Actually, in some ways, Amber is a very sweet girl. She's always been nice to us."

"What about the three stooges, Tom, Charlie, and Matt?"

"Who knows?" Rosemary answered. "They're all busy, but Matt told us he's had a job offer from a software company in San Francisco, I think."

"You think he'll accept it?"

"He might. He's still single and there's not much to keep him in Philadelphia. He's well-grounded and will do what he thinks is best for him. I think when you left for a different area it gave him a sort of freedom to move as well. We'd miss him, of course, but we don't expect any of you to stay tied to us."

Colleen sat quietly with her parents for a while. She needed to talk to her mother privately, but would have to wait until they could find a time to be alone.

"I should check the roast," Rosemary said as if reading Colleen's mind. "They can burn before you know it. Would you help me, Colleen?"

"Of course."

When they returned to the kitchen, Rosemary pulled a short stool from the breakfast bar. "The roast is fine, but I get the feeling you need to talk to me about something personal," Rosemary said as she sat on the stool and wiggled a little to get comfortable.

Colleen laughed. "You're a marvel, Mom. How do you always know when I need to talk?"

"Years of practice, darling. What's up?"

"I'm not that comfortable discussing this, but I'm having a little problem with my social life."

"This isn't about Rusty, is it?" Rosemary frowned.

"God no! I haven't seen or spoken to her since the trial and don't plan to. As far as I know she's still in prison. It's about a woman at my new job. She hosts an all-night program. In fact, her program is mostly what I'm working on. She has a very large audience in the Midwest and I recently sold her program in Charlotte and Savannah. She has an amazingly seductive voice, a natural for radio. I wish you could hear it."

"And obviously you like her," Rosemary said with a smile.

"I do. But she doesn't want anything to do with me."

"Why? You're a wonderful woman. You and Rusty had problems, but those were mostly hers."

Colleen cleared her throat before continuing. "The problem is that Marsha refuses to have anything to do with me because...well... she thinks I'm *too* attractive. How did she put it?" Colleen thought for a moment and snapped her fingers. "She believes she's below my standards."

Rosemary thought about Colleen's statement for a moment. "Tell me a little about her."

Colleen took a deep breath and closed her eyes. "Her name is Marsha Barrett, but her on-air name is Desdemona. Her program caters to the lonely. You know, those who don't have any other way to fill their nights."

"People like herself, in other words," Rosemary murmured.

"I don't know. I guess they're simply lonely. Anyway, she's shorter than I am, about five-seven or eight. In my opinion she could gain a few pounds. She's got the cutest hair," Colleen said with a smile. "Incredibly curly, like springs almost, the color of rich milk chocolate. She wears glasses and her eyes are brown around the edges and lighter in the center, very unusual looking. Beautiful, soft bedroom eyes." Colleen paused for a moment before continuing and cleared her throat. "I don't know what happened to cause it, but she has a scar on her upper lip."

"So, you, a tall, slender blonde with blue eyes and a flawless complexion, who dresses like a fashion model, are interested in a skinny woman with brown hair, brown eyes and a less than perfect face. And you can't understand why she isn't interested in you. Does that about sum it up?"

"Yeah, I guess so."

"Why can't you understand her hesitation?"

"She's a woman, I'm a woman. I've made it pretty obvious that I like her and would like to know her better. Why is that a problem?"

"I'm not questioning your motives, dear. I know you wouldn't deliberately hurt anyone, but it's obvious to me this Marsha has no desire to be hurt and believes she will be...by you. She may have already been hurt by someone she perceived as attractive. She thinks, for whatever reason, that you're lowering your standards, at her expense."

"But that's not true. Isn't there any way I can convince her it's not?"

"Persistence, I suppose, but that can become extremely tiring after a while. Patience hasn't always been one of your better qualities, honey. If, while you're pursuing Marsha, a beautiful woman came into your line of sight and you were attracted to her, who would you choose?"

"Rusty was a beautiful woman, Mom, and we all know how well that turned out."

"Rusty was, and probably still is, a user, not to mention an abuser. You should have left sooner, but you were young and naïve enough to believe she was in love with you. Are you willing to make the same commitment to Marsha or do you think she'll never leave you?"

Colleen stared at the counter top. "She said the same thing, or something pretty damn close."

"It's a valid concern. We all have egos, honey. Some bruise more easily than others. A lot of our self-esteem is tied up in how someone we care about sees us. I didn't really believe your father when he said he loved me."

"He worships you."

"I think I was always afraid he'd be like his brother."

"Uncle Jack?"

Rosemary nodded. "I tutored Jack for a few months. He was a big man on campus and for a while I was the envy of the other math tutors." Rosemary stared off for a moment as if lost in her memories,

"You've never told me that before." Colleen said.

"Your uncle hasn't changed much over the years. He was devilishly handsome, a true ladies man. With his blonde hair and sky blue eyes, and the talent to flirt shamelessly, he could have his choice of beautiful young women. But he was open and friendly."

"Did you date him?"

Rosemary shook her head. "He asked me out once, but his reputation scared me a little. I liked him, but couldn't see a future with him. Besides, after a month or two he introduced me to his brother." Rosemary smiled. "And the rest, as they say, is history."

"Have you ever regretted your choice?"

"Not for a moment. When Quentin said he loved me, it took me a very long time to believe that here," Rosemary said, tapping her head. "He could just as easily have destroyed me. When he was a young man, and before his hair abandoned him, I thought he was the handsomest man I'd ever met, even more handsome than Jack. To me, he's still handsome. I've always been a cripple, but I didn't think he'd have the courage to stay with me. For all I knew, he only wanted to know what it would be like to sleep with a woman with a handicap."

"You couldn't possibly have believed that about Daddy!"

"I think Quentin knew how I felt and that's why he's always been so tender and gentle with me. I love him for that. Beautiful people terrify people like me and your friend Marsha. We may secretly admire them from a distance, but will always suspect their motives if they try to get too close too quickly."

When Colleen seemed to hesitate, Rosemary asked, "Have you been...intimate with her?"

"Not really," Colleen answered softly. Tears hovered in her eyes as she brought them up to meet her mother's. "She kissed me. When I stopped her and woke her up she claimed it was a dream and she was kissing the woman who lives in her mind, a fantasy lover."

"She must have a very vivid imagination."

"I didn't want to stop her, Mom. I returned the kiss for a moment. It's been a long time since anyone kissed me the way she did. Like I was special."

Rosemary patted her daughter's hand. "Be patient, dear. Perhaps you're seeing Marsha as a challenge. You don't meet many people who don't want to be with you."

The doorbell chimed. "Oops, better check that roast now," Rosemary said. "Will you carry it to the table for me?"

Colleen hopped off her stool and slipped potholders onto her hands. She opened the oven door and lifted the large rib roast out. "It looks and smells wonderful, Mom. Thanks for the talk. I think I understand a little better how Marsha feels now."

"She's afraid. Easing her fears is up to you if you think she's really worth it."

"She is to me," Colleen said with the wide smile Rosemary hadn't seen in years. "Maybe I'll bring her with me the next time I come home."

"We'd love to meet her," Rosemary said.

"Hey, Trigger!" a man's voice boomed out from the kitchen doorway.

"Hey, Studly!" Colleen returned the greeting when she saw her brother, Rick.

"Have you gotten taller since the last time I saw you?" he asked as Colleen hugged him. "I know a basketball team looking for a new center provided you've learned to dribble without looking at the damn ball."

"Not my thing, buddy," she said with a laugh.

Chapter Eleven

AT ELEVEN-FORTY, twenty minutes before show time, Marsha made her way down the corridor to the studio. She laughed as the host of the show preceding hers pointed to the watch on his wrist and flashed the fingers of both hands twice to indicate she had twenty minutes left before she had to be seated in the chair he was now occupying. Gary, the G-Man, Lombardi was a throwback to the eighties, but his show featuring the greatest hits of that era was popular in the station's listening market.

It's a damn good thing no one in our audience can see the person behind the voice, Marsha thought. Gary was a short, pear-shaped man. However, Marsha had met his wife. Jody Lombardi was an elegant looking woman who made friends easily. She was a few years older than Gary and had three children from a previous marriage. But the G-man must have done something she found irresistible because they had been married almost fifteen years.

Gary leaned back in his chair and watched Marsha go through her nightly routine. She reached around him, planting a light kiss on his balding head, and set her cup on the side console. She keyed up the music that would signal the beginning of her all-night request line and slipped her headphones on at the end of Gary's last selection for the night. She waited for his usual brief, upbeat sign-off monologue before turning the soundproof, glass-enclosed room over to her. On the hand signal from the night technician and switchboard operator, Marsha began her night.

"Good evening, O-ma-haaaa," she groaned in the low, sultry voice that had brought her a loyal following. "It's a beautiful evening made for sharing with that someone special in your life. If you're still awake and listening, I promise not to interfere with your playtime. If you're in that lull between tender touches, I'll start our night together with one of my personal favorites." She punched up the first tune of the evening. "Ah, yes. It brings back many memories of lazy intimate nights," she purred.

As the song began Gary said, "Well, that's disgusting enough to gag a maggot."

"You're just jealous, G-Man. Go home and get a little," Marsha chuckled.

"I'm off tomorrow and believe me, baby, now that all the kiddies have flown the nest, tomorrow night I won't be listening to you." He laughed and pulled his coat on, tossing her a wave as he exited the studio. The lights on the telephone system began to blink. Marsha punched the first line.

"This is Desdemona," she said, dragging out the last syllable to sound like a moan of satisfaction. "What can I do for you on this fine night, darlin'?"

"If I answered that question, I'd lose my girlfriend for sure," a man's voice said with a laugh.

"What's the lucky lady's name?"

"Lilah."

"As in Deee-lilah?"

"As in deee-licious."

"Be still my heart. What can I play for you and Miss Deee-licious tonight?"

Marsha queued up the requested song and moved on to the next caller.

A more or less steady stream of requests continued through the night. Marsha had been surprised and didn't know whether to be satisfied or dismayed by the number of people who apparently stayed up all night. Since the day she'd sold the idea for the show to the station manager, there hadn't been many nights when she had to make selections on her own. Even over the busiest holidays, there were individuals either looking for love or celebrating having found it, at least for one night. There were nights Marsha found herself jealous of her listeners who seemed so happy and fulfilled to have that special someone everyone was looking for in their lives. She wished she could make the same claim, but there was no one other than the voices of strangers to fill her long, lonely nights. The only time she'd taken a chance on someone else had ended disastrously, leaving her traumatized and lonelier than before her fleeting fling with happiness.

AT FIVE IN the morning Marsha leaned back in her chair and rubbed her eyes. It had started out as a promising night, but within a few hours had disintegrated into a night where everyone had a complaint. "I hate nights like this," she said to Boomer. "Everyone's got a freakin' problem and thinks the whole world wants to hear about it. You workin' next weekend, too?"

"Yeah. Maybe it'll be another Lonely Hearts weekend. How about you?"

"You'll probably be stuck with Minuteman. You know, someone should write a tune called 'Nobody Gives a Shit about Your Piddly-Ass Problem'," Marsha said with a grin.

"I think someone did. Remember 'My Give a Damn's Busted'?"

"Should have been a bigger hit. I didn't find it offensive, did you?"

"Nope, and I liked that Toby Keith song about puttin' a boot up somebody's ass, too. What the hell is more American than that?"

The song playing was beginning to fade and Marsha switched on her headphones. "This is Desdemona, filling the midnight hour and beyond. Still looking for an early morning lover to take us higher." The phone line lit up and Marsha pushed the button on her phone. "What can I give you in the pre-dawn hours, baby?"

"Can't say unless you want to lose your license," a woman's voice chuckled. "How about 'Take me Higher'?"

"Good choice. Call me later and let me know what I can really do for you," Marsha whispered seductively.

"You got it, baby."

Switching her headphone to speak to Boomer again, she said, "Don't know what I'll do if that one calls back."

"You really need to get laid, Dez, if you're desperate enough to hit on a denizen of the night."

"Just my luck. Probably a fuckin' vampire," she sneered as she sorted through a small stack of mail.

A light on her phone blinked and she paused to punch the button. "This is Desdemona. How can I make your night better?"

"You ever been cheated on, Dez?" a sniffling woman asked.

"Afraid so." Marsha rolled her eyes. Another caller with a problem.

"It's a bitch, you know? You think you know someone so well and then they turn out to be someone you never dreamed they could be. They lie, knowing you'll believe them because you love them."

"I hear ya, girlfriend," Marsha commiserated. "Anything I can play to make you feel better?"

"How about 'Give Me One Good Reason'?"

"Sounds like a winner, honey. Remember there's someone out there for you and only you."

A moment later Boomer let out a long, low wolf whistle. "Well, lookie who's here. Nothing wakes me up like a hot, sexy blonde in the pre-dawn hours," he said. "And if she's a vampire, she can suuuck me dry any time." He waved at a figure walking down the hall toward the studio.

Marsha leaned to one side and her heart stuttered when she saw Colleen carrying a tray. She stopped at the control room and waited as Boomer swung the door open. She stepped inside and wrapped a napkin around his neck and set a plate and cup in front of him. Boomer's eyes shined at the plate of food in front of him as Colleen left the booth and closed the door. She crossed the hall and quietly tapped on the studio door.

Marsha unlocked the door and motioned Colleen in before they went live again. Colleen nodded and quickly closed the door behind her, relocking it. Marsha caught the scent of fresh coffee as she spoke to the next caller. She started the requested song and switched the headphones to silence any chatter from Boomer. Colleen set a plate and cup in front of Marsha and took a seat on the other side of the console.

"What's this for?" Marsha asked.

"Thought you might be hungry. If you're not, I'm sure Boomer will take seconds," Colleen answered.

"Where'd you get it? I'll reimburse you."

"I made it. I do know how to cook, remember? At least scrambled eggs and bacon."

Marsha saw Boomer making various hand signals to show his appreciation for the meal.

"I assume what we say in here can't be heard. It's either that or Boomer's having a seizure of some kind. You don't have to worry, Marsha. I won't do anything to embarrass you...or myself," Colleen said as she exhaled. She leaned back while running her hands through her hair, letting the blonde strands flow through her fingers like water. Colleen cleared her throat. "Did you get a haircut while I was gone? I like it."

"Thanks. I told Hershberger to do something with it that didn't require much effort on my part," Marsha answered as she chewed. "The food is great, by the way. Thanks. I was about to doze off."

"You're welcome. I wanted to talk to you and didn't think you would come to my place again unless drugs were involved."

"Probably right," Marsha said with a grin. "Unless it's about business, which we can discuss here at the station, we don't really have anything to talk about."

"I sold your show to a station in Philadelphia while I was out of town."

"Ken said you took a few days off."

"I did. I visited my folks outside Philly and decided to mix business with pleasure."

"You know, maybe you're moving too fast."

"Possibly, but I'm one of those women who knows what she wants and goes after it."

"Sometimes the fast approach doesn't work. Sometimes you have to move slowly and let each move have a chance to settle in. Otherwise you risk over-saturating...uh...the market."

"Yeah, that's what my mother said. She told me to be patient."

"Sounds like a wise woman. Hang on a sec." Marsha welcomed the next caller of the night. "Dez has been waiting to hear your voice all night, sugar, so lay it on me."

"What a provocative thought," a voice purred over the line.

"Only if you've got a provocative reply."

"I need to hear something to put me in the mood. Any suggestions?"

Marsha looked at Colleen and shrugged. "I've got plenty of suggestions, but the feds frown on porn radio, honey. What would you like to hear?"

"How about 'Georgia on my Mind'? I returned from a trip down south recently."

"Sounds like a winner. Sure you don't want to hear 'Another One Bites the Dust'?"

"You remember. I'm flattered."

"I never forget a sexy voice. Stop talking to me and make the lady happy," Marsha said.

"Oh, I will. Talk to you again real soon."

The caller disconnected and Marsha punched in the woman's request. When the music began, she looked at Colleen. "Okay," she said.

"Repeat offender?" Colleen asked.

"Yeah. She started calling around the time you arrived at the station and has been a steady caller ever since. Personally, I think she's a trucker. Always calls late in the show."

Colleen leaned forward. "Here's the deal, Barrett. I want a chance to know you better. I'm willing to wait, but not forever. I won't beg. If you tell me to take a hike, I will, even though I think you'd be making a huge mistake. I don't give a rat's ass what other people think. I'm not ashamed of who I am or who I'm with. I've been hurt before and won't let it happen again."

Marsha smiled crookedly. "Is there some reason I need to know all that?"

Colleen stood and shrugged. "Just thought you should know." She stopped next to Marsha and leaned down. "I don't like to play games," she whispered before walking out of the studio without looking back. Marsha flipped the headphones back to live and glanced at the studio clock. She still had a couple of hours to kill.

"What was that all about?" Boomer asked.

"Nothing important," Marsha said abruptly.

Two long hours later she impatiently snatched the headphones from her head and dropped them on the console as she packed up a few things. She threw a wave at Boomer and walked briskly down the hallway. "She in?" she asked Colleen's secretary.

"She sure is. Want me to ask her if she has time to talk to you?"

"No, thanks. I think I'll take the risk." She turned the doorknob and walked in. She pressed the lock on the door, dropped her backpack, and stared at Colleen who was seated behind her desk, her reading glasses perched halfway down her nose. Colleen looked serious as she removed her glasses and stood. She walked around her desk and leaned against the front edge.

Marsha took two quick steps forward to stand in front of Colleen. "I don't play games either," she said.

"Yet you're pretending you aren't interested in me," Colleen said calmly.

"Maybe I'm not," Marsha said even though her eyes had drifted down to Colleen's tempting lips.

"Liar," Colleen replied softly.

Marsha shrugged. "I like you, but friendship is the best I can offer."

"It's a start." Colleen turned and wrote on the back of a business card. "This is my private phone number. I hope I'll see you later this evening. If you can be there around seven, I'll fix that dinner I owe you. We can just talk if that's what you want. If you don't show up," she said with a shrug, "I guess I'll have to keep waiting." She tapped the tip of Marsha's nose with the card and smiled.

Chapter Twelve

COLLEEN SMILED WHEN she opened the door of her condo a little before seven that evening. Marsha shuffled from foot to foot as she handed Colleen a bouquet of flowers.

"They're beautiful. Thank you." Her eyes scanned Marsha and she said, "You look nice."

"I wasn't sure how I should dress. Sorry," Marsha mumbled. "I don't do dates." Her mouth felt as dry as the Gobi Desert.

"Don't apologize. As long as you're comfortable, that's all that matters." Colleen rested her hand on Marsha's shoulder. "I always want you to be comfortable when you're with me. Don't try to become what you think I'd want."

"What do you want?"

Colleen looked over her shoulder. "I thought I knew once, but now I'm not sure. Does it matter?"

Marsha pressed her hands against the front of her black slacks and made sure her Oxford, button-down shirt was neatly tucked into her slacks as she followed Colleen into the kitchen. "You look beautiful," Marsha managed. "But you already know that."

"Thank you. I'm glad you think so. I couldn't wait to get home and into something more comfortable." Colleen found a vase in a top cabinet and arranged the flowers in it. "I apologize for dinner. It's not home-made. I left work too late to actually cook myself, but I hope you like Chinese."

"I do. I'll eat just about anything that doesn't eat me first," Marsha said with a chuckle.

Colleen looked at Marsha, the corners of her mouth curling into a grin. "What an interesting remark. I'll have to remember it. Why don't you go into the living room and relax while I reheat a couple of things?"

"Do you mind if I look around? I didn't have much of a chance to look around the last time I was here."

"Feel free. I don't have any deep, dark secrets to hide."

Marsha raised her eyebrows. "No hidden stash of sex toys?"

"Are you into that?" Colleen asked, meeting Marsha's gaze.

"Never had the guts to order them from the catalog," Marsha said with a shrug. "I'm kinda fond of the old-fashioned way," she added as she felt her face redden. "I've always been a very tactile person."

"That sounds...fascinating," Colleen said with a smile.

Marsha wandered back toward the living room, starting at one end and working her way slowly around the room. You could tell a lot about a person from their knick-knacks and, if nothing else, they might give her a topic of conversation for later. She examined the books on the built-in bookshelves on either side of the small fireplace centered in a far wall. Colleen's taste in reading seemed relatively eclectic. Marsha had read a few of the same books. What she didn't see were any lesbian novels. Perhaps they were in the bedroom or in one of the closed cabinets near the bottom of the bookcases. She smiled as she looked at the DVD cases. Colleen's tastes ran toward older, classic films, such as the *Wizard of Oz, Gone with the Wind, Rebecca*, and apparently she had a particular fondness for Alfred Hitchcock films. Her CDs were primarily instrumental and New Age with an occasional album of oldies, but goodies. "May I put on some music?" Marsha called out.

"I don't have much of a selection, but if you see something you like, feel free," Colleen answered from the kitchen.

Marsha pulled out two or three CD cases and inserted them into a small bookcase stereo sitting nearby. As the melodic piano tones of Suzanne Ciani poured from the speakers, she lowered the volume and continued her examination of knick-knacks. In the middle of the longest wall, two bay windows with cushioned seats framed another slightly larger built-in shelving unit. Tastefully framed pictures were interspersed with delicate blown glass pieces. One by one, Marsha carefully took down the pictures and examined them. Colleen was in many of the pictures, always blonde and beautiful, always smiling and happy. As Marsha gazed at a picture she thought might be a family portrait, she couldn't help but notice how much Colleen stood out. The older woman and the five men all had dark hair and a somewhat Mediterranean look about them. Colleen, with her blonde hair and blue eyes, stood in the rear with her arms draped across the shoulders of the men on either side of her. An older man and woman were seated comfortably in front of their children, holding hands.

"That was taken not long after I graduated from college," Colleen rested her chin on Marsha's shoulder and looped her arms loosely around her waist.

"You...you don't look like the rest of your family."

"I'm adopted." Colleen brought a hand up and pointed to each person in the picture "That's my mom and dad in the front, of course. Quentin and Rosemary. Behind them are my brothers. Tom is an attorney, Charlie is a doctor, Rick, the stud, is a football coach at a high school in Philadelphia, and my youngest brother, Matt, is a software engineer. Then there's me in the middle. After four boys, my mom really wanted a girl. When they adopted me, of course, they had no idea I'd be so much taller than everyone else."

"Was your birth mother tall?"

"I have no idea. I was only a few days old when she decided she didn't want to be bothered with me." Marsha detected a slightly bitter tone in Colleen's voice. "I couldn't have asked for better, more loving parents." Colleen took a picture from the top shelf. "This is my mom and dad on their wedding day."

"They look very happy."

"It took my dad nearly two years to convince mom to marry him. She didn't want to be a burden and didn't trust my dad's motives, something you and she have in common."

"What...I mean..."

"Mom had polio as a child. It left her body misshapen, but I'm here to tell you it didn't stop her from snatching one of us up and busting our butts when we needed it," Colleen said with a laugh. "Dinner's ready if you are," she said and placed the picture on the shelf.

"Your father's a handsome man."

"Only now with glasses and less hair," Colleen said softly.

When they were seated Colleen passed various containers to Marsha. "I didn't know what you liked, so I got a little bit of everything," Colleen said. "I like the spicier dishes personally."

"I like sweet and sour," Marsha said.

"Then we should be able to finish most of this off."

"Why did you think you needed to explain your family to me?" Marsha asked as she added fried rice to her plate.

"I guess because you judge me by the way I look and think I have some kind of ulterior motive for enjoying your company. I don't. I love my family very much and it isn't because of how they look. It's because of who they are and how they've treated me. I talked to my mom about you when I was home. She actually sort of took your side. She understood your reservations and told me to be patient."

"I'll have to meet your mom someday."

"She would like that," Colleen said with a smile. "I miss them so much. What about your family?"

Marsha frowned. "I don't really have a family. They took one look at the thing they'd produced and threw me away."

"What!" Colleen said, the look on her face disbelieving.

Marsha cleared her throat and hesitated. "I...I was born with a defect. A...harelip and cleft palate. I nearly starved to death before the state took me away and placed me in the first of a long series of foster homes. Whoever was willing to deal with my needs, for a price."

"And that's what caused the scar on your lip," Colleen stated.

"You could have asked me about it sooner. You don't have to pretend it's not there."

"I wasn't. I knew you'd tell me when you wanted me to know the story behind it." Colleen shrugged and took another bite. "Besides, it gives you a rather roguish smile."

"You think so?" Marsha asked, looking pleased.

"Oh, yeah," Colleen said.

Marsha fingered the scar and stared at the plate in front of her. Colleen reached over to touch her finger against it as well, but Marsha leaned away. "I don't want to discuss my defect anymore," Marsha said. She could still hear the venom in her mother's voice telling her she should have died at birth, so she wouldn't be around to torment her parents. Colleen placed a hand over Marsha's and lightly squeezed.

Marsha pulled her hand away from Colleen's warmth. She couldn't stand the way it made her feel, pathetic. She laid her napkin on the table and pushed away to stand.

"You don't have to leave, Marsha," Colleen said. "I appreciate what you've told me and it doesn't change the way I feel about you in the least. I'd still like to spend time with you."

"Doing what?" Marsha asked.

Colleen waggled her eyebrows. "We'll think of something." She laughed when she saw the look on Marsha's face.

Together they cleaned up the kitchen before finally retiring to the living room. Marsha looked around the room again and changed the CDs in the stereo. When she turned, Colleen was standing behind her.

"Dance with me?" Colleen asked. "You probably don't remember the last time."

"Then you know I'm not very good," Marsha said.

"Doesn't matter."

Marsha shook her head and took Colleen into her arms, moving with the slow rhythm of the music. Gradually, thanks to the way Colleen stroked her back and played with her hair, Marsha began to relax. She liked the way Colleen's body moved against hers and closed her eyes.

When the music finally stopped Marsha stepped away self-consciously and stared down at the floor. Colleen moved to the sofa and patted the place next to her.

"Why don't you sit here?" she asked with a smile. "I promise not to bite...much."

Marsha wiped her sweaty palms on her pants and joined Colleen on the sofa. She was glad to be with Colleen, but wasn't sure what she was supposed to do once they were past dinner. She felt embarrassed, like a kid on her first date. What did normal people do on dates?

"Don't be nervous," Colleen whispered close to her ear. Marsha's body stiffened. She placed a light kiss on Marsha's jaw and sat up, entwining their fingers. "Do you mind if I hold your hand?"

Marsha shook her head and leaned it against the back of the couch. "I don't understand you, Colleen," she said. "Why? Why me? I'm nothing. If you want to spend time with an unattractive woman, there's something wrong with your wiring." She shrugged. "I suppose I should be grateful, but I'm not because I'm too damn scared I'll fuck up and the dream will end."

Colleen took a deep breath and squeezed Marsha's hand. "Who hurt you so deeply?"

"Nobody. Everybody."

"Maybe you're doing it to yourself by convincing yourself you're not worthy of being happy. Everyone deserves that, Marsha."

"I can't make you happy."

"You already do. I wish there was something I could do to convince you."

Tears formed in Marsha's eyes and wavered along the edge of her eyelashes. "All my life I've wanted someone who...when she looked at me I knew she desired me, someone so filled with love for *me*," she said poking her fingers into her chest, "that she couldn't contain it. Someone who cared if I was happy." She blinked her eyes rapidly to clear them. "Is that too much to want?"

Colleen leaned forward and wiped the tears on Marsha's cheeks with her finger. "It's what we all want, but I understand why we can't trust our feelings. I...um...thought I was in love once."

"What happened?" Marsha asked.

Colleen frowned and shook her head. "It was a painful period in my life. I've put it behind me and would rather not discuss it, if you don't mind."

Marsha nodded and decided to change the subject. "If you're still interested, I'm planning the end of school barbecue in a couple of weeks for the kids you met."

"When? I'll make sure I don't schedule anything else. How much can I donate? What can I bring?"

Marsha laughed and held her hands up. "Wait, wait. I don't have it all figured out yet. Trish's new significant other has offered to grill, if she's off that weekend. Trish is bringing something and my neighbors have all agreed to bring a dish. Now I have to recheck a few stores about chipping in hamburgers, hot dogs and buns."

"Why don't you let me do that for you?" Colleen volunteered. "I've got a few contacts who might throw in some free stuff."

Marsha glanced at her wristwatch. "I'd rather just have a nice dinner for them and their families, I think. Look, I need to get going. Maybe catch a short nap before the show tonight." She stood up. "Dinner was great. Thanks."

Marsha waited for Colleen to escort her to the front door. She was surprised when Colleen took her hand again. "We should get together before the barbecue to make sure you have enough food. You didn't say when it will be."

"I'm thinking the last weekend in May. Jacobi's checking to see when classes end. Depending on what he finds out I might have to change it to the first weekend in June. Still kind of in flux."

Colleen leaned close to Marsha to open the door and rested a hand on her shoulder. Marsha felt her body tremble from the close contact and hoped Colleen hadn't felt it. Colleen turned her head slightly to look at Marsha and smiled. Her mouth was so close that Marsha licked her lips. She cleared her throat before speaking. "Um...give me about a week to compile a list of what we'll need. Then maybe we can meet and make a final list. I know I'll have to buy a few things, but hopefully it won't be too bad."

Marsha looked uncomfortable and debated whether she should do what she was thinking about. It would be a risky move for her.

"Are you all right?" Colleen asked, running her hand down Marsha's back.

"I'm fine," Marsha said with a frown.

Colleen started to say something, but Marsha blurted out suddenly, "Would you go to the club with me some Saturday? I totally understand if you say no, I just thought–"

"I'd like that," Colleen said quickly. "Of course I will. This coming Saturday?"

"Really?" Marsha asked. "You will?"

Colleen nodded and smiled. "I'd like that very much."

"Great!"

MARSHA TRIED TO relax as she paid the cover charge and led Colleen into The Queen's Court. The woman she was in her own mind stood straighter and acted more confidently, as if she belonged there with Colleen. She looked around casually before spotting Trish.

"There they are," Marsha said.

"Do I look all right? I want to make a good impression on your friends," Colleen said.

"You look good enough to eat," Marsha answered with a smile. She took Colleen's hand, guiding her toward the darkened booth along the far wall.

"I'll remind you of that later," Colleen whispered.

"You won't need to."

Trish was snuggled against the shoulder of the woman Marsha had met briefly the last time she'd been at the Court. When Marsha and Colleen stopped next to the table, Trish smiled. To Marsha, Trish looked happy, actually more than happy. She removed her hand from Colleen's to allow her to slide into the booth first before joining her. A waitress stopped briefly to take their drink orders. Colleen's hand rested easily of Marsha's thigh and squeezed it lightly.

"Colleen, this is my best friend Trish Longoria," Marsha started her introductions. "And this is her date, Mattie. I'm sorry, but I don't know your last name."

"Scott. Mattie Scott," the younger woman said as she extended her hand to Colleen.

Marsha continued, "Trish, Mattie, this is Colleen Walters. She works at the station with me."

"The goddess," Trish said with a grin.

"What?" Colleen asked.

"It's what we called you before we knew your name," Marsha explained with a blush.

"Thank you, but it's a little embarrassing," Colleen said.

They all sat back slightly when the waitress returned with their order. Marsha frowned as she tried to dredge up a memory from the first time she'd met Mattie. Finally, she snapped her fingers and said to Colleen, "Mattie's a firefighter."

"I'm shocked you remember that," Mattie said with a friendly laugh.

"A lot about that night shocks me," Marsha said, blushing slightly.

"Especially when she woke up in my bed," Colleen added. She leaned against Marsha's shoulder. "Now we can both be embarrassed," she whispered.

"They didn't need to know that," Marsha said with a frown.

"Why not?" Mattie asked. "Nothing to be ashamed of. Colleen's a great looking woman and you," she pointed at Marsha, "are one lucky dog." She wrapped her arm around Trish's shoulders and drew her into a tight hug. "But not as lucky as I am."

"Why, thank you, Mattie," Colleen said. She turned to Marsha and placed her hand on her forearm. "I like this song. I could be talked into a dance."

Marsha slid out of the booth and held a hand out to Colleen. "You do remember I'm not a very good dancer, right?" Marsha warned.

"You'll do fine," Colleen replied as she took Marsha's hand. They walked to the elevated dance floor and joined several other couples who apparently also liked that particular Shania Twain tune.

Marsha sucked in a breath and took Colleen into her arms, counting the beats of the song silently a moment before stepping into it. Marsha was afraid to talk much in case she lost the beat and made a misstep.

Colleen leaned closer and caught Marsha's eye. "Don't think about it so hard. You're doing great. You're supposed to enjoy dancing."

"I suck unless I'm three sheets to the wind," Marsha mumbled.

"We'll have to work on that because I really like to dance. Now relax," Colleen chuckled as she brought both arms up to encircle Marsha's neck and looked into her eyes. "Pretend there's no one else out here and it's just you and me alone on this big empty dance floor. No one matters except us." She pulled Marsha against her and let her fingers stroke Marsha's hair. Marsha rested her head in the hollow of Colleen's neck, feeling all of her apprehensions fall away. The feel of Colleen's fingers threading through her hair brought out Marsha's feelings, no matter how much she fought them. Colleen kissed down the side of Marsha's face to reassure her until the song ended. When Marsha took a step back to leave the floor, Colleen's hand slipped to the back of Marsha's head and she leaned forward slightly to kiss her. Marsha tried to back away, but Colleen's hand held her in place, her tongue demanding to enter Marsha's mouth. As much as Marsha wanted what Colleen was offering, she knew she couldn't trust what she was feeling. She had trusted her feelings before and been hurt. She wouldn't allow it to happen again. She couldn't.

Chapter Thirteen

BY THE LAST weekend in May Marsha's house was stacked with food for her annual children's barbecue. She had combined some of her own money, as usual, with Colleen's and been forced to use her neighbors' refrigerators to hold all the meat. This year Mattie had collected some money from the other firemen at her station, so in addition to the usual hamburgers and hot dogs, there was chicken as well. Her neighbors and the parents of some of the children were bringing potato salad, deviled eggs, iced tea, lemonade, and, of course, wings. Marsha was amazed at how much they had gathered in a relatively short time. She had taken off Friday, as well as the weekend, to get everything gathered for Saturday's party for the kids. Trish promised to get Mattie up early to deliver the grill Saturday morning. Marsha poured herself a glass of iced tea and plopped down on the couch. She was exhausted.

The front door buzzer sounded and Marsha pushed herself up from her couch. She flipped on the porch light and was surprised to find Colleen standing on the porch holding a huge stack of hamburger and hot dog buns.

"What the hell?" Marsha laughed as she pushed the screen door open, just in time to catch two packages as Colleen lost control of the precariously stacked items. She juggled them for a moment before carrying them into the kitchen and returning to relieve Colleen of more. "Where did you get these?" Marsha asked.

"I made a deal with a bakery near my apartment," Colleen said. "They donated what they had left over from today." She shrugged. "And they threw in a few loaves of French bread for the heck of it."

When Marsha finished stacking the packages and making sure they wouldn't slide she turned to find Colleen leaning against the refrigerator.

"There's tea in the fridge if you want some," Marsha said.

"Have anything stronger? It's been a long, busy day."

"Beer, for the grown-ups."

"That works for me."

Colleen moved away to let Marsha remove a bottle and twist the cap off. "Glass?" Marsha asked.

"Bottle's fine."

Marsha wrapped a paper towel around the bottle and handed it to Colleen.

"Is there anything else that you need before tomorrow?" Colleen asked as she took a healthy swallow of beer.

"I don't think so." Marsha walked into the living room. "Have a seat and catch your breath. I really appreciate the help."

Colleen was casually dressed in Capri pants and a sleeveless shirt. She slipped out of her sandals before she sat down, drawing her legs under her.

"God, this feels so good," she said, letting her head fall back and running her hand through her hair.

Marsha couldn't tear her eyes away from Colleen's relaxed body. Or her long, elegant neck. She knew she should say something, but her mind was a blank. Colleen brought her arm down and rested it across the back of the couch. Marsha repositioned herself on the couch and was startled when Colleen's hand began playing absently with the dark curls along her neckline.

"Are you all right?" Colleen asked, concern on her face.

"Yeah, I'm fine. Just thinking. Sorry."

"What are you thinking about?"

"Nothing important," Marsha mumbled.

"I could torture it out of you, you know?" Colleen said easily.

Marsha grinned as she turned to face her. "Oh, really. And how would you do that, Wonder Woman?"

Colleen set her bottle down and said, "If I had my golden lariat, I could throw it around you so you couldn't resist me, but since I left my lariat at home, I guess I'll have to just say please."

Marsha took another drink of her tea and chewed on her bottom lip. "I...I lied before. I do remember...touching you," Marsha said. "I liked it," she said softly.

When Colleen stopped playing with her hair, Marsha wished she'd said nothing. She leaned forward and rested her arms on her thighs and stared at the floor.

Colleen leaned closer and ran her fingers through Marsha's hair. "So did I," she said. "You were my Desdemona."

Marsha frowned and turned her head to look at Colleen. "Desdemona is the kind of woman you really want, not me." There was a hint of anger in her voice.

"You are Desdemona! My God! Don't you know how sexy you are?"

"Desdemona's only an act. She's not me," Marsha protested.

"She's *all* you. That beautiful voice comes from inside you." Colleen shook her head. "You're beautiful in here," she said, tapping Marsha over the heart. "Where it counts. Oh, never mind. You'll never believe it."

Colleen turned away and sat up. Marsha reached out and hesitantly brought her hand up to touch Colleen's face. She closed her eyes, then spoke softly, allowing Desdemona to say what she wanted to say. "I long to feel your skin beneath my fingers. I want to feel you shiver as they move over your body, begging me to...slip inside you. I long to feel your muscles tighten as they draw me deeper into the flame that burns inside you. I want to hear you call out my name as release claims you, urging me to continue driving you to the boundaries of ecstasy, toward the precipice from which there is no escape."

Colleen's breathing became heavier as Marsha described what she wanted her to feel. She wrapped her arms around Marsha and pressed her body against Marsha's. "Oh, baby," she whispered as her hands stroked Marsha's hair. "Take me there. Please. Let me fall with you, safe in your arms."

Marsha hesitantly took Colleen's face in her hands and gazed into her eyes, trying to see what message was there before she kissed her tenderly. Colleen's hand entwined itself in the curls on Marsha's head and deepened the kiss, her lips parting in an invitation to enter. When they broke apart to breathe, Marsha brought her eyes up to meet Colleen's again, searching for the rejection she knew would be there. She kissed along the edges of Colleen's mouth before moving down along her jaw and near her ear.

"It only lasted a few seconds, but I remember everything. I remember every touch, every smell, every feeling," Marsha whispered.

Colleen pulled her head away to see Marsha's face. "Why did you pretend you didn't remember?"

"I didn't want to be hurt," she said, knowing she risked being hurt on so many levels.

"Oh, baby," Colleen murmured as she kissed the top of Marsha's head.

Slowly Marsha allowed her hands to travel up Colleen's back and move down again to skim smoothly along the top of her thigh. Colleen's thighs parted slightly as Marsha's hand moved lightly up her inner thigh. "Please touch me, baby," Colleen groaned, the hot breath from her mouth flowing over Marsha's ear.

"You're so beautiful," Marsha whispered. "So beautiful." She kissed Colleen's neck, finding the strong pulse there. She teased Colleen's lips with her tongue before drawing her into a probing kiss, not caring if she ever breathed again. She would gladly die rather than lose the feeling of being joined with Colleen.

Colleen wrapped her arms around Marsha's body, shivering when Marsha's lips moved along the tender skin of her collarbone. She gasped as Marsha's hand caressed her breast.

Colleen took Marsha's mouth aggressively. Colleen's shirt fell away when Marsha sought more contact, burying her lips in Colleen's tempting cleavage. Through the fabric of her bra, Marsha's fingers teased her nipple. "Take me to bed, baby," Colleen urged. "Don't think about it, just do it. I want to feel you on me, under me, beside me...in me."

Marsha stood and held her hand out. When Colleen took it, Marsha turned and looked at her. She felt her control slipping when she saw the look in Colleen's eyes. She had never lost control before, but knew she was teetering on the edge now when they entered the bedroom and Colleen kissed her before pulling Marsha's t-shirt over her head. Following a few minutes of visually exploring the landscape of one another's body as they removed their clothing, Colleen gently pushed Marsha onto the bed. She leaned over Marsha and kissed her as her breasts dragged over Marsha's belly and chest. Marsha reached up and brought Colleen down to join her, their limbs entwining around one another.

This was what Marsha had dreamed of and she gave her mind and body permission to let go. She rolled Colleen onto her back and hovered over her, lightly kissing her eyelids, her cheeks, and her neck before her hips settled between Colleen's legs. She felt Colleen's legs part and wrap around her hips, drawing her down until Marsha felt her heated center pulse beneath her. Colleen began moving against her and Marsha could feel her slickness as she lavished attention on her breasts. She slid her hands beneath Colleen and lifted her from the mattress slightly as she sucked on the now taut nipples. Colleen pressed her nails into Marsha's back, pleading for more.

"Please, baby," Colleen gasped. "Make me yours now."

Marsha moved her hand down Colleen's hip and into her heated center, gliding into the wet pulsing opening. The muscles drew her fingers in and caressed them as she began thrusting slowly, increasing her depth with each one. She felt Colleen's body open to greet her. Colleen threw her head back, grasping the sheets as she gyrated against Marsha's hand until her release came. Marsha couldn't stop driving into Colleen's body, the feel of her release continuing to flow over her hand. Finally, Colleen pulled her down into a fevered kiss. Not waiting to catch her breath she rolled Marsha onto her back and wiggled between her legs.

"I need to taste your desire, baby," she said as she scooted lower.

The moment Colleen's tongue touched her clit, Marsha almost jumped off the bed, but Colleen held her tightly to prevent her escape. It had been so long. Marsha ran her hands into Colleen's hair as every thought fled her brain. There was only the touch of Colleen's tongue and her fingers, nothing else as Marsha began to squirm beneath her lover.

"Oh, my God!" she managed as she felt herself being taken to the edge of an ecstasy she'd never felt before. "Yes, baby, yes," she said, giving her body permission to surrender. Her abdomen sank into itself as her release built. Colleen's hand found her breast and pinched the nipple when Marsha arched her body, allowing Colleen's mouth to feast on the proof of her satisfaction.

Chapter Fourteen

MARSHA AWOKE AS pinkish fingers of light threaded into the gray of the sky. She stretched her body and smiled when she felt Colleen snuggle closer to her. If it was a dream, she hoped it turned into a coma so she would never have to awaken, never lose this feeling. But how long would it last? Long enough to shatter her heart when it ended? She let her hands skim over the softness beneath them and lightly kissed the tender skin along the back of Colleen's neck. Colleen rolled onto her side and blinked her eyes open. Marsha was in awe of what she saw there. Her own image reflected back at her in Colleen's still sleepy, but satiated eyes. Had she really caused that? Colleen's hand floated over Marsha's side and encircled her nipple, lightly pinching.

"Good morning, baby," Colleen mumbled as she rubbed her face against Marsha's shoulder.

She leaned over Marsha and kissed her. "Last night you let me experience all of you, body and soul. It was more than I ever dreamed of."

Marsha nuzzled against her. She saw her bedroom clock and groaned.

"What's wrong?"

"We have to get up, but the only thing I want to do is spend all day in bed with you, feeling you. I love how your body reacts when I touch it."

Colleen ran her index finger down Marsha's face and torso, teasing her. "Well, there is always tonight."

"That's more than twelve long hours away." She kissed the crook of Colleen's arm and squeezed her butt cheek. "You shower while I make some coffee."

Colleen pulled her close for another kiss. "We could save water and bathe together after we make the coffee."

Colleen crawled over Marsha, eliciting a groan. Straddling her, Colleen wagged a finger at her. "Not yet, sweetie," Colleen said.

Marsha grinned, letting her fingertips stroke the breasts that hovered temptingly above her. "You don't need a shower, baby. You're already wet."

Colleen looked insulted, but a smile tugged at her lips. She leaned down for a quick kiss and hopped off the bed.

Marsha followed her into the kitchen and watched as she poured water into the coffeemaker. She walked up behind her and let her fingers run down Colleen's back. Colleen turned in her arms and brought her hands up to run them through Marsha's hair, pulling her closer. Marsha buried her face between Colleen's breasts and inhaled deeply. Marsha looked up and her knees almost buckled when she saw the look in Colleen's eyes. "Do you know how much I want you at this moment?"

"Just this moment?"

Marsha shook her head slowly. "Every moment I'm near you."

AT TEN O'CLOCK the front door bell buzzed. Marsha answered it with a cup of coffee in her hands.

"You'd better have one of those for me, Marsh," Trish announced as Marsha opened the front screen. Colleen walked up next to Marsha and placed a hand on her shoulder. She gave a large mug to Trish as Marsha wrapped her arm around Colleen's waist. Trish took a sip and let out an appreciative sigh. "What time did you get here?" she asked, looking up at Colleen.

Marsha and Colleen smiled at one another. "About eight o'clock last night," Colleen answered.

Trish reached out and turned Marsha's head slightly to the side with her index finger "Looks like a fun time was had by all," Trish smirked as she sipped her coffee and touched the mark on Marsha's neck.

"Where's Mattie?" Marsha asked, rubbing the tip of her ear, certain it had turned red.

"She's backing into the driveway. Probably could use a little help."

Marsha looked out as Mattie was backing her old pickup into the drive. A large grill was tied in the back. Trish joined Marsha on the porch and said, "She borrowed the big grill from the station for the day." Trish leaned closer to Marsha. "She loves to grill. Go figure."

Colleen joined them and handed Marsha another mug of coffee. Marsha took it and went down the steps to help Mattie with the grill. Mattie and Marsha sat on the tailgate of the truck for a few minutes chatting.

"That's a cool grill," Marsha said.

"My dad and I welded it together for the station. They won't be using it this weekend."

Marsha examined it for a moment and ran her hand over the welded joints. "Nice job."

"Thanks. You got any boards? We can roll it down easier than lifting it."

Marsha jumped from the rear of the truck and trotted around to the back of her house. She returned a few minutes later with two two-by-sixes. She leaned them against the tailgate. "I used them when I moved in here and that was probably the last time, but they should still be good."

Mattie pressed down on each board to test its strength and nodded. "Should work."

Several minutes later they set up the grill in a shady spot along the side of the front porch. When they entered the house, they found Trish and Colleen standing in the kitchen, chopping hard-boiled eggs and onions while chattering away.

Mattie helped herself to another cup of coffee. "Whatcha cookin', sweet pea?" she asked Trish with a kiss on her shoulder.

"I'm learning to make macaroni salad." Trish answered.

"I love macaroni salad," Mattie said, picking up a slice of egg white and dropping it in her mouth.

Trish smacked her hand when she reached for a second slice. "You'll get plenty later, chow hound. God, if I ate like you, I'd be as big as a...never mind."

"You're perfect to me, sweetie," Mattie said, wrapping her arms around Trish's full figure and planting a kiss on the side of her neck.

Colleen laughed and stuck a spoon into the macaroni. "Want a bite?" she asked as she brought it to Marsha's mouth.

Marsha took it and nodded. "That's great." Then she moved closer and whispered into Colleen's ear. As Colleen blushed, Marsha laughed and gave her a quick kiss.

As Mattie finished her coffee and rinsed out her cup, Marsha patted her on the arm. "I need to check with my neighbors. They usually set up a table so they and the kids and their families can eat together. I need to see who still needs a table and some chairs."

WHILE MARSHA AND Mattie were gone to make their table and chair count, Trish looked at Colleen and said, "So it looks like things are coming right along between you and Marsh."

"It's fine, so far. She seems a lot more comfortable now than she did a couple of months ago."

"She looks flat out enamored. I don't think I've ever seen her smile so much before. At least not since I've known her."

Colleen paused for a moment. "I think I'm falling in love with her, Trish. I hope she'll believe that." She shrugged. "At first I admit I was just attracted to her, but it's so much more than that now. She does things to me that I never believed possible." Colleen shivered thinking about the night before.

"Does she trust you?"

"I hope so. I'd never do anything to hurt her. I couldn't."

"You know her self-esteem sucks, right?"

"I'm working on that. Do you know why?"

"Not for sure, but it might involve a woman she knew in Chicago before she moved to Omaha. I almost got her to talk about it once."

"She's never mentioned another woman to me. How do you know about her?"

Trish shrugged. "Not too long after I met Marsh we were sharing a particularly shitty evening at my place. We drank quite a bit, twenty Jell-O shots a piece and chased them down with a couple of Margaritas." She grunted and shook her head. "Lethal combination. Anyway we started discussing women we'd been attracted to and how each turned out to be the biggest mistake we'd ever made."

"Unfortunately, we've all been there," Colleen sighed.

"Ain't that the truth," Trish said with a laugh. "You're the first, well, only one really, to get even semi-close to her since I've known her. She's got a pretty serious inferiority complex thing going on. She's a nice person, but is always waiting for the other shoe to drop. Unfortunately it always has."

"Hopefully, not this time," Colleen said. She washed her hands and dried them on a kitchen towel. "I'll go see if they're ready to start all this meat."

"Don't let her push you away, Colleen. Believe me, she'll try to."

"I won't."

Colleen walked onto the front porch and smiled when Marsha glanced up at her. "Got the charcoal ready? We've got a ton of meat inside ready to grill."

"Hey!" Mattie said. "Tell Trish to melt a stick of butter and squeeze about a dozen lemons into it. Then we can start the chicken. It'll take the longest to grill." She turned to Marsha. "You got a brush I can use to baste the chicken."

"Yeah, I'll get it." She ran onto the porch and stopped to give Colleen a hug and a kiss. "You about ready with everything else?"

"We're good," Colleen answered.

"Then come on out, grab a drink, and sit on the porch in the shade while we slave away."

Colleen laughed. "Looks like Mattie's the one slaving away, hot stuff."

Marsha stopped and turned around. She smiled as her eyes slid down Colleen's body. Taking a couple of quick steps back, she pulled Colleen into a deep kiss. When she ended the kiss, her hand cupped Colleen's cheek. "I slaved away last night," she said.

"And I certainly appreciated your efforts on my behalf. I'm looking forward to a repeat performance." Colleen bit her bottom lip.

"Later, baby," Marsha said with a wink.

The remainder of the afternoon was filled with Marsha and Mattie playing games with the children while Colleen and Trish visited with Marsha's neighbors and the parent of each child. Most of them had already met Colleen, but looked at Trish in amusement. To everyone's surprise, Trish proved to be an excellent chess player who easily defeated anyone who challenged her. Except for Jacobi. By the time the final clean-up began Trish was sitting on Jacobi's porch deeply engrossed in her game strategy.

As each family began to wander off, stopping to hug or shake hands with Marsha, Colleen stood behind her, periodically letting her fingers wander around Marsha's waist or massaging her shoulders. When she said her farewell to the last of the kids, Marsha turned and stared at Colleen.

"Are you deliberately trying to arouse me?" Marsha said with a grin.

"Is it working?" Colleen asked.

"Let me help Mattie load her grill and I'll let you know. Need any help in the kitchen?"

Colleen shook her head. "There wasn't much left to put away. I packed some chicken, potato salad and a few deviled eggs for Mattie and Trish. If we ever get hungry again there's still plenty left for us."

"Why don't you see if you can blast Trish off Jacobi's porch while I help Mattie?"

Colleen lowered her head, giving Marsha a soft kiss before walking across the street to get Trish.

Mattie tied rope to the legs of the grill and ratcheted it slowly onto the truck bed, then tied it securely to large eyelets welded onto the sides of the truck. Marsha couldn't believe how easily it moved up the two-by-sixes. A few minutes later Trish accompanied Colleen across the street.

"That old boy is a chess hustler," Trish muttered as she stood beside Mattie who was leaning against her truck.

"Did you whup his ass, sugar?" Mattie asked as she wrapped an arm around Trish's shoulders and kissed the top of her head.

"Next time," Trish said, patting Mattie on the stomach. "You still full, baby?"

"I left a little room for dessert," Mattie grinned, leaning down to kiss Trish's neck.

"I'm pretty sure there was a message in there somewhere," Trish laughed. "All that food made me sleepy. I think I can go home and take a nap without much trouble." Trish stepped away from Mattie long enough to give Marsha a bear hug. "It was fun, Marsh."

"Glad you both could make it. And thanks for the use of the grill. It was a lifesaver, Mattie."

"The fire department aims to please. Let me know any time you need it again," Mattie said, extending her hand for a firm shake.

Marsha and Colleen held hands as they made their way up the steps to the porch and waved as Mattie pulled out of the driveway.

"I've been waiting hours for everyone to leave," Marsha said. She pushed Colleen against a side wall of the porch and stepped close to her body. She buried her face in Colleen's cleavage and took a deep breath. She looked up and smiled. "You smell like barbecue smoke. Delicious."

As Colleen wrapped her arms around Marsha she glanced around the now quiet neighborhood. She saw movement down the block that looked like someone standing between two houses near the corner.

Whoever it was seemed to be watching them, sending a shiver down Colleen's back.

"Cold?" Marsha asked.

"Just chilly," Colleen answered, continuing to stare at the person. They were too far away to identify. "A warm shower would help. Join me?"

They walked into the house. While Colleen went into the bedroom to begin undressing, Marsha checked the doors and windows to make sure they were all locked.

Colleen smiled when Marsha stepped behind her and the soft touch of Marsha's hands on her skin drove away the feeling of uneasiness she'd felt earlier. Marsha kneaded Colleen's ass as she leaned over the bed. "You feel so good," Marsha said as she slid her hands along Colleen's sides and caressed her breasts from behind.

"If you keep that up, we'll never make it into the shower, baby," Colleen groaned as Marsha's finger flicked across her nipples and her thigh pressed between Colleen's legs.

"Do you want me to stop?" Marsha asked.

"Oh, no," Colleen murmured as she brought her body up and slowly slid her wetness along the top of Marsha's thigh and covered Marsha's hands with her own. Marsha kissed and sucked along Colleen's neck as the blonde ground against her.

"I need to feel you inside me. Now!" Colleen panted.

"Get on the bed on your knees for me, baby," Marsha breathed heavily.

Colleen crawled onto the bed with Marsha behind her. She leaned forward onto her elbows. Marsha brought her mouth down and slid it the length of Colleen's sex. As Colleen moaned from the feel of Marsha's tongue, Marsha entered her with two fingers and pressed them as deeply as she could.

"Oh, yes, baby," Colleen said as the movement of her hips matched the deep thrusts of Marsha's fingers. "More, baby. Harder," Colleen urged as she began to move faster. She covered her eyes with her hands as her sex opened to take in a third finger. "Yes, yes, yes!" she screamed.

Marsha's movement slowed, but didn't stop as Colleen's body pushed back against her one final time, periodically shuddering when Marsha withdrew her fingers slowly and wrapped her arms around the exhausted woman. Marsha kissed her way up Colleen's arm and along her neck.

"You're so beautiful when you come," Marsha whispered as she held her.

Colleen rolled over partially and threw her arm around Marsha's neck and brought their lips together in a hungry kiss. "No one's ever made me come that hard before," she sighed.

Chapter Fifteen

COLLEEN SAT BEHIND her desk Monday morning and sipped a cup of coffee as she perused an advertising contract in front of her. She'd read the same clause five times and still couldn't remember what it said. She set her cup down and leaned back in her chair. She wasn't really tired. She felt relaxed for the first time in a long time. She smiled. She knew the reason for her relaxation. Marsha. Her skin tingled as she remembered the feel of Marsha's hands moving across her body. Last night Marsha hadn't made love to a fantasy woman. She had made love to Colleen and Colleen had never known such tenderness or satisfaction, although she was a little sore from their marathon lovemaking.

Colleen rested her chin on the heel of her hand and smiled, reliving the weekend she and Marsha had spent learning and appreciating one another's body. The phone on her desk rang. She answered it on the third ring, forcing her mind to leave her pleasant memories. "Colleen Walters," she answered. After a few moments of silence, no one responded. "This is Colleen Walters. Can I help you?" The only response was the sound of metal clanging in the background and men's voices. Finally she placed the receiver back on its cradle. Obviously a wrong number. Before she could turn back to the contract she was supposed to be examining, the phone rang again. She frowned at it, but snatched it up. "Walters," she snapped.

"You sound like you're all business today," Marsha's voice said. "I didn't mean to disturb you."

"You didn't, baby. Just had an annoying wrong number right before you called." Colleen lowered her voice. "How are you feeling this morning, sweetie?"

"I'm fine. A little tired though."

"Really?" Colleen replied, her lips curling into a smile. "I can't imagine why."

"I was with a woman last night."

"Oh? Anyone interesting?"

"She was...insatiable."

"And she's a little sore this morning too. Are you sure you can trust her?"

"Working on it. I want to, but–"

Heather, Colleen's assistant, opened the door and stuck her head inside. "Sorry to interrupt you, Ms. Walters, but you have a call waiting on the other line."

"Okay," Colleen said. "I'm sorry, honey, but I have another call. I'll talk to you later, okay."

"I'll probably be asleep until around three."

"Call me when you wake up. Sweet dreams, honey."

Colleen pushed the button to answer the other line. "Colleen Walters. Sorry to keep you on hold." Again all she heard was metal clanging. "Hello. Who is this?" The sound of heavy breathing drowned out the background noise and startled Colleen. She slammed the receiver down hard and stood. She marched around her desk and flung open her office door.

"Who was that call on hold from?" she snapped as she stood over Heather's desk.

Heather looked up. "Uh...I...Well, I don't know, Ms. Walters. They didn't leave a name, just said you were expecting their call."

"Can you retrieve the number the call came from?"

"Sure. Let me call up the memory. Should I call them back for you?"

"No. Just give me the number. I'll call myself." She snatched the piece of paper containing the number from her assistant's hand. She paused before stomping back into her office and smiled at the young woman. "Sorry, Heather. The call was a surprise that's all. Not your fault."

Colleen looked at the number as she sat. It didn't look familiar. She fisted her hands and stared at the phone. For some reason she felt uneasy, but forced herself to pick up the receiver and dial the number.

"Milo's Paint and Body," a man answered gruffly.

"I'm sorry to bother you, but I received a call from this number a few minutes ago and we were disconnected. Did you see who made the call?"

The man's voice faded as he yelled at someone. "Hey, Eddie! Did anyone come in to use this phone a little while ago?"

Colleen couldn't hear the other man's reply, but the man who had answered was back on the line. "Yeah. Some woman made a couple of quick calls about five minutes ago."

"Can you describe her, please?"

"Eddie! Come're!"

A second man was on the line a few seconds later, panting slightly. "Yeah!"

"I'm sorry, but can you describe the woman who used the phone there about five or ten minutes ago? I was expecting her call," Colleen lied.

"Tall, kinda skinny. Dark, curly hair. Short. Dressed kinda fancy, like for business, ya know. She was wearin' sunglasses so I didn't see her eyes. Looked too rich for my blood, if ya know what I mean," Eddie chuckled.

"Is she still there or nearby?"

"Nope. Jumped into a car and took off like she was being chased by the devil."

"All right. I appreciate it, Eddie. Goodbye."

"Sure thing," Eddie said as he hung up.

Colleen leaned back in her chair and took a deep breath. Strange, she thought. Probably nothing more than a wrong number. Then again she had never heard of a heavy breather willing to be placed on hold.

A COUPLE OF hours after lunch, a tap at Colleen's office door drew her attention away from the preliminary contract lying in front of her. She smiled when the door cracked open and Heather, the station intern who was serving as her temporary secretary, poked her head in. "Mail's here," she said with a smile.

"Just lay it on the desk," Colleen said. "I'll check it in a few minutes. Thanks."

Heather crossed the carpeted floor and set a small stack of envelopes and a manila envelope on the corner of the desk. "How do you like your job so far, Heather?"

The young girl grinned. "So far you're the only one who remembers my name, but it is my first week here."

"In case no one's said it already, welcome to KLEW," Colleen said. "What do you want to do in radio in the future?"

"I'd love to have a show like Desdemona's. But I don't think my voice is provocative enough." Heather shrugged.

"What made you pick radio instead of television?" Colleen asked. "You're an attractive girl."

Heather thought for a moment. "I personally like the anonymity of it. The listeners can imagine the person behind the mic any way they want. Plus, someone like Desdemona doesn't have to worry about her wardrobe or squealing fans hounding her when she goes out. Lots of my classmates are looking toward television." She shrugged. "Guess I don't want to become known as Heather the Weather Girl."

Colleen laughed. "All very good reasons."

"Why did you choose radio?" Heather asked.

"Pretty much the same reasons, except I have no desire to be behind the mic." Colleen picked up her mail and glanced through the envelopes. "Thanks again, Heather."

Once Heather was gone, Colleen took a letter-opener from her desk drawer and methodically cut each envelope open. Most were tossed into the trash can next to her desk. She picked up a slightly larger manila envelope and turned it over. No return address. A handful of five by seven photos slid onto her desk and she dropped the envelope. She stared at an assortment of color pictures and shivered as she thumbed through the series of snapshots of her with Marsha. She looked closely at each picture before she realized they had been taken during the weekend barbecue. There was a shot of Trish, one of Mattie, and a few of Marsha's neighbors. One was obviously taken in the evening when

Marsha had kissed her after Trish and Mattie left. A picture of Marsha alone had a target superimposed over her face. *First you'll watch her die,* was written along the bottom of the picture. The next picture was a close-up of Colleen's smiling face, also with a message across the bottom: *Then I'll watch you die.* Colleen squeezed her eyes shut for a moment before sweeping them into the trash. Then she reached for her phone and quickly dialed a number.

"JACK WALTERS," HER uncle's voice answered after two or three rings. His deep voice was soft, as usual.

"Uncle Jack, Colleen."

"Hey, what's up, sweetie?" he asked jovially.

"She's out, Uncle Jack." Colleen wrapped an arm around her waist to calm the fluttering in her stomach. "And she knows where I am."

"That's not possible, baby. She's barely halfway through her sentence."

"I'm telling you she's out," Colleen insisted.

"Let me make a couple of calls, Colleen. Stay calm."

"She threatened to kill me again, Uncle Jack."

"I know," he said softly. "Let me call you right back. You at home?"

"No. I'm at work," Colleen answered.

Colleen paced back and forth in front of her desk waiting for her phone to ring. She carried her coffee cup into her office restroom and rinsed it out before preparing a new cup. Another knock at her office door distracted her for a moment. Heather entered carrying a large crystal vase holding a dozen pinkish-orange roses surrounded by greenery and baby's breath. As she walked toward Colleen's desk, the cloying, spicy scent of the roses struck Colleen's nose.

"A delivery guy just dropped these off for you," Heather said. "Aren't they beautiful?"

Colleen stared at the roses and barely managed to acknowledge Heather as she began to feel sick to her stomach. She wanted to scream and throw the flowers and vase across the room. They had once been her favorites, but now only brought back painful memories. She needed to remain calm. She needed to warn her parents that the psycho who had tormented them for over a year was loose again.

"There's a card," Heather said as she pulled a small yellow envelope from the cardholder stuck among the roses. "Must be a secret admirer."

"Just leave it there, please. I'll look at it later," Colleen said with a slight tremble in her voice.

As soon as Heather closed the office door behind her Colleen slowly approached the desk as if fearing the roses would spring from the vase and attack her. She sat down and slid the envelope closer before picking it up. She opened the flap and withdrew the card. She recognized the handwriting and read the message the card held: *Deepest sympathies for your loss.*

The phone on Colleen's desk rang and startled her as she stared at the offensive floral arrangement. Her hand shook and she almost dropped her coffee cup. She pressed the button for the ringing line without looking at the number, "What did you find out?" she asked.

"Hello, baby. Do you like the roses? I'm looking forward to touching you again...sooner than you know," a soft voice purred, leaving a hint of laughter in Colleen's ear before the call disconnected.

A minute later the phone rang again. Colleen looked at the number before answering as she struggled to keep her hand from shaking. "Jack?"

"You were right, Colleen. How did you know?"

"She sent me a present." She cleared her throat. "And she just called me. I thought it was you."

"Call the police."

"And tell them what?" she snapped. "That my ex-lover sent me a bouquet of roses?" She rubbed her forehead.

"Do you still have a restraining order?"

"Yes. But you know as well as I do that the restraining order only works if she harms me and then it would be too late. Warn Mom and Dad. I don't know what she might do. She's crazy."

"Do you still have the gun I gave you?"

"Yes. When did she get out?"

"Apparently a couple of months ago. Overcrowding and good behavior. Apparently a model prisoner."

Colleen laughed without humor. "You know the definition of model, don't you?"

"What's that?"

"An imitation of the real thing. Thanks, Uncle Jack. I love you."

"I love you too, honey. I won't let anything happen to you. I promise. Since you met Rusty because of me, I owe you that."

Colleen placed the phone back onto its cradle. She had to think. Marsha! Rusty had to have seen them together over the weekend. She had to warn her. How long had Rusty been watching them?

Colleen grabbed the phone again and dialed Marsha's number. The cell rang several times, but no one answered. She located her car keys and left her office. She hurried to the attached parking garage and jumped into her vehicle. She redialed Marsha's number on her cell. "Come on, come on. Wake up, Marsha," she mumbled as she quickly glanced up and down the street before accelerating onto the road. She didn't want to frighten Marsha, but it was time to tell her about Rusty.

Chapter Sixteen

MARSHA STEPPED OUT of the shower and ran an over-sized towel briskly over her skin. As usual, the hot water made her sleepy and she yawned as she tried to brush her wet hair into some semblance of order. She had just pulled her old terry cloth robe on when she heard the buzzer at her front door. She was surprised when she was greeted by a young man dressed in a brown uniform and a bicycle helmet.

"Marsha Barrett?" he asked.

"Yes."

"Sign here, please," he said, thrusting a clipboard and pen forward.

As soon as Marsha handed the clipboard back to him, he opened his messenger bag and withdrew a large white envelope.

"Thanks," she said, taking the envelope and flipping it over looking for a return address. She carried it to the couch and sat down. She leaned back as she slid a finger under the flap and pinched the metal clasp open. She stuck her hand inside and slid out an eight-by-ten photograph. She frowned as she stared at the color picture. She instantly recognized the woman. It looked like it had been taken inside a dance club somewhere. In the middle of a seemingly pulsing crowd Colleen's arm was wrapped around the shoulders of her dance partner. The woman's hand cupped Colleen's breast as her mouth was pressed into the hollow of her neck. Colleen held the woman's head in place, seemingly enjoying the touch of the woman's hand and lips. The look on Colleen's face was sheer ecstasy, eyes closed, head thrown back. Marsha flipped the picture over. A label attached to the back read: *She belongs to me!*

COLLEEN RAN UP the front steps to Marsha's house nearly half an hour after she left the station. She punched the doorbell and heard it buzz, but no one answered. She pressed the buzzer again and held it a few seconds in case Marsha was asleep. Something was wrong. Marsha's door buzzer should wake the dead. She paced on the front porch before pounding on the door with her fist. "Marsha!" she called out. "Please open the door!"

She thought she heard a sound from inside and pressed her ear against the door. She stumbled and almost fell when the door flew open unexpectedly. Without looking at Marsha's face, Colleen grabbed her and pulled her into a tight embrace, running her hand over Marsha's damp hair.

"Oh my God, sweetie," Colleen breathed. "I was so worried. There's something I have to tell you."

Marsha pushed Colleen away roughly. "You're a fuckin' liar!" Marsha shouted. "Get the hell out of my house! I never want to see you again!"

Colleen was stunned. "What..." she started. Then she saw Marsha's face. Her eyes were red and swollen as if she'd been crying...crying a lot. Colleen reached out to comfort her, only to have her hand slapped away.

"Don't touch me!" Marsha screamed. "You're just like every beautiful woman I've ever known. Now get out before I call the cops and have you removed." Marsha drew herself up and marched to the door, opening it for Colleen.

"I don't understand, Marsha. What's wrong?"

Marsha shifted her eyes and narrowed them slightly. "You lied. You let me believe you cared. You let me believe I was someone you could care about."

"You are! I care about you more than I thought possible. Please tell me what's wrong."

Marsha strode to her coffee table and snatched up something. Before Colleen could say anything else, Marsha brought her hand up quickly, holding the picture she'd received earlier.

Colleen glanced at it and her voice sounded weak when she spoke. "Where did you get that?"

"What's the difference? This is you, right?" Colleen opened her mouth to speak, but nothing came out. "Is it you?" Marsha repeated loudly.

"Yes," Colleen forced out.

Marsha turned the picture and stared at it again briefly. "And the leech attached to your neck?"

After their eyes met briefly, Colleen saw the depth of Marsha's pain and anguish. Colleen shook her head and stared at the carpeting. "Would you believe me?"

"Depends on what you say," Marsha said as she frowned.

"She was my lover," Colleen answered, her voice catching. She looked at the ceiling, refusing to meet Marsha's eyes again. "I trusted her." She shook her head. "It was a mistake."

"Did your family know her?"

"Yes." Colleen said. "They hated her, but I...I chose her."

"Why?"

"Why did I choose her?" Colleen turned her eyes away and stared out the front window. "She was attentive, wealthy, and..."

"Beautiful," Marsha said flatly.

"Yes," Colleen rasped forcefully. "She was the most beautiful woman I'd ever seen." She turned to face Marsha. "I didn't know how much ugliness lay beneath all that beauty. I was young and stupid and naive."

Marsha frowned. "Is that why you've chosen me? You think there is some kind of beauty beneath all this ugliness?" she asked, sweeping her hand down her body. She shook a finger at Colleen and laughed. "The truth finally rears its ugly head, pardon the pun."

"That's not true, Marsha."

"The hell it isn't!" Marsha shouted. "Beautiful people attach themselves to less attractive mates because they know it's safe. There's no chance in hell their mate will ever leave them for someone more beautiful."

"That has nothing to do with us."

"Why are you telling me now?"

"To protect you. Rusty threatened to kill me, my family, and anyone close to me." Colleen paced in the small room. "She was released from prison early. She's probably been following me for at least the last month. She knows who you are and where you live. You're not safe if she knows we're seeing one another. I...I think she was here the night of the barbecue. I saw someone, but it was only a shadow."

"That's too fuckin' bad because I'm not leaving my home because of some whack-job bitch you used to fuck." Marsha's face twisted as it filled with anger.

Colleen ignored the cutting comment. "Come home with me. You'll be safer there."

Marsha barked a laugh. "I seriously doubt that."

"I'd feel safer if you were with me, sweetie."

"Go home. I can take care of myself."

Colleen reached out to touch Marsha's cheek, but she turned away. "Please, Marsha," she said. "Don't do this."

"Just go home," Marsha said, feeling the crushing weight of despair choking her. "It was great while it lasted. More than I deserve."

Colleen paused at the front door and looked back at Marsha. "You're not the only one with scars, you know. At least you can see yours."

Marsha stared after her as the door closed, tears running down her cheeks.

MARSHA STEPPED OFF the bus a little before eleven-thirty and walked the half block to the radio station. She saw Colleen moments before she pushed the door open. She took a deep breath and strode into the lobby, hoisting her backpack farther up her back.

"Marsha," Colleen said.

"Get away from me," Marsha snapped as she shouldered past Colleen.

"Marsha, please."

"Leave me alone," Marsha shot over her shoulder. She threw a wave at Boomer and went into the studio. Gary looked at his watch as if to ask what Marsha was doing there. Colleen stopped outside the soundproofed room and stood there until Gary gave his sign-off and prepared to leave. Marsha followed him to the door and locked it behind him. She took her seat and arranged her headphones comfortably on her head.

"What's happenin', *chica*?" Boomer asked.

"Nothing that involves you, Boomer. Leave it alone, okay? Let's go," she said as the intro music for her show began.

"This is Desdemona, here to hold your hand and hear your feelings. Feelin' kind of lonely myself tonight so I'll grant my own request to start us off while you dial in. Give it your best shot tonight, Omaha." She lowered her voice seductively. "I'm waitin' for ya."

As the music began Boomer's mic broke in. "Please let me talk to you, Marsha."

"Talk's cheap, baby," Marsha said, glaring at the sound booth. "The sex was great, by the way. Thanks for that at least."

"It wasn't about the sex, dammit!" Marsha saw Colleen's face redden slightly as she looked at Boomer. She turned away for a semblance of privacy. "I love you," she said in nearly a whisper.

"Afraid someone will hear you?"

Colleen glowered at Marsha from the sound booth. "I love you, Marsha Barrett," she said boldly. "Would you like me to say it on air too?"

Boomer's mouth fell open and he shook his head. He reached up and took his headphones from Colleen. "You can't say that on the air, Marsh," he said. "The switchboard's lit up like a fuckin' Christmas tree."

"Send the calls through," Marsha said.

One by one she handled each call and request until a lull came nearly an hour later. She hit the mic button to Boomer. "Tell Ms. Walters to leave. She's in violation of FCC rules and regs by being in the sound booth. Call security if you have to."

Satisfied that Colleen had left the booth, Marsha spoke to Boomer again. "Hey, Boomer. Sorry about that."

"You dumpin' a fox like Colleen? That's brutal, woman."

"Life is brutal."

COLLEEN LEFT THE radio station a little after one in the morning. She had gone to her office after the confrontation with Marsha in an attempt to calm done, but she was still angry. Marsha had jumped to a conclusion and not given Colleen a chance to explain. That hadn't been fair and Colleen frowned as she approached the parking garage and felt around in her purse for her damn car keys. She had to find a way to speak to Marsha and make her understand the danger she was in. Rusty had promised to kill Colleen and anyone close to her and Rusty never made a promise she couldn't keep.

Frustrated as she searched for her keys, she paused at the entrance to the parking garage. "Where the hell are you?" she muttered. She relaxed for a moment as her fingers located the elusive keys. Colleen made her way down the short flight of concrete steps to the first small landing. She glanced down before stepping onto the first step, but was stopped when an arm wrapped around her throat and pulled her back.

"Hello, baby," a low, familiar voice said as a second hand moved slowly over Colleen's chest. "Miss me?"

Colleen struggled against the arm covering her throat. She wanted to scream, but the choking hold prevented anything from leaving her mouth.

Rusty's arm continued to tighten as her hand groped Colleen's breast. "Damn, I've missed the feel of you." Her breathing became raspier as she fondled Colleen roughly.

Colleen's struggles grew weaker and she could feel her brain beginning to spin from lack of oxygen. Her hands still clung to Rusty's arm, but there was no strength in them. Her knees felt like Jell-O and she tried to push against Rusty in order to take just one breath.

"How does it feel to have the life being squeezed out of you, Colleen? That's how I felt for three long, suffocating years," Rusty hissed into Colleen's ear. "I lost everything because of you and now you're going to know how that feels." She pinched Colleen's nipple hard through her clothes. She released Colleen's throat and pushed her sharply forward into the metal rail surrounding the landing.

Colleen grabbed the railing with one hand while the other grasped at her throat. She tried to turn to face Rusty, but her feet were at the edge of the small landing. She lost her footing and fell down the final steps to the lower level of the garage. She was momentarily dazed when the back of her head struck the pavement and bounced. Pain shot up her leg as her ankle buckled when she tried to push her body up. She managed to sit up and attempted to crawl away. She could hear Rusty slowly and deliberately walking toward her.

Colleen was breathing hard and bit her lower lip against the pain in her throbbing ankle. Finally, she stopped to gather her breath. "What do you want?" she wheezed.

Rusty smiled down at her. It was the same smile Colleen had seen before she lost consciousness five years earlier. Rusty took a gun from her jacket pocket and pointed it at a terrified Colleen. "I made you a promise, sugar, and you know I always keep my promises. No matter how long it takes."

Colleen fought back tears and her lips trembled as she spoke. "I don't care what you do to me, but leave my family alone," she begged.

"That's going to be half the fun." Rusty knelt down next to Colleen and cocked her head as she smiled and stroked the side of Colleen's face with the gun's cold barrel. "So you're safe for a while, but you'll be begging me to kill you as everyone around you dies first."

Rusty stood, staring down at the injured Colleen as she shoved the gun back into her pocket. "By the way, darling, how is that sweet mother of yours? *Dying* to see her again." She threw her head back and laughed as she walked away.

AN HOUR LATER, Marsha was in the process of lining up the next fifteen minutes of requests. The number had been enough to keep both her and Boomer busy. Not many of her listeners were interested in chatting, but each caller had a song in mind for either a current lover, a prospective lover, or a former lover. If the request line stayed as active as it currently was, Marsha knew it would be a short evening.

A little after three-thirty in the morning, Boomer sent through another request. Marsha blew out a deep breath before answering the line.

"And what can I play to make your night a little happier, baby?" Marsha asked in her usual welcoming voice.

"My evening has already been remarkable, darling. Better than anything I could have imagined. What I want to hear right now is the theme from *Jaws*. Caio, darling."

"Sounds like you're ready to take a bite out of someone. Anyone who needs to be warned?" Marsha asked.

"She's already been warned," the woman said, her laughter cut off when she disconnected.

"That was sweet," Boomer said sarcastically.

"Really." It had only been a few days earlier that Marsha thought she'd found someone special, but had realized she'd made a mistake. Maybe she'd overreacted to the picture of Colleen in another woman's arms. After all, she hadn't known Colleen then and really hadn't given her a chance to explain. If she saw her in the morning perhaps they could talk.

"Hey, when you taking your break?" Marsha asked.

"In a few. Why? Ready for a pick-me-up?"

"I was kinda thinkin' about a fresh cappuccino, now that you mention it."

Boomer left the main control room and waited as she stepped out of the studio. "My treat," she said as she handed him a five. "Don't skip the country on me, okay?" she said with a laugh.

TWENTY MINUTES TICKED away with no sign of Boomer. Not long after that Boomer interrupted her conversation with a listener and motioned for her to open the studio door. She ended the conversation and keyed up a public service announcement.

"What took you—" she started.

"Colleen's hurt, man," Boomer said, his eyes shifting up and down the hallway. "I got her back to her office, but she won't let me call an ambulance."

"Okay," Marsha nodded. "I'll check on her. I'll take my break now. Everything's already lined up."

"I got it," he answered. "Forgot about the cappuccinos though."

Marsha tapped on Colleen's door, but there was no response. She finally turned the knob and stuck her head into the office. Only the light on Colleen's desk was on. Marsha waited for her eyes to adjust, but still didn't see Colleen.

The door into Colleen's private bathroom opened and the blonde hobbled out, drying her face and hands. She saw Marsha, but refused to meet her eyes. "What do you want?" she asked, her voice sounding irritated.

"Boomer said you were hurt. What happened?"

"I...uh...had an accident. Missed a step in the garage and twisted my ankle."

"Will you be all right?"

"Why do you care? You made your feelings perfectly clear earlier," Colleen snapped. Then her face crumpled as she tried to bite back tears. Limping badly, she began making her way toward the office couch.

Marsha reached out to assist her, but Colleen jerked her arm away and almost lost her balance. She was forced to catch her weight on her injured ankle and bit back the pain as she winced "You can go back to work. I'll call a cab to get home. I don't need your assistance. I don't want your sympathy."

Marsha frowned. "You're lying."

Colleen's head flew up. "Nothing I've told you has been a lie, dammit. You wouldn't give me a chance to explain anything because you'd already made up your mind that you couldn't trust me. I gave my body and soul to you completely, but all it took was one picture to make you forget everything without even giving me a chance to explain."

"Tell me now."

"Why should I? You don't want to hear the truth."

"Make me believe you then," Marsha challenged.

"I didn't fall down the damn stairs," Colleen said, exhaling loudly. "I was pushed."

"Did you see who pushed you?"

Colleen looked increasingly uncomfortable. She rested her hand on the back of the sofa. "It was Rusty, my former lover."

"The redhead in the photograph?"

"If you want to hear the truth then shut the hell up and let me tell this," Colleen said firmly. She glared at Marsha. "Yes, Rusty. She was very beautiful. Possibly the most physically beautiful woman I've ever met or ever will meet. Does that make you fucking happy? It's what you really want to know, isn't it?" She waited for Marsha to say something, but she didn't. "She's still beautiful on the outside, but ugly on the inside," Colleen continued, her voice catching. She looked at the ceiling, refusing to meet Marsha's eyes again. "I loved her and I trusted her." She shook her head. "I was too young, too trusting, too naïve, too easily impressed by a façade, too everything."

"If it's too hard for you, I understand," Marsha said, reaching out to touch her arm.

Colleen slapped her hand away and glared at her. "No. You wanted to know. You don't trust me or my motives. I know better than anyone where misplaced trust can lead." Colleen paused and seemed to gather herself. "The last time I trusted someone outside my family had terrible consequences. My lover was an important woman in the financial community of Washington." Colleen closed her eyes, remembering the past. "Rusty was a few years older than I was, but pursued me anyway. She was tall, slender, and the most gorgeous woman I'd ever met. She was charming, considerate, generous, attentive, everything I thought the perfect partner would be. I felt special because she wanted me. When we entered a room, heads turned." She opened her eyes and looked at Marsha. "But it was all because she felt important with me on her arm."

"You don't have to go on," Marsha said as she turned to leave. "I get it."

Colleen grabbed Marsha's hand and held it tightly. "You don't get shit! We argued. We had argued before, but suddenly words weren't enough. She slapped me. When she saw the disbelief and fear on my face it empowered her somehow. She couldn't stop and beat me until I was unconscious. When I regained consciousness I called the police. She was sentenced to five years for assault and battery. That was three years ago." She took a deep breath and exhaled it forcefully. "She stole my self-confidence and self-esteem in one horrible night. I haven't told anyone here what happened because I was ashamed and humiliated. Only my family knows."

Marsha ran her thumb over the top of Colleen's hand. "I'm sorry you were hurt," she said.

"She threatened me and every member of my family at the end of her trial. Our supposed friends stopped talking to me and accused me of cheating and stealing her money. Only the jury believed me. Now she's back. She'll kill me and everyone in my family. Everyone I care about."

Colleen buried her face in her hands and wept as Marsha sat next to her and took her in her arms.

Colleen gradually gathered herself and pushed Marsha away. "No one saw what happened and I can't prove Rusty was there."

"I believe you," Marsha said, stroking Colleen's cheek.

"Don't," Colleen said. "Leave me alone, Marsh. Please go away."

"Colleen –" Marsha started.

"Go away!" Colleen said as loudly as she could. "I've already accepted that she's going to kill me, but I won't be responsible for anyone else's death."

"I have to get back to work right now, but if you wait until I'm off I'll take you to the hospital and then home. Promise me you'll wait."

Colleen shook her head and started to say something, but Marsha stopped her.

"Promise you'll wait."

Taking a deep breath Colleen nodded.

"I'll put some ice on your ankle. Then just rest." Marsha helped Colleen lie down and get comfortable. She ran to the break room, found a discarded sandwich baggie, and filled it with ice. By the time she returned to Colleen's office, Colleen was asleep. Marsha draped the baggie over Colleen's swollen ankle and pulled the quilt off the back of the couch and arranged it gently over her, brushing hair from her face. She went toward the office door to leave when she heard Colleen say, "I'm sorry I disappointed you, Marsha."

Marsha didn't respond.

MARSHA WAS EXHAUSTED when she opened the door to Colleen's condo after two hours in the emergency room and held it as Colleen slowly made her way inside on her hospital-issued crutches. Although her entire body ached, the x-ray had shown Colleen had a badly sprained ligament, nothing was broken. A few days rest and she would be fine.

"Let's get you into bed," Marsha said after she closed and locked the front door. She gently guided Colleen into the bedroom and helped her sit on the edge of her mattress.

"I'm a little hungry, Marsh," she said. "I haven't eaten since around noon yesterday."

"I'll make you something and then give you one of these spiffy pain-killers," Marsha said.

Colleen blew out a long breath and ran a hand down her slightly swollen leg. She reached up to pull her top over her head, but struggled with it. "Fuck!" she snapped.

Marsha helped remove the top and said, "Lie down. I'll be back in a few minutes." She helped Colleen recline and removed her shoe before reaching up to ease her skirt and slip off. Colleen didn't put up much of a struggle, but caught Marsha's wrist. Although her eyelids were beginning to droop, she said clearly, "I know you don't trust me anymore and I don't blame you, but I loved you with everything I had, Marsha."

"I know." Marsha shrugged. But sometimes love just wasn't enough, she thought.

Colleen frowned. "You could be killed because of me." Tears began to fill her eyes. "I'm not worth dying for."

Marsha draped a quilt over Colleen, swept her hair back, and kissed her forehead before going into the kitchen. She opened a can of soup and prepared a grilled cheese sandwich. She helped Colleen sit up and eat. By the time they were finished, it was obvious that Colleen couldn't keep her eyes open much longer, claiming excellent drugs were responsible. Marsha cleaned up the kitchen before she rejoined Colleen.

Colleen rolled onto her side. "I'm sorry, Marsha. This isn't working out the way I wanted."

"Roll over," Marsha said softly. She wrapped an arm around Colleen's waist and drew her closer to spoon against her. "Just rest."

Chapter Seventeen

TWO WEEKS AFTER her run-in with Rusty, Colleen was finally able to get around with a slight limp. While recuperating, Colleen had little to do other than think. She tried reading, but nothing seemed to grab her attention for more than a few minutes. Thankfully, she hadn't heard from Rusty and there'd been no further threats against either herself or her family. She also hadn't heard from Marsha. Colleen remembered falling asleep the night she injured her ankle with Marsha's arm around her, but Marsha was gone when she woke up the next morning. By the time Colleen returned to work Marsha didn't seem angry any longer, she also wasn't as friendly and went out of her way to never touch Colleen. It seemed that Marsha had erased any memory of the weekend they had spent together at the end of May. Gradually Marsha began to seem comfortable enough to meet Colleen in her office to discuss possible changes to the format of her show, which was doing well in the new southern and Philadelphia markets.

Periodically, Colleen touched Marsha when they were alone and going over paperwork, but Marsha refused to acknowledge any interest. Marsha hadn't initiated intimate contact with Colleen since the night of the neighborhood barbecue and seemed content for their relationship to remain nothing more than a friendship. Colleen hungered to be touched more as time passed and couldn't understand Marsha's reticence.

Colleen looked forward to seeing Marsha, hearing the soothing softness of her voice, or catching her subtle scent long after she'd left a room. She fantasized about holding Marsha in her arms again while stroking her body. Colleen knew Marsha felt safe within her fantasies, knowing her fantasy lover would never betray her and she would always be romantic and desirable. For a weekend, Colleen had been that lover and she wanted to be again.

MONDAY NIGHT MARSHA leaned back in her chair in front of the studio console and let the strains of the last request wash over her, adding to the intensity of her fantasy. It had been a relatively quiet night with very few new listeners calling in to make requests. Marsha hoped they were all with their perfect fantasy lovers, seeking satisfaction at least in their own minds. In between the haunting strains of a Kenny G request Marsha opened her mic, closed her eyes, and spoke softly, her lips nearly touching the microphone cover.

"Let your mind drift away to that first perfect moment your lover came to you. The first time your fingers touched and the nerves of your fingertips sent pulses of desire into every part of your body. Can you still feel the tenderness, the heat, the passion, the desire simmering just beneath your skin ready to erupt?"

The light weight of hands on her shoulders startled her and Marsha's eyes opened. She would have fallen from her chair if her hand hadn't gripped the edge of the console. Her body knew the hands touching her without looking. She cleared her throat and segued from her sultry soliloquy.

"This is Desdemona on KLEW-FM in beautiful Omaha, Nebraska reminding you to play nice and be safe, especially when your thoughts turn to someone...special." She punched in the next song which, thankfully, was less seductive. She used the console to turn her chair around and look up at Colleen. When their eyes met, Marsha suddenly had trouble breathing. Colleen's eyes were filled with longing.

Marsha flipped her headphones off so Boomer wouldn't overhear their private conversation.

"I would have sworn the studio door was locked," Marsha said.

"Why are you doing this, Marsha?"

Marsha couldn't look into Colleen's eyes any longer. "I don't know what you mean. I'm not doing anything."

"And that's the problem." Colleen took a deep breath and exhaled slowly before continuing. "When you talk like that to your listeners, it feels like you're touching me. I want to be with you again so much. I want to crawl inside you and possess you. You're the lover *I* dream about. Surely you know that. You have to know I want more than merely friendship."

Marsha opened her mic and spoke, her eyes returning to Colleen's. "Boomer, I need a moment. Bring up a thirty-second spot. The next two requests are already in the queue. Follow with another thirty-second. How long?"

"About six, seven minutes."

"Long enough," Marsha said. She pushed a button on the console and heard a muffled click as the door to the studio locked. Marsha removed her headphones and stepped closer to Colleen, guiding her toward the studio door. Colleen's lips glistened in the low lighting as she ran her tongue over them.

"Please don't hurt me," Marsha whispered as Colleen brought their lips closer. "I couldn't survive it again."

"Never," Colleen said against Marsha's mouth.

Colleen let Marsha lead as the kiss deepened, tongues probing and bodies aching for more. When the kiss came to an end, Marsha swallowed hard. She reached for her headphones and slipped them over her ears. After some light flirting with the next caller, she began the next selection.

"Can you meet me for breakfast?" she asked Colleen. "Please."

"Of course. The usual place?"

MARSHA PUSHED OPEN the front entrance to International House of Pancakes and scanned the restaurant.

"Table for one, Marsha?" a harried-looking hostess asked.

"I'm meeting someone," Marsha answered, still looking around. Finally she spotted Colleen and smiled. She could feel Colleen's cool blue gaze on her as she made her way to a booth near the back of the restaurant and imagined her walk as smooth and debonair.

"Hi," Marsha said when she stopped next to the booth and slid in across from Colleen. There was already a carafe of coffee on the table and Colleen poured Marsha a cup while she got settled.

"Thank you," Marsha said in acknowledgment as she added cream and sugar.

"What did you want to talk about?"

Marsha took a deep drink of her coffee and looked at Colleen. "Do you have a clue how beautiful you are?" Marsha asked. "You are just...just so heartbreakingly gorgeous." She watched as Colleen's face turned a brighter pink with embarrassment. She reached across the table and took Colleen's hand, turning it over and stroking a finger across her palm. "You scare the shit out of me, Colleen, because you give me hope that someone could care for me in a way I've never thought possible. You have to know I want to be with you, but I'm afraid. I want to, but..."

Colleen withdrew her hand from Marsha's grasp and frowned. Finally she glared at Marsha and said, "So you aren't interested in a more intimate relationship with me."

"I didn't say that. Of course, I want to be with you, make love with you." Marsha smiled. "You make me feel alive for the first time in a long time."

"I know how you make me feel. I love the woman you are."

"You wouldn't say that if you knew the real me." Marsha stared into her coffee cup and spoke so softly Colleen could barely hear her.

"Then tell me."

"I trusted another woman once," Marsha said as she played with her napkin. "I wanted to believe she cared about me." She took a deep breath and exhaled before continuing. "I didn't have the right to be angry because of your former...lover. I was guilty of the same thing. Paulina was lovely, but not too sophisticated, certainly not wealthy." Marsha smiled. "We lived together for a while, just until her modeling career was established. The more successful she was, the farther apart we grew, but God she was beautiful. Next thing I knew she began using drugs occasionally. Said it helped her keep her weight down. Guess I was so afraid of losing her I didn't make a big deal out of it. We were only together about a year when one night I came home from work early and found her in our bed with another model she'd met during a shoot that day."

"After just one day?"

"Paulina claimed it was an instant attraction," Marsha said with a bitter laugh. "So I told her it meant an instant eviction. The next day the cops were at my door and arrested me for assault. Paulina claimed I had been stalking her. She claimed I beat her up when I saw her with another woman. She did have a black eye, but I didn't give it to her."

Marsha saw the look on Colleen's face and shook her head. "I would never hit a woman, no matter how angry I was, Colleen, so please don't compare me to Rusty. I'm far from beautiful, but I wouldn't hit anyone."

"I know," Colleen said quietly.

"I couldn't afford the bail and didn't really know anyone I could contact, so I stayed in jail for about three months." Marsha rubbed her eyes and couldn't look at Colleen. "When my fellow inmates found out the charge against me, life became...difficult."

Colleen reached out and placed her hand over Marsha's. "You don't have to go on if it hurts too much."

Marsha laughed. "You told me everything, so it's only fair you know." She took a deep breath. "I became the victim of jail payback. I wasn't a virgin when I went in, but it took me almost six months to get over being sexually assaulted on virtually a daily basis. I couldn't stand to be touched."

"How did you get out?"

Marsha shrugged. "Paulina died of an overdose. One day they opened my cell and said the charges had been dropped. I took what I could and split the next week. I haven't been with anyone...until I met you."

"Did it bother you when I touched you?"

"A little at first, but I got used to it. I enjoyed touching you though, more than I thought I would."

"Please feel free to touch me more. I do like it."

"Yeah, I noticed. I'm sorry, Colleen. I over-reacted. And after what you told me about your ex, I didn't want you to think I was no better."

Colleen shrugged. "I confess it concerns me and brings back my fear of being hurt again a little."

Marsha squeezed Colleen's hand. "I swear I would never hurt you, Colleen."

"I know."

Marsha left a tip on the table for their waitress. She slid out of the booth and held her hand out to Colleen, who didn't hesitate to take it. They walked hand-in-hand out of the restaurant and hailed a cab. Colleen gave Marsha a quick kiss before they climbed into the vehicle.

THAT NIGHT, AFTER a delicious meal of chicken parmesan on a bed of seasoned vermicelli, Colleen put the leftovers into a container for Marsha to take to work for her middle of the night snack. They sat close on the couch and Marsha hesitated before she touched Colleen, each time waiting for her to object. But she never did,

Later Colleen drove Marsha to the station and as they walked from the parking garage to the entrance of the station, Marsha slid her arm around Colleen's waist and leaned slightly against her. It was such a simple act, a natural act, but for both it was an enormous hurdle. To Marsha, allowing herself such an understated and easy familiarity with another woman felt amazing. Colleen stopped at the bottom of the steps into the entrance. Marsha stood one step above her.

"Thanks for a great dinner and the ride to work."

"Do you want me to pick you up in the morning? You could sleep at my place," Colleen said with a waggle of her eyebrows.

"Not if I really wanted to get any sleep. There's no sense in you making two trips. I'll see you when you come to work and then catch the bus."

"Dinner tomorrow?"

"I'll cook this time and have it ready when you get home from work."

"Will my car be safe?"

"Pull it around back. It should be safe there. You have insurance, right?" she asked with a grin. She turned to push the station door open, but stopped and returned to Colleen. She took a step closer and smiled as she leaned forward and took Colleen's face in her hands, kissing her deeply.

"Wow," Colleen breathed as they separated. "Where have you been hiding that?"

Marsha stepped back with a laugh and pushed the door open. "See you in the morning."

"Have a great show," Colleen said as she turned to walk back to her car.

MARSHA SMILED AND waved the next morning when she saw Colleen through the glass of the studio. She glanced at the clock on the wall opposite her. Colleen was at work almost two hours earlier than usual. It had been an uneventful night, but she had enjoyed her phone flirtations. Somehow, to her own ears, she sounded happier, less melancholy. She and Boomer had tossed a few friendly barbs back and forth and shared the food Colleen had packed. She was scheduled to be off the coming weekend and was looking forward to the three days to rejuvenate. Although she had decided to allow the relationship with Colleen to continue, while praying her heart wouldn't be broken, she was actually looking forward to spending time with the willowy blonde. Nothing physical, just spending time getting to know her better. Well, maybe a little physical.

A tap on the studio door brought Marsha back to the present. She pushed the console button to unlock the studio door. Alicia quietly opened the door and slipped inside when the last request began.

"Where's Geoff?" Marsha asked.

"Flu. I get to do a solo this morning," Alicia answered, setting her backpack down.

"I can stay and help, if you need me," Marsha offered.

"Thanks, but I'll be fine. It'll give me a chance to try a couple of things I've been wanting to do."

Marsha keyed up her mic and brought an end to her night. She waited until Alicia began her welcome to listeners before she packed up her things and left the studio. Boomer stepped out of the control booth and gave her a high-five as they walked down the hallway. Before they turned down the main corridor leading to the front door, Colleen stepped out of her office.

"Could I speak to you for a moment, Marsha?" Colleen asked.

Boomer gave Marsha a knowing wink. "I'll see you Monday night, Marsh. Enjoy."

"Thanks, Boomer. Give my regards to your wife," Marsha said as he continued down the hall.

A warm hand grabbed Marsha's arm as she entered Colleen's office. As soon as the door closed, warm lips pressed against hers. She slid her arms around Colleen's waist and deepened the greeting.

"Good morning to you, too, baby," Marsha said when their lips parted.

"I've waited all night to do that," Colleen said, holding Marsha close. "Can you stay a few minutes? There's something I need to talk to you about."

"Only if you have coffee."

"Just made a pot. Have a seat while I pour."

Almost before Marsha could get comfortable in a chair facing Colleen's desk, a mug of steaming aromatic coffee appeared in front of her. Instead of going behind her desk, Colleen sat in the chair next to Marsha.

"My mother called early this morning," Colleen said. To Marsha she sounded a little nervous.

"Is everything all right?"

"You're off this weekend, right?"

"Yeah," Marsha answered, dragging the word out.

"Fly to Philadelphia with me for the weekend."

"Is something wrong?"

"No. It's my folks' anniversary, but I want to spend the weekend with you to get us back on the right track. It would give you a chance to meet my parents."

Marsha almost choked on her coffee as she swallowed around the lump that had instantly formed in her throat. Colleen thumped Marsha on the back until she could catch a breath.

"But..."

"Don't worry, darling. I told them about you when I was home last time." Colleen stared at her hands. "I know it sounds ridiculous for a woman my age, but I tell my mother pretty much everything that's happening in my life. I always have. She wants to meet the woman who's become very special to me."

"That sounds like forever, Colleen." Marsha stared into her cup. "Forever is a long time."

"It's what *I* want, but, of course, I can't speak for you."

Seeing Colleen's eyes mist, Marsha reached out and took her hand. When Colleen looked up, she said, "I'm willing to give it a shot if you promise to pick me up if I faint when I meet them."

"Just be yourself and they'll love you as much as I do," Colleen said, throwing her arms around Marsha.

MARSHA WAITED NERVOUSLY to deplane in Philadelphia a few hours later, shifting from foot to foot. She looked down to check her clothing every few minutes until Colleen laughed.

"You look fine, honey. You're making me nervous and they're *my* parents."

Probably worrying about what your parents will think when they see me the first time, Marsha thought. The plan was for Colleen's parents to pick them up and then take them out for a late lunch before driving to their home on the outskirts of the city. Marsha felt as if a rock were in the pit of her stomach already and was certain she would throw up if she was forced to eat while attempting to make light conversation with two complete strangers as they examined her like an insect under a microscope, trying to decide if she was good enough for their daughter.

Colleen grabbed Marsha's shoulder and pointed toward the exit from the gate area. "There they are!" she said excitedly.

A man standing behind a woman using arm crutches smiled and waved when he saw Colleen moving closer to the exit to greet them. Marsha followed Colleen and took a deep breath, but it didn't help her churning stomach. Colleen bent down to hug the woman before turning her attention to the man who was apparently her father. They stepped to the side of the concourse and Colleen looped her arm through Marsha's.

"Mom, Dad, this is Marsha Barrett." Colleen looked at her and smiled. "Sweetheart, these are my parents, Rosemary and Quentin Walters."

Marsha extended a hand toward Rosemary, who promptly took it and pulled Marsha into a hug. Quentin gave her a firm pat on the back.

Marsha stepped back and took the rolling carry-on from Quentin. Her mind wasn't past hearing Colleen call her sweetheart. The idea that she could be anyone's sweetheart filled her with happiness and she couldn't take her eyes off the beautiful woman gripping her hand. She was still adjusting to it when she realized Quentin Walters was speaking to her.

"I'm sorry, sir. What did you say?"

"I asked if you had a comfortable flight," he repeated with a smile.

"Yes, sir. I don't travel much, so I suppose it was about average. Loud though."

Colleen had warned her she might feel as if she was enduring a job interview once she and the Walters met. She tried to think of clever things she might say if the right question came up.

"Colleen tells us you're from the Chicago area," Quentin said as they waited for the rest of their luggage in baggage claims.

"Near there. Haven't been back in over twenty years. I'm pretty sure it's changed since I left."

"Are your parents still there?"

"No, sir. They're deceased," she lied. For all practical purposes they were dead as far as she was concerned. She let out a quiet sigh of relief when she saw Colleen's bag fall onto the carousel.

"Better let me get that," Quentin said with a smile. "I almost got a hernia the last time and have been lifting weights since she told me she was coming home again."

"Probably all the stuff she needs to look so beautiful all the time," Marsha said with a grin.

"No doubt," Quentin said with a grunt as he hoisted the bag from the carousel. "Thank God it's got wheels."

While Quentin and Marsha wrestled with the luggage, Colleen sighed, "My heroes."

"You can engrave that on our tombstones," Marsha said, looking over a small stack of bags in her arms.

"I'll remember that, baby."

Rosemary chuckled. "I hope you don't mind, but I prepared lunch at home. I thought you girls might be tired."

"Sounds wonderful, Mrs. Walters," Marsha said as she shifted the items in her arms. She looked imploringly at Quentin. "You brought a U-Haul, I hope."

Colleen grinned at Marsha. "Are we at the U-Haul stage already, sweetie?"

OVER LUNCH THE heat from Colleen's hand on her thigh was distracting. Marsha answered every question without hesitation, but noticed Rosemary looking at her several times as if there was something she wanted to say or ask, but held back. Marsha liked the Walters, especially the way Quentin seemed to fawn over his wife. It was obvious everything he did was because he loved her and had nothing to do with her handicap.

"My daughter tells me she loves you," Rosemary finally said, looking directly at Marsha.

Marsha turned her head to look at Colleen. "She's told me that, too, but I haven't quite figured out why yet, ma'am," Marsha responded.

"Perhaps it's merely a healthy sexual attraction," Rosemary said with a shrug.

"Mother!" Colleen hissed.

"Could be something fleeting, like the flu or food poisoning and she'll eventually get over it," Marsha said.

"Marsha!" Colleen fumed. "You two are a laugh a minute."

Rosemary sat back in her chair and returned her attention to Marsha. "Do you believe Colleen loves you?"

After a moment of thought, Marsha answered. "I believe *she* believes it." She cleared her throat. "It's a simple thing to say. Harder to believe."

"And you're afraid of being hurt," Rosemary said.

Marsha swallowed and nodded slightly. "Aren't we all? Colleen's a beautiful woman. I am...less attractive. People are naturally drawn to beauty, so I'm a little hesitant to believe anyone would choose a dandelion over a rose."

"Is that how you see yourself? As a pesky weed?"

"Perhaps."

Rosemary smiled, nodding slightly. "You remind me of myself when I met Quentin. I was able to overcome my fears, thank God. Otherwise I would have missed a wonderful life." She turned to gaze at her husband and Marsha could see the adoration that passed between them. Finally, Rosemary took a deep breath. "Well, I'm sorry to say it, but I need to get busy. The boys and their families will be descending on us in a few hours."

"I can't believe you're going to cook tonight, Mom. It's *your* anniversary," Colleen said as she stood to gather plates and glasses.

"Your father and I discussed it and decided we'd be happier and much more comfortable at home. Besides, I know you girls will clean up," Rosemary said with a smile.

"Lunch was excellent, Mrs. Walters," Marsha said as Quentin helped Rosemary stand and adjust her arm crutches.

"I'm glad you enjoyed it, dear."

Colleen hugged her parents, then took Marsha's hand. "Help me?"

"Just tell me what you want me to do," Marsha answered.

"Oh, I will," Colleen said in a low voice. "But it has nothing to do with washing dishes."

Rosemary winked at Colleen. "We changed the sheets in your room, dear, so everything should be clean and fresh. I'm going to take a short nap before I start preparing dinner." With Quentin's hand resting in the small of her back, Rosemary set off toward their bedroom on the first floor.

Marsha finished clearing the dining room table and followed Colleen into the kitchen. The dishwasher was open and Colleen was loading glasses into the top rack. "Just set them in the sink," she said, rinsing another glass.

Marsha turned on the hot water and ran it over a small plate. Before she could hand it to Colleen, hands slid around her waist and caused her breath to hitch as she was pulled against Colleen's body. She started to protest, but was enjoying the heat against her back too much.

"You feel so good," Colleen whispered as she moved her body against Marsha's back. "How about a nap after we finish in here?"

"But your parents..."

"I'm pretty sure they know we've already slept together," Colleen smiled, lowering her voice to a whisper the last two words.

Marsha sighed. "I like your parents, Colleen. I don't want to take advantage of their hospitality. Doesn't it bother you?"

"The only thing that's bothering me right now is why *you're* so concerned about my parents knowing we sleep together. Are you ashamed to let others know?"

"No, of course not," Marsha said.

"I can make up the bed in the guest room if that would make you happier." There was an unmistakable edge in Colleen's voice as she closed and started the dishwasher. "I'm going upstairs to unpack."

Marsha rubbed her hands up and down the sides of her thighs. Why was this so hard? She went quickly up the stairs toward Colleen's second floor bedroom. She stopped when she saw her duffle in the hallway. Oops. She brought her hand up and hesitated a moment before tapping lightly on the door. When the door finally swung open, Colleen left it open and stepped away. "Well?" she asked.

Marsha entered the room and looked around. Faded mementos from high school and college filled a large corkboard over a white French Provencal writing desk near the window. Lace doilies covered the nightstands and chest of drawers. Soft yellow chintz curtains covered the windows, making the room decidedly feminine.

"Nice room."

"It was my sanctuary. I don't think Mom has changed anything since I left," Colleen said.

"It's very....feminine," Marsha observed with a smile. "Like you."

"I'm tired and am sure you are as well. We should get some rest before the thundering herd arrives."

"Hang on," Marsha said. "I have to investigate some of these knicky-knacky things. I want to know all the little secrets from your past."

"It's junk from a million years ago, Marsha," Colleen groaned.

Marsha gazed at old ticket stubs and pictures pinned to the

corkboard. She leaned closer to one of the pictures

"Is this you?" she asked as she pointed to it.

"Unfortunately, yes," Colleen stood behind Marsha, resting her chin on her shoulder and kissing her neck.

"You were a fuckin' cheerleader!" Marsha smiled as she turned to look at Colleen.

"I'll have you know I was an excellent cheerleader. Very flexible."

"And did you date the captain of the football team, too?" she asked in a low, teasing voice.

Colleen blushed. "Once. The boy was an octopus."

Marsha drew Colleen closer to nibble at her bottom lip. "I can be."

Colleen was breathing heavily as she leaned in for a deeper kiss. "But I like the feel of your hands on me. Do I still need to make up the bed in the guest room?"

"I don't care where I sleep as long as you're there." Marsha drew Colleen into a searing, hungry kiss as her hands caressed her body. "I want you so much," she breathed into Colleen's ear.

THREE HOURS LATER, with a smile on her face, Marsha stood over the kitchen sink peeling a small cluster of potatoes. Basically, Rosemary stood at a long counter, issuing directions. Colleen and Rosemary chatted, occasionally soliciting a response from Marsha. She had always longed to have such a relationship with her mother or even a foster mother, but she had been a shy, silent child. From time to time, one of her foster mothers would attempt to teach her how to cook. All that usually meant was they could later foist off preparing meals on her while they watched soap operas.

Once everything was cooking, Marsha shared a drink with Colleen and her parents. The conversation was light and never turned to personal topics. She was comfortable with the feel of Colleen's fingers stroking the back of her neck lightly.

"The boys will be here in about an hour," Rosemary said, setting her drink down. "I'm going to take a shower and change before they arrive."

"Sounds like a good idea," Colleen said. She reached out and took Marsha's hand.

When they reached Colleen's former bedroom, Colleen said, "You shower first, sweetie."

Marsha pulled clean underwear from a drawer in the dresser and waited until she was alone in the bathroom to undress. She ran the water until it was an acceptable temperature, then stepped under the spray. She had just shampooed her hair when she felt a cool draft. Slender fingers finished working the shampoo into Marsha's hair. She turned and leaned her head back. Colleen ran her hands over Marsha's head, forcing the suds to run down her back. As rivulets of warm water ran down Marsha's face, Colleen's lips met hers in a kiss that promised so much. Colleen pulled her into a gentle embrace and Marsha rested her forehead above Colleen's warm left breast. They stood enmeshed in their feelings until Colleen took a step back.

"I'd never showered with anyone before I met you," Marsha admitted as she looked at Colleen.

"Do you like it?" Colleen asked with a smile.

Marsha nodded and her mind floated back nearly ten years, probably the last time she had been intimate with anyone, but they had never showered together. "Let me wash your hair."

Colleen handed her a bottle of shampoo. Marsha flipped the top up and squirted a handful into the palm of her hand, raising it to her nose to smell it. Jasmine combined with a hint of lavender. Colleen let the water run over her head and bent her neck forward to give Marsha access. At first Marsha rubbed the shampoo through Colleen's hair vigorously. After she determined Colleen's hair had been thoroughly covered she changed to a gentle massaging motion with her fingertips, occasionally sweeping suds away from the top of her lover's head. Satisfied no shampoo would fall into Colleen's eyes, she let her hands slide onto her neck to massage the muscle along the nape. She could feel Colleen's body relax.

"I love the way your skin feels," Marsha said. She dipped her head to suck a warm nipple into her mouth and felt it harden against her tongue. "And the way you taste."

Colleen brought her hands up to press Marsha closer against her. "Don't stop, baby. Please don't stop," she rasped.

MARSHA WAS CERTAIN she was blushing as Colleen introduced her to the other members of her family when they arrived. She was amazed at how relaxed and comfortable Colleen seemed. No one in Colleen's family looked at her as if there were anything strange about Colleen bringing another woman home with her. She wasn't treated any differently from the young woman Matt brought as his date for the evening. Marsha busied herself by setting the long dining room table and setting up a separate table for Colleen's youngest nieces and nephews near the main table.

"You don't have to do this, sweetie," Colleen said as Marsha placed a plate on the table. Her hand rested lightly on Marsha's back.

"It's okay. Makes me feel useful," Marsha said.

Colleen leaned down slightly and whispered in Marsha's ear. "I found you extremely useful not that long ago."

Marsha knew she was blushing furiously. She wanted nothing more than to trust Colleen, but wasn't quite there yet.

Over dinner, Marsha had a hard time keeping up with the various conversations going on around the table. She answered several questions about her job, how she and Colleen met, her family, and her background. She answered the questions about herself and how she and Colleen met truthfully, however, as usual, she avoided anything dealing with her family or past.

"Don't you have four brothers?" Marsha asked.

"Yeah, but Studly called while we were in the shower. He told Mom his summer baseball team had a make-up game tonight so he and Amber wouldn't make it. They'll be here early tomorrow morning instead. The Prom Queen usually won't come alone. Says she feels outnumbered."

"I know the feeling," Marsha mumbled.

"Aunt Colleen!" a teenage-boy called out while she was looking at Marsha.

"Yes, Kirk," Colleen answered, turning a smile toward the boy.

"Pass the potatoes," he said.

"Please," his mother said with a nudge.

"Pass the potatoes, please," he repeated.

Colleen reached in front of Marsha and picked up a mostly empty bowl and extended it to him. He took it and shoveled the remaining potatoes onto his plate. His mother nudged him again.

"Thank you," he said, handing the bowl back.

"You're welcome," Colleen replied.

"You'd think I never feed him judging from how much he's put away," His mother, Karen, said.

Marsha laughed. "He's just a teenage boy with a bottomless pit." She looked at the boy. "Actually, he's saving us from having to make a place in the fridge for more leftovers."

"See," the boy said. "I told you no one would care how much I ate."

"You kinda skipped the Brussels sprouts though," Marsha said. "They were good."

"They're green," he answered around a mouthful of potatoes.

"They're healthy," his mother said.

"They're still green," he shrugged. "I'm not a cow, Mom."

Quentin and his sons made their final plans for an early round of golf the next day and Rosemary invited her daughters-in-law to a few rounds of bridge. By ten that evening everyone was gathering children and exchanging their goodbyes until the next day. Marsha excused herself and went into the kitchen to see if there was any coffee remaining. She poured a cup and added cream and sugar before finding an apron and tying it around her waist. She walked into the dining room and began gathering plates and utensils. It seemed the least she could do while waiting for her meal to digest. Colleen walked into the dining room and picked up a couple of plates. As she walked past Marsha, she dropped a light kiss on her lips. "Thank you, darling," she said.

"For what?"

"For tolerating the clan."

"They're nice people."

"I've always thought so."

Marsha followed Colleen into the kitchen. "Rinse or stack them in the dishwasher?"

"You rinsed lunch. Let me rinse this time."

"Okay."

"Colleen, do you and Marsha want a nightcap? Your father's pouring," Rosemary asked as she stuck her head into the kitchen.

Colleen looked at Marsha. "A drink to relax before we head to bed?"

"I'd enjoy a beer, if you have any," Marsha said.

"Two Heinekens," Colleen told her mother.

"We'll be in the den," Rosemary said before she disappeared again.

About an hour later they were all attempting to stifle yawns. When Rosemary finally announced she was going to bed, Marsha felt relieved to have completed her first day with Colleen's family. Everyone had been friendly.

Marsha sat on the edge of the bed to remove her shoes while Colleen went into the bathroom to brush her teeth and comb out her hair. She turned off the bathroom light and lowered the lights in the bedroom. Marsha looked up and her mouth went dry. Colleen was indeed a goddess. She had changed into a light green, floor length negligee with white lace accenting the bodice. Her blonde hair fell smoothly over her shoulders. Marsha tried to open her mouth and express her appreciation of the sight moving toward her, but closed it without saying a word. What could she say? She had never seen anyone so magnificent in her entire life. And Colleen was offering all that magnificence to her. Before she could stand, Colleen sat on her lap and kissed Marsha. A deep probing kiss. When the kiss ended, Colleen ran a finger down Marsha's cheek and trailed it down her neck stopping just above her bra.

"Tired?" Colleen asked demurely, but there was no mistaking the look in her eyes.

"It's been a long day, but I've never seen anyone as sexy as you are at this moment," Marsha answered as she leaned forward to nibble along Colleen's throat, pausing when her lips found Colleen's pulse point and felt her heart rate increase.

Chapter Eighteen

MARSHA ROLLED OVER the next morning and glanced at the clock on the nightstand. Colleen was gone. Marsha hurried through a quick shower, hating to wash away the scent of Colleen left on her body after several rounds of lovemaking. She smiled, remembering how she had felt wrapped in Colleen's arms. She felt loved for the first time in a very long time, but realized she would have to take a chance. Happiness demanded sacrifices. She had to believe what Colleen said. Of course, she could be hurt, but she probably wouldn't die from it, simply be badly bruised. But to have this feeling of unconditional acceptance, even temporarily, would be worth the risk.

She dressed and made an attempt to tame her curly hair. The scent of frying bacon and fresh coffee brewing wafted up the stairs and filled her nose as she moved quickly toward the source of the delicious smells. She stopped outside the kitchen door at the sound of Colleen speaking to someone.

"So what time will the Prom Queen be here?" Colleen asked.

"I wish you would all stop calling her that," a deep male voice said.

"I've never called Amber that to her face, Studly," Colleen said with a chuckle. "I wouldn't do that to any twelve-year-old."

"So where's the flavor of the month you brought home this time?" the man asked, changing the subject.

"I'll wake her in a minute, but thought we'd catch up before I threw her to the wolves again."

"How was dinner last night? Sorry we missed it."

"It was good. Everyone seemed to like Marsha."

"I hope she's better than that last viper you dragged home," he said.

"She's nothing like Rusty," Colleen snapped.

"Does she know about Rusty?"

Colleen's voice became subdued. "Yes. Rusty's already paid me a visit, but I have no proof she assaulted me."

Marsha brought her hand to her face and traced the scar on her upper lip. She turned to go back to Colleen's bedroom, but was startled by Rosemary who was standing quietly behind her. Marsha hadn't heard her approach and wondered how long she had been standing there.

"Ready for breakfast, dear?" Rosemary asked.

"Sounds great and smells wonderful," Marsha said as she pasted a smile on her face.

"Then let's get you fed before the others arrive. You'd be lucky to find a scrap after that. I swear they're worse than locusts."

Marsha pushed the kitchen door open and held it while Rosemary entered. "Look who I found," Rosemary announced.

Colleen rose from her chair at the kitchen table and cast a quick glance at her brother before she hugged Rosemary and leaned down to kiss Marsha.

"Did you sleep all right, honey?" Colleen asked.

Marsha tried to read what she saw in Colleen's eyes. "Just dandy, thanks."

Colleen rested her arm on Marsha's shoulder. "Honey, this is my brother Rick, better known to us as Coach Studly. Studly, Marsha Barrett."

"The DJ, right?" Rick asked as he extended his hand.

Marsha nodded as she took his hand firmly.

"Good grip," Rick said with a smile.

"Unlike most queers?"

Rick studied Marsha for a moment while he sipped his coffee. "Yeah, but you're a dyke like Trigger, right?"

"Totally," Marsha said.

"Very subtle, Studly," Colleen said as she placed her hands on Marsha's shoulders. "Have a seat and I'll get you a cup of coffee. How do you prefer your eggs?"

"Thanks. Over medium, please," Marsha answered quietly.

"So, Marsh," Rick said as he exhaled. "You play football?"

"Some. Mostly flag with the kids in my neighborhood."

Rick rubbed his hands together and smiled. "Then that settles it. With Mighty Mouse here and Trigger we'll have enough for two teams." He looked around Marsha and asked, "You gonna be our cheerleader, Mom?"

"Aren't I always?" Rosemary answered.

"Why do you call Colleen Trigger?" Marsha asked as she accepted a mug of coffee from Colleen.

Rick laughed. "She was so damn blonde as a kid she reminded us of Roy Rogers' horse, that palomino with the long blonde tail. You got a nickname?"

"Not unless you count 'Hey you'."

"Then Mighty Mouse will work," Rick said as he took another sip of coffee.

Halfway through her breakfast the kitchen door popped open and a thin blonde wearing her hair in a high ponytail entered. She looked like a teenager and headed immediately for the coffee pot. She returned to the table and plopped down before lightly kissing Rick's cheek and taking a long drink of coffee.

Marsha saw Colleen smirk before she spoke. "Morning, Amber."

"Sorry I'm running late. I had to run a couple of errands." Amber stopped talking as if she'd just noticed a stranger at the table. She stuck her arm out over the plates. "Hi. I'm Amber Walters, the coach's wife."

"Mighty Mouse, Trigger's friend," Marsha answered around a mouth full of food.

Amber turned to her husband and asked, "What's the game plan today, Coach?"

Marsha looked at Colleen and shrugged as she continued to eat. After breakfast Marsha insisted on cleaning up the kitchen. While the others went into the living room, Marsha rinsed off dishes and handed them to Colleen to place in the dishwasher.

"Let's take a walk to burn off some of that lumberjack breakfast before your brother blows his whistle for the beginning of the first quarter," Marsha suggested.

Even though it was the end of summer, it was a brisk, overcast day. Marsha pushed up the sleeves of her long-sleeve t-shirt and took Colleen's hand as they walked across the large back yard and onto a well-worn path through the wooded area behind the Walters' home.

"I'm having a nice time," Marsha said. "Thanks for inviting me."

"You're welcome. Hopefully this will be the first of many visits. Mom really likes you. She thinks you're honest and realistic."

"Your family is the one every kid wants. A kid's wet dream, I guess."

"You too?"

Marsha shrugged. "Despite everything, I've always wished I had a normal family. Every kid I've ever known wished their friends' family was their own. I'm no different."

Colleen stopped and pulled Marsha to her. "I love having you here with me."

BY THE TIME Marsha and Colleen entered the back door of the house, it was filled with laughing, jabbering people. Marsha noticed a tall, blond man standing in the middle of the living room, surrounded by Colleen's family. He looked up and saw Colleen. A smile spread across his face, exposing dimples in both cheeks.

"Uncle Jack!" Colleen said as she released Marsha's hand and rushed toward the man. He swept her into his arms and spun her around in a full circle before lowering her back to her feet. He held her at arm's length to look at her.

"I swear, Quentin, your daughter gets more lovely every time I see her," Jack said. "You're a lucky man. A beautiful daughter and a gorgeous wife." Then he added, "Not to mention four handsome sons." He extended his arm and touched each of them on the cheek with his fingertips.

Colleen took her uncle's hand and pulled him to where Marsha was standing. "Uncle Jack, this is Marsha Barrett. Honey, this is my uncle, Jack Walters."

Marsha stared at the tall, blond man in front of her. She was certain she had seen him someplace before, but couldn't remember where. She extended her hand as she continued searching her memory.

Jack smiled and shook Marsha's hand, but his smile didn't extend to his eyes. Instead, he shifted his eyes to look at Colleen again before returning to the rest of the family.

Almost before Marsha knew what was happening, the teams were chosen. Colleen was on the opposing team and winked at Marsha as they set up seats for Rosemary, Quentin, and Jack. One of the children had attached plastic pom-poms to the bottoms of Rosemary's crutches so she could raise them into the air without having to stand. Bottles of water were set on a table for the participants and two of the youngest children were responsible for running them to the players. Rick and his youngest brother, Matt, were the quarterbacks. The game consisted mainly of throwing passes and hoping someone caught them. The game was punctuated with groans and laughter as each side tried to score. Marsha had to laugh when she watched Rick's wife Amber scurry across the back yard, waving her hands. She runs like a girl, Marsha thought.

Marsha lined up and ran down the yard, suddenly discovering she was alone. She looked back at Matt and watched as he heaved a pass in her direction. The ball practically floated into her arms and everyone saw the surprised expression on her face when she caught it and began running. Moments before she would have crossed the goal line, hands grabbed her from behind and pulled her to the ground. She turned her head and saw a laughing Colleen.

"Hey, I thought this was *flag* football," Marsha protested. "Where's a referee when you need one?"

Colleen crawled to her knees and straddled Marsha's waist. "It is," Colleen said. "But I love the feel of you between my legs, sweet thing." She wiggled her butt slightly.

Marsha grinned and shook her head. "God, you are shameless, woman," she said.

Colleen leaned closer and placed her hands on either side of Marsha's head, dropping a kiss on her lips before pushing her body up. "Fess up, Barrett. You know you love it."

Marsha lifted an arm and Colleen pulled her up.

"You're faster than you look," Colleen said. "Whew! I need a break."

Marsha tossed the ball back to Matt and jogged to the water table. She reached for a bottle, but was stopped by a girl who looked about five. "Open," the girl ordered.

Marsha laughed and fell to her knees in front of the child. "What's your name again, sweetie?" she asked

"Amy." With Rosemary's help, the girl opened the tip of the water bottle and squirted a stream of water, most of it missing Marsha's mouth and soaking the front of her shirt.

Marsha wiped excess water from her face. "You're my hero, Amy," she said.

The little girl beamed at Marsha before she scampered away to take water to another player.

"You're very good with children," Rosemary observed.

"Kids aren't judgmental," Marsha said as she stood and rested her hands on her knees. "At least until they get older."

"Ready, hot stuff?" Colleen asked as she joined them at the table and playfully patted Marsha's ass.

"How much longer?" Marsha asked as she glanced at Rosemary and blushed. "I've already had my allowance of exercise for the next six months and I'm wiped," she said. She noticed Jack studying her as if he were also tugging at a deeply buried memory.

"Let me catch the next pass and the game will be over. Then we can all get cleaned up and take a nap," Colleen said, waggling her eyebrows suggestively.

Marsha rolled her eyes and felt her face flush before following Colleen back onto the field.

When the game finally ended, Marsha plopped into a deeply cushioned chair in the den to cool off. Colleen came in and fell into her lap. She opened a bottle of cold water and shared it with Marsha. Marsha wrapped her arms loosely around Colleen's waist and closed her eyes for a moment. Colleen drew her legs up and rested her head on Marsha's shoulder. Marsha didn't know how long they had been dozing when a hand shook Colleen's shoulder, waking them both.

"Your father, Jack, and the boys have already left for their round of golf and the girls have taken the kids home. I was going to fix us some sandwiches, but don't have enough bread. Can you run to the store for me, sweetie," Rosemary asked.

Colleen rubbed her eyes. "Of course, Mom." She looked at Marsha. "Wanna join me, honey?"

Before Marsha could answer, Rosemary quickly added, "Let Marsha stay here to help me get everything else ready, will you, dear?"

Colleen placed her hands on the arms of the chair and pushed her body up. "Okay. What do you need?" she asked her mother.

"Get a wheat and a white. And you might want to grab another bag of chips. Let me get you some money."

"That's all right, Mom. I have enough for that. Be right back."

Marsha stood and Colleen gave her a quick kiss before picking up a set of keys from a bowl near the door and leaving.

"Sit down, Marsha. I wanted to talk to you when Colleen wasn't here," Rosemary said as she made her way to the nearby couch.

"About?"

"Has Colleen spoken to you about Victoria...er...Rusty?"

"A little bit," Marsha answered. "Enough to let me know how their relationship ended."

"So you know she's been released early?"

Marsha frowned and studied her hands for a moment. "I know

she's already hurt Colleen. According to Colleen, this Rusty shoved her down a small flight of stairs. I took her to the emergency room."

Now Rosemary frowned and rubbed her forehead with her thumb and index finger. "Colleen didn't tell me that."

"It scared her more than anything else."

"Victoria Manning is a cruel and abusive woman, Marsha. I wish Jack had never introduced them. Unfortunately, Colleen was mesmerized by her for quite a long time. When I met Victoria, I was afraid that Colleen was in over her head." Rosemary pushed herself up and went to an oak secretary against the far wall. She lowered the drop leaf front and withdrew a manila envelope. She carried it back to her chair and handed it to Marsha. Marsha opened the envelope and withdrew a stack of pictures. She glanced through the photos, barely recognizing the woman in them. Her eyes met Rosemary's. "Colleen almost died from the beating Victoria gave her the last time she was out of control. Colleen came here with us to recuperate, but it was months before she would allow even Quentin or myself to touch her. Her eyes were swollen shut for nearly three weeks and she flinched at even the slightest movements around her. She woke up almost every night screaming because of another nightmare," Rosemary explained. Then she smiled as she looked at Marsha. "She doesn't seem to object when you touch her now. I'm glad to see that, but am concerned now that we know Rusty has been released. You have to try and protect her, Marsha."

"I can't imagine anyone harming her, ma'am. She's a special woman."

"She seems to care about you very much, Marsha."

Marsha shrugged. "Like I've already said, I don't know why."

"You're actually quite attractive in your own way, my dear."

"You mean in a plain way," Marsha said with a laugh.

Rosemary shrugged. "In an average way perhaps, but Colleen is definitely smitten. All I can ask is that you don't hurt her. She's only been on her own about six months and I wouldn't want her to relapse. Feel free to contact me any time she seems different to you."

"We don't live together, Mrs. Walters. I don't think either of us is quite ready for that step yet."

"But you've been intimate, haven't you?"

"That's something I'm not prepared to discuss. Too personal. Colleen might tell you. She says she tells you everything."

"Even for a mother and daughter we're very close."

"I wasn't lucky enough to have that closeness...with anyone. I know you and your husband adopted her as a baby."

"We were very lucky to get her, especially since we had other children."

"My parents abandoned me when I was about eighteen months old. I've spent virtually my entire childhood in foster care or hospitals.

Never was adopted...just housed."

Rosemary reached out and took Marsha's hand. "I'm so sorry to hear that. No child deserves to spend their childhood unwanted." Rosemary dropped the pictures back into the envelope and returned it to the secretary.

Marsha shrugged. "It happens. I survived childhood and am working on surviving adulthood. I've learned that others can't be trusted to do the right thing."

Rosemary leaned over slightly and looked out the den window. "Colleen's back. Thank you for listening to the worries of a concerned parent." She winked at Marsha and smiled. "I trust you to take care of my daughter."

"Thank you."

Colleen came bounding into the den a minute later. "I put the bread in the breadbox, Mom."

She helped Rosemary stand and kissed her on the cheek.

"Come fix a sandwich when you're ready," Rosemary said as she hugged Colleen and left the room.

Colleen dropped onto Marsha's lap and brought her arms up to encircle her neck. "So did Mom finish her interrogation?" she asked with a laugh. "I drove around the block three times to give her more time."

"She's just worried about you and wanted to know my intentions," Marsha said with a grin.

Colleen's eyes widened. "Really? And what are your intentions, if I may ask."

"I told her I didn't plan to hurt you even though we might have disagreements from time to time. Then to make up I planned to drag you into the bedroom and make love to you until you died from satisfaction."

"You did not!" Colleen squealed and then covered her mouth with her hands.

Marsha laughed and Colleen grabbed her by the shoulders and shook her. "That was mean, unless you plan to actually do it."

"Planning my attack even as we speak," Marsha grinned. "But I might wait until we get back to Omaha."

"You're such a tease!" Colleen exclaimed as her mouth devoured Marsha's in a heart-stopping kiss.

LATE AFTERNOON, QUENTIN and Jack walked into the Walters home, arguing about their day golfing although their comments were laced with humor.

"You're supposed to hit the ball where it was lying, Jack," Quentin said.

"Well, excuse me, brother, but I left my snorkel at home," Jack retorted.

"I could see the damn ball! You just didn't want to get your feet wet."

"Do you know how much I paid for those shoes?"

"If I know you, and I do, it was twice as much as you needed to. Unlike you, I win because of my skill and technique, not my fashion sense," Quentin laughed.

"You cheat!"

"Do not!"

"Do too!"

In the midst of their discussion, Rosemary entered the kitchen. She stared at the two men and shook her head as she made her way to the refrigerator. She lifted a pitcher of iced tea out and set it on the counter. "Would either of you children care for a glass of tea?" she asked mildly.

"I would, dear," Quentin said with a smile. He patted Jack on the arm and joined Rosemary at the counter. He leaned over and kissed her on the cheek. He glanced over his shoulder at his brother. "Jack?" he asked.

"Yeah. All this arguing made me thirsty," Jack answered.

"Don't pout, Jack," Rosemary said. "It's not that becoming on a man your age."

"It used to work," Jack said as he joined them. "Let's sit down for a minute, okay."

Quentin held a chair for Rosemary and they all sat at the kitchen table,

"Tell me about this Martha," Jack said as he took a drink of tea.

"Marsha," Rosemary said.

"Whatever," Jack shrugged. "What do you know about her?"

Quentin leaned forward and rested his forearms on the table. "We just met her, Jack, but she seems nice enough."

"Colleen loves her," Rosemary added. At the surprised look on Jack's face, she added, "And I believe her, even though I'm not sure Marsha does."

"Where is she from? Where did they meet? Who are her parents?" Jack asked.

"Why the Inquisition?" Quentin asked. "She makes Colleen happy."

"You know why, Quentin. I feel guilty that my only niece met Rusty through me. I wasn't careful enough and Colleen paid the price. I won't let it happen again...ever." Jack blinked rapidly.

"Have you found Rusty yet?" Rosemary asked quietly.

Jack shook his head. "Harold's still looking, but apparently she's flying well below the radar. He'll keep an eye on Colleen when she goes back to Omaha. I'll see what I can find out about this Marsha." He took Rosemary's hand and squeezed it lightly. "I promise I'll keep our girl safe, Rose."

Chapter Nineteen

AT THE END of the long weekend, Colleen and Marsha picked up their luggage and took them to Colleen's Mazda in long-term parking. They had dozed most of the flight back to Omaha. At Marsha's request, Colleen drove her back to her own house and dropped her off.

"Sure you don't want to come home with me?" Colleen asked as she helped Marsha carry her things inside. "You can wash clothes there, you know?"

"If I went with you I'd never get anything useful done."

Colleen rested her hands on Marsha's hips and leaned in for a kiss. "I think keeping me satisfied is extremely useful, don't you?" she ended haughtily

"But as satisfying as that is, I do have to work tonight. I'll see you in the morning before I leave the station," Marsha answered with a grin and another kiss.

Marsha waved as she watched Colleen drive away and felt as if she were floating as she stepped into her house and closed the door. As she stood in her living room and looked around, something felt wrong, but everything looked the same as the day she left. Maybe it was because she was alone for the first time in three days. The house smelled musty, probably from being closed up. She opened a living room window and another in the kitchen to allow fresh air to flow through the rooms.

She was exhausted and exhilarated. She leaned against the wall, using her toes to pull her sneakers off. She wandered into her bedroom and dropped her duffle on the floor before she fell onto her bed. It didn't take much to convince her to get a few hours of sleep and take a shower later. She stripped out of her shirt, bra, jeans, and socks, dropping them to the floor before wriggling beneath the covers wearing only her panties. The cool sheets beneath her felt good and within minutes she was snoring soundly.

The sun was going down when Marsha smacked her lips and opened her eyes again. She rubbed her hands over her face and sat up slowly. She bent over and gathered the clothes she had dropped earlier and carried them into her small bathroom. She sat on the toilet to relieve herself and deposited her clothes in the hamper. She removed her panties and reached into the shower to turn the water on, waiting until it felt hot enough against her arm. It wasn't long before steam formed in the small room. She turned to get a clean towel and stopped in her tracks. The steam from the shower covered the mirror over the sink, revealing words written in deep red lipstick. She looked around as she approached the mirror.

The words virtually glowed against the rest of the mirror. *Stay away from her!* Marsha grabbed her pants and shirt from the hamper and pulled them on haphazardly. She opened the bathroom door and glanced carefully up and down the hall. She was certain the words hadn't been there earlier. The wooden floor felt cold against her bare feet as she looked into her bedroom, the small office, the kitchen and living room. Nothing had been disturbed. She exhaled a nervous breath and closed the windows and checked the locks on the doors. Everything was as she'd left it before falling asleep, except the message on the bathroom mirror.

Eventually Marsha returned to the bathroom. She snapped a couple of pictures on her cell phone, then used an old wash cloth to remove the words. She had planned to take a longer shower, but the water was little more than lukewarm by the time she stepped in. When she left the shower she was shivering from being forced to rinse her hair in cold water. As she dressed she tried to figure out who'd left the message, even though she had a hunch and didn't like it.

COLLEEN HATED TO admit it, but she was exhausted. She dug in her shoulder bag for the keys to her condo. She located them at the bottom of her bag. No matter what she was looking for, it always seemed to be at the bottom. She tossed her garment bag over her shoulder and lifted the retractable handle of the rolling suitcase. She probably could travel with less stuff, but she liked to be prepared for anything when she traveled. She shoved the key into the lock and turned it. She leaned in and disarmed the alarm system. Pulling her suitcase into her bedroom, she opened the closet to hang the garment bag. She sat on the edge of her bed and picked up the telephone, speed dialing a number.

"I'm guessing you both made it home safely," Rosemary's pleasant voice answered.

"We did. Now all I have to do is unpack and wash all this stuff," Colleen sighed.

"Is Marsha with you?"

"I dropped her at her place. She has the same things to do and has to work tonight."

"I hope she had a pleasant time considering all the activity over the weekend."

"She said she enjoyed her visit."

"She handled your brothers better than I expected."

"What was up with Uncle Jack? He seemed to glare at Marsha all weekend," Colleen said.

There was a pause before Rosemary answered. "You know how Jack is, honey. He's always been overly protective where you're concerned. He feels responsible for Rusty and doesn't want anyone to hurt you again."

"Tell him to relax. Marsha would never hurt me physically," Colleen said with a smile.

Colleen stood and wandered into her kitchen. She took a bottle of water from the refrigerator, twisted the cap off, and swallowed a long drink as she leaned against the counter. When she set the bottle down her eyes came to rest on a vase holding two intertwining roses sitting in the middle of her dining room table.

"Umm, I really need to use the bathroom, Mom," she said. "Can I call you back after I change and put everything away?"

"Of course. I'll talk to you later. Love you," Rosemary said as she disconnected.

"Love you, too," Colleen mumbled, moving closer to the table. Posed in the center of the table for two was a tall, light pink vase. Inside were two of her favorite roses, their stems twisted around one another until the blooms formed one huge blossom. Colleen had first seen the Disneyland Floribunda Rose at a botanical garden in Washington, D.C. The blooms were a striking combination of pink, yellow, and apricot. As the flower blossomed the tips evolved into a deep shade of orange. They were identical to the roses delivered to her office a month earlier. Colleen's hand almost touched the soft petals until she stopped and fisted her fingers. She needed to be calm. She walked quickly into her bedroom and caught a familiar scent. She shoved her suitcase onto the floor. Her hand was shaking as she grabbed the bedspread and yanked it back. Breath caught in her throat when she saw a heart-shaped piece of Godiva chocolate, wrapped in bright red foil, resting in the center of her bed. She leaned down closer to the sheets and inhaled. The unmistakable smell of Rusty's favorite fragrance lingered on the material. She slept here! How had she gotten past the alarm and gotten into the condo without anyone noticing?

Chapter Twenty

THE FOLLOWING MORNING Marsha was more than ready for a hot shower followed by seven or eight hours of peaceful sleep by the time she got home. She stopped by Colleen's office before leaving the station. Colleen's assistant, Heather, told her Colleen wouldn't be in. As soon as Marsha entered her house, she removed her clothes and carried them into the bathroom, depositing them in the hamper. She leaned over and turned on the water and ruffled her hair vigorously as she started to step under the water. She leaned over to the small linen closet next to the tub. As she turned to place the towel on top of the hamper she glanced toward the mirror over the sink, half expecting to see another message scrawled on the bathroom mirror. She released a sigh of relief seeing nothing there.

Her body relaxed under the warm water and after toweling off she wandered into her bedroom. She threw back the bedspread and sheet and climbed into bed. She rolled onto her side and stuck her arm under her pillow as always. "Ow!" she said, jerking her hand from beneath the pillow. A drop of blood oozed from her finger and she stuck it in her mouth. *What the hell?* She lifted the pillow and found a picture pinned to her bedding. She removed the pin and picked the wallet-sized photo up by its edges to examine it more closely. She didn't recognize where the picture had been taken, but the photo was of her with a bright red bull's eye super-imposed over her face. She never allowed anyone to take her picture, but there was something familiar about it. Then it struck her like a punch to the gut. It was taken while she and Colleen were walking in the woods behind the Walters' home in Philadelphia. It was slightly grainy, as if it had been taken from a distance then cropped and enlarged.

Marsha slid from beneath the covers and pulled on her jeans and a t-shirt. She left the house and jogged across the street to Hershberger's. If anyone had noticed anything unusual it would be Jacobi. The man was practically the national poster boy for paranoia. She scanned the street while she waited for the old man to open his front door. When she heard him unlocking it, she whirled around.

"I was wondering when you come for coffee," he said, his deep voice rumbling as he pushed open the screen door.

Although she wanted to start questioning her neighbor right away, Marsha waited until they were seated at his small kitchen table. "Anything unusual happen last night, Jacobi?"

"Nah," he answered between slurps. "Quiet. How work?"

"Same as usual, I guess." She took a couple of sips then asked casually, "You didn't see anyone around my house, did you?"

"No one I not already know."

"What do you mean?"

"That pretty blonde lady who helped us with plants was there a few minutes, but I–"

"What time was that?"

"I don't know. Hang on." Jacobi pushed himself up and shuffled to a table next to the front door. He returned with a small tablet and sat down heavily as he licked his fingers and thumbed through its pages. He ran his index finger down a page and nodded. "I have trouble sleeping last night. Let's see, ah, here it is. Two this morning. Blue and silver Mazda in front of your place. Driver a tall, blonde. Entered at two-ten and left at two-thirty. Nebraska plate number was," he paused for a moment, readjusting his glasses. "Damn, can't hardly read my own writing. Looks like AVM-298Z." He handed the tablet to Marsha. "That look right to you?"

While Marsha re-read the information, Jacobi said, "Was dark on porch. She had trouble getting key in lock."

Because she didn't have a key, Marsha thought. "I don't suppose you took a picture?"

Jacobi shrugged. "Why would? I knew who was."

Marsha finished her coffee faster than normal and left Jacobi's house, running across the street as fast as she could. She quickly dialed Trish's work number.

"Nebraska Motor Vehicles," Trish answered. "How may I assist you?"

"That's a really loaded question," Marsha answered.

"Marsh!"

"I need a huge favor, Trish."

"How huge?"

"I have a license plate number. I need to know who it's registered to."

"Give me the number and I'll have to call you back in a few."

Marsha closed her eyes and said the number from memory. Until Trish called back there wasn't much she could do. When her phone rang several minutes later, she lifted the receiver, but didn't say anything.

"Marsh?" Trish's voice came over the line.

"Yeah, sorry. What did you find out?"

"You really need to write down important information. That plate is registered to the goddess."

"Colleen?"

"You have more than one goddess?"

"Of course not. Are you sure?"

"Records don't lie, my friend, so relax. What's up?"

"She was here last night while I was working, I think."

"Probably wanted to leave you a surprise."

"She succeeded. Listen, I just got home about an hour ago and am wiped. Thanks for the info. I'll call you later, okay?"

"Sure thing. I've got a line of pimply-faced teens, eager to become menaces on the highway, standing in front of me anyway. Later."

MARSHA KNOCKED ON the door of Colleen's condo and shuffled her feet. She rubbed her forehead, trying to think of the best way to tell her about the picture beneath her pillow. She should have called before storming over to Colleen's condo. Too late, she thought when she heard the deadbolt click and then Colleen standing in front of her. Her hair was disheveled and there were dark smudges beneath her eyes as if she hadn't slept. Despite that, she was still beautiful to Marsha.

"Hi, baby. What up?" Colleen asked wearily.

"Are you okay?"

"I'm okay, but feel like I'm coming down with a cold or something," Colleen answered as she swung the door farther open.

"We need to talk," Marsha said as she stepped inside.

"About what?"

Marsha handed Colleen the picture. "That was pinned to my bed this morning. I think it was taken while we were in Philadelphia."

Colleen stared down at the picture without speaking.

"Jacobi saw a car in front of my house early this morning." Marsha cleared her throat before continuing. "He wrote down the plate number and Trish confirmed that it belonged to you."

"I wasn't there, Marsha. I swear."

"I know. He wrote the time down and at two-ten you should have been sound asleep."

"We should go down to the garage and check my car," Colleen said.

The two women made their way around the blue and silver Mazda, looking both inside and beneath it. Colleen checked the GPS. Nothing indicated the vehicle had left the parking garage the previous night. Marsha used a flashlight to check for scratches on the screws holding the license plates. All she noticed was that the screws looked cleaner than the area around them.

"Jacobi told me the woman was a tall blonde. He thought it was you."

"Could have been wearing a wig," Colleen said.

Marsha took a deep breath as she scanned the garage around them. A shiver ran up her spine. She was certain they were being watched. She rested her hand on the small of Colleen's back and motioned toward the elevator. "Let's go back upstairs," she said.

Once they were inside the condo again, Colleen said, "She was here. Inside my apartment." She walked into the kitchen, opened a drawer, and removed an object wrapped in a paper towel. She dumped the item onto the kitchen table. "It used to be my favorite brand of chocolate. I found it in my bed when I returned from Philly." Colleen's face twisted and she said, "She...she slept in my bed while I was gone."

"How do you know that?"

"The sheets and pillows smelled like the cologne she always wore. I was sleeping on the couch until I can get the smell out of the bedroom."

Marsha glanced over her shoulder at the blankets and pillow jumbled on the couch. "You can stay with me for a while if you don't want to stay here."

"She knows where we both live. Unless I leave Omaha, there's no place to hide," Colleen snapped. She took a deep breath and said, "I'm sorry, honey. This isn't your fault. I'm sorry she's involved you in her sick game."

"We could go the police," Marsha suggested.

"I already have a restraining order, but unless she physically harms me, there's nothing the police can do," Colleen said. "Now she's threatening you as well. I should have known better, but I thought I had more time."

"I don't blame you for any of this, Colleen," Marsha said as she stepped closer to wrap her arms around Colleen's waist.

THAT EVENING MARSHA walked the short distance between her favorite late night coffee shop and the radio station. She had slept in late that day, but awakened fresh and rested. She convinced Jacobi to trim her hair and felt better than she had in a long time. She hadn't heard from Colleen and hoped she'd gotten some rest, too. Like everyone else, Colleen had been attracted to a beautiful woman. Part of what attracted her to Colleen was her beauty, probably from reading too damn many lesbian novels in which every woman, even the fucking cleaning lady, was a raving beauty and secretly an heiress.

Marsha smiled, wondering where the people in those fantasies lived. It was a target-rich environment filled with tall, beautiful, wealthy women who never bothered to look down at the gnomes and dwarves they stepped on along the path to finding blissful romance. She couldn't really blame them though. Who wanted to read about a couple of ordinary women who were only attractive to one another getting it on? She supposed it helped women like her escape the reality of their lives for a few hours and that wasn't much different from what she did for a living five out of seven nights.

She pushed through the front doors and sipped her coffee as she wandered toward the studio. She laughed out loud when she watched G-Man boogie to whatever song he was playing. As he began to settle down and move into what he called the "cool down" portion of his high-energy program, Marsha heard voices coming from the break room. She backed away from the studio and raised her hand in the air to give G-Man a thumb's up. She was still laughing when she entered the break room and saw Boomer and Colleen sharing a table.

"Hey, Dez!" Boomer said. "Heard you had a great weekend!"

Marsha saw a light blush work its way up Colleen's cheeks. "Kiss and tell time?" she asked.

Before Colleen could respond, Boomer added, "I didn't know you liked football. That's awesome, dudette."

"Now you know two things about me that you didn't know before," Marsha said.

Boomer gave her a blank look as if wondering what she was talking about.

"Indiana," Colleen said softly. "Her birthmark looks vaguely like Indiana."

Boomer looked back and forth between the two women.

"You win, Boomer. I owe you ten," Colleen said

Marsha shifted her eyes to Colleen. "Working a little late, aren't you?"

Colleen shrugged. "Paperwork. I'm leaving soon."

Boomer awkwardly stood and stretched his long frame. "I'll go check the sound board. No telling what that jackass Frankie did to it this time."

Marsha glanced at the large red clock hanging on the break room wall. "Can I walk you to your car?" she asked.

"It's a free country."

The tone of Colleen's voice hurt Marsha, but she figured she probably deserved it. Marsha hurried to keep up with Colleen's long strides as they left the station and walked toward the parking garage. Unable to stand the silence, Marsha said, "I'm sorry."

Suddenly Colleen reached out and grabbed Marsha around the shoulders, pulling her closer to her side. "Anything unusual happen since I last saw you?"

"All's quiet on the low-rent front."

Colleen found her keys as they entered the garage. She opened the car door and tossed her purse and briefcase inside before turning to lean against the side of the vehicle.

Marsha played with a pebble on the ground with the toe of her sneaker. "I did have a good time in Philadelphia."

"What was your favorite part?"

Marsha rubbed her cheek and couldn't bring herself to look at Colleen. She cleared her throat. "Falling asleep with you in my arms."

"Really?"

"Yeah, football couldn't hold a candle to that. What was yours?"

"That cute little sound you made when you snuggled against me during the night."

"You'll have to record these strange sounds you claim I make."

Colleen brought her hand to Marsha's cheek and stroked it tenderly. "Are we still okay?"

"Yeah. I'm sorry. I'm not used to being threatened."

"You never get used to it, but you don't have anything to apologize for."

Marsha waited until Colleen slipped into her vehicle, then leaned in and kissed her lips, pulling Colleen's tongue deeply into her mouth until Colleen groaned.

"I'm so–" Marsha started as she broke apart from Colleen.

"Don't you dare say you're sorry after a kiss like that," Colleen said breathlessly.

Marsha laughed and pecked Colleen's lips quickly before stepping away. "See you in the morning," she said. "Sleep well."

Colleen backed up and turned toward the garage exit and Marsha trotted back toward the sidewalk peeking at her watch. Damn, Boomer is probably having a hernia. She turned onto the sidewalk quickly and ran into a woman, almost knocking her down. She grabbed her by the arm to prevent her from falling.

"Omigod. I'm so sorry," Marsha panted with fright. "Are you all right?"

"Late for a hot date?" the woman asked with a friendly smile.

"Late for work." Marsha turned and continued walking backward. She pointed back toward the stunning redhead. "Sure you're okay?"

"Never better," the woman assured her.

Chapter Twenty-one

AMBER WALTERS STEPPED out of her car in front of the Walters' home. She unlocked the passenger door and opened it, making sure the seat was back far enough to accommodate Rosemary and her crutches. She jogged up the front steps to the large home and rang the doorbell. She had promised to take Rosemary to a doctor's appointment a few weeks earlier to allow her father-in-law to keep a golf date with old friends who would be in town. Amber liked her in-laws, but knew they had their reservations about a woman her age marrying their son. No one believed that she and Rick had not known one another until years after she graduated from the high school where Rick taught. They had actually met at a bar when she had accompanied some friends from high school to celebrate her graduation from college. She had applied for a teaching position back in her hometown and was waiting to hear from them. Despite what anyone thought, Amber was an intelligent young woman. She may be a blonde, but she wasn't a dumb blonde. When Rick asked her to marry him six months after they met, her parents tried to talk her out of accepting his proposal. The truth was she did love the man everyone called The Coach.

Her only regret was that after several years of marriage, she still had not become pregnant. She loved children and would gladly have as many as Rick wanted and they could afford. Oh, well, she was still young. They had discussed adoption, but she wasn't ready to stop trying to have a child of their own. She knew Rick's sister had been adopted and Amber liked Colleen very much, even if she was gay. After all, no one's perfect, she thought as she waited for Rosemary to get to the front door. Finally the door opened and Rosemary seemed ready to go. After a few pleasantries, Amber helped her mother-in-law down the stairs.

Rosemary handed her crutches to Amber and used her arms to pull her body into the passenger seat and adjust it in a comfortable position before fastening her seat belt.

Amber hopped into the driver's seat and buckled her belt.

"I like your vehicle, Amber," Rosemary noted.

"Thanks," Amber said as she paused at the end of the Walters' semi-circular drive to check the traffic. "When Rick decided we needed a new car, I told him we needed something a little bigger that would hold a car seat in the back."

"Still planning for children?" Rosemary asked.

"Still planning," Amber answered with a smile, turning her head toward her mother-in-law. "I think we just need to relax and learn to enjoy one another. A friend of mine from college and her husband adopted a baby a few years ago and, I swear, a month later she was pregnant. The doctor told them they had just been worrying about it too much."

"Anything's possible, my dear. I didn't think I was capable of having children, but apparently my fears were unfounded."

"I don't have any qualms about adopting, but hope, if we're lucky, we can also have a child of our own. And I know Rick wants that as well."

Rosemary chuckled. "I'm sure he does. For some reason men think they're a failure if they can't or don't give their wife a baby. With Quentin, getting pregnant wasn't the problem. It was all those boys. I love them all, but I think women want a little girl almost as badly as a man wants a son."

"I confess, Rosemary, I would really like a girl, but either one is fine with us."

"Colleen was such a good baby. Hardly ever cried and it took her about ten seconds to wrap Quentin around her little finger," Rosemary said with a laugh. "He practically slept in the nursery with her, afraid his little girl wasn't strong enough to make it through the night without her Daddy."

"Female babies are always stronger, aren't they?" Amber asked.

"That's why so many of them survive after birth. Women are simply physically stronger as babies. Look at me! I don't know for a fact that a male baby could have survived everything I went through, but I had excellent parents to help me along."

"Polio isn't hereditary, right?"

"Nope. It's a disease."

"So I wouldn't need to be tested, genetically?"

"I wouldn't think so, but you can ask your doctor to be safe."

"We're both planning to be genetically tested, but no matter what the tests showed, I don't think I could ever terminate a pregnancy."

"Is that a religious conviction?"

"Not really. More of a personal one."

Amber signaled and turned into the parking area at the hospital where Rosemary's doctor was on staff. "We made it with time to spare," Amber announced.

"I've enjoyed talking with you, Amber," Rosemary said as she released her seat belt. "It made the trip pass quickly."

Amber slid out of the car and trotted around to open the passenger door and hand Rosemary her crutches before escorting her inside.

"You can either wait in the waiting room or go in with me," Rosemary said. "Your choice, dear."

"You don't mind if I go in with you?"

"Maybe when I was younger, but very little embarrasses me at my age. It's only my annual physical." Rosemary leaned closer. "Honestly, I could use a little help on a test or two."

A little over an hour later Rosemary and Amber made their way back to Amber's car. The tests on Rosemary had been routine and detected nothing new.

"I don't know about you," Rosemary said after a deep breath. "But I'm a little hungry. Are you?"

"I could use a snack, but I'm more thirsty than anything else. There's a drive-thru up ahead or there are a couple of restaurants farther down the road. We can stop wherever you want," Amber said.

"My treat to repay you for taking me to my appointment," Rosemary said.

"You don't have to pay me for that," Amber protested.

"I want to. I've enjoyed our conversation very much."

"If you can wait, there's a nice seafood place on the far side of the bridge into the city that overlooks the river," Amber suggested. "Rick and I have gone there a few times. We can watch the boats."

"That's fine," Rosemary said. "I can wait that long."

They drove along for several minutes and the traffic became heavier as they approached the city. It was only a few more miles to the restaurant and no more than twenty miles to the Walters' home after that. Amber checked her rearview mirror. She was traveling in the slow lane, but a car was approaching them at a high rate of speed. She tapped her brakes to alert the driver she was there, but he brought his vehicle close enough to almost touch her rear bumper.

"Go around, you idiot," she muttered.

Rosemary turned as far as she could and saw the car riding their bumper. "Are you speeding?" she asked.

"No, and the passing lane is open. He can go around me any time."

"Maybe you should pull over if he insists on staying in this lane," Rosemary suggested.

"Probably some teenager trying to be cute, but I can't pull over here. The shoulder ends just ahead on the curve."

Amber felt a light tap on the rear bumper and sped up slightly. As she entered the curve, the vehicle swung from behind her at the last second, barely missing her left rear quarter-panel. Rosemary exhaled audibly once the car began passing them. Amber flashed her a quick smile.

"There's a pad and pen in the glove box," Amber said. "I'll slow down a little. See if you can write down his plate number. Someone needs to report him."

Rosemary pulled the glove compartment open and reached in for the pad and pen. The car stayed even with them, even though Amber reduced her speed to let the driver pass her.

"What the hell is he doing?" Amber wondered aloud. "See if you can contact the highway patrol, Rosemary. I don't like this at all."

Amber couldn't see the driver. The windows were tinted darkly and didn't allow her to see the interior of the vehicle. Finally, the driver accelerated and brought the rear of his car even with the front side of Amber's vehicle. With no warning, the car swerved into her lane and struck her on the driver's side, forcing her into the metal guardrail. He held her there and her eyes widened as she saw the end of the rail approaching. She would leave the road and her car would have no place to go except down the embankment. She didn't know how steep the embankment was or what was at the bottom. They were close to the river and her greatest fear was that the car would end up in the water. Amber struggled to keep her car as even as possible and accelerated moments before the guardrail ended. She shot past the other vehicle and brought her car back onto the road for a moment. She reached into the back seat and found a pillow she kept there. She dragged it into the front and shoved it at Rosemary.

"Bury your head in this and hold it as tight as you can!" she yelled at Rosemary.

Seconds after she accelerated, she slammed on her brakes. The vehicle behind her swerved, but struck the rear of Amber's car on the back left quarter panel, pushing her to the right and over the edge of the embankment. They bounced down the rough terrain and Amber threw her arm across Rosemary's chest in an attempt to protect her. She kept her foot on the brake, hoping to stop the car, but its forward momentum increased and the car went airborne for a moment, before slamming into the ground and hitting a tree near the bank of the river. Amber's head struck the side window and the glass cracked. She felt her arm snap from holding Rosemary's seat belt. Blood ran into her left eye, but she managed to glance across the front seat at her mother-in-law.

"Rosemary!" Amber called.

The only response was a low moan. The pillow lay on the floorboard. Amber pushed against the driver's side door and fought the airbag in front of her, attempting to get out and make her way to Rosemary. The door groaned, but failed to open. The pain in her arm was excruciating. She leaned back to get it under control mentally before making a second attempt. She saw her purse lying near the brake and strained to reach it. It was too far away. She used her left arm to lift her right arm closer and stretched as far as she could. A scream left her, but she managed to get a single finger around the strap of her purse. Slowly she dragged it close enough to reach inside and feel for her cell phone, praying it still worked and could pick up a signal. She couldn't stop her tears as she touched the phone and secured it between her index and middle fingers. After dropping it three times, she was able to bring it to her lap. It didn't appear to be damaged and she punched in 9-1-1.

A LIFE FLIGHT helicopter waited in the middle of the highway into Philadelphia as work crews struggled to pull the partially submerged vehicle from the grip of the river. Amber leaned against the tree that had temporarily stopped their vehicle. Her left arm was wrapped around Rosemary. Amber glanced down at her arm and felt a wave of nausea. The sight of her bone protruding through the skin just below her elbow scared her. She was still conscious and asking about her mother-in-law. A paramedic worked on what was apparently a cut to Amber's scalp. She managed to tell them what had happened, but the only description she could provide was of the car itself.

Rosemary hadn't regained consciousness since Amber had managed to pull her from the car, but her moaning tore at Amber's emotions. The rescuers had called for the helicopter and used Amber's phone to contact Rick and Quentin, who would be waiting for them at the hospital when they arrived.

"Take my mother-in-law in the helicopter," Amber pleaded. "I can go by ambulance."

"You've got a pretty nasty head wound, ma'am. I'm sure you have a concussion, but I don't know how severe, okay. And we have to immobilize that arm."

"Why?" Amber asked as she began to cry. "Why would anyone do this?"

"Lotsa crazies out there, ma'am. We'll probably never know."

Suddenly Amber's eyes rolled back in her head and her body began twitching uncontrollably. "She's seizing!" the paramedic yelled.

Paramedics worked to stabilize her before strapping her to a gurney and guiding it up the embankment, followed by a second gurney carrying Rosemary.

RICK WAS OBSERVING members of his backfield run through a new set of plays that afternoon and blew his whistle to stop the action. He ran onto the field and grabbed a lineman's practice jersey. "What did I tell you about keeping your eyes on the safety, son?" he asked, getting in the teenager's face.

He walked backwards toward the side and blew his whistle again to restart the play. His boss came up to him and placed a hand on his shoulder. "Rick," the older man said.

"Just a sec, Coach. Let this play run first," Rick answered.

"It's Amber, Rick," the coach said, squeezing Rick's shoulder. "There's been an accident."

Rick whirled around to face his boss and grabbed his arm, an unbelieving look on his face. "How bad?" he asked.

"I don't know. She and your mother are being flown to County General."

"What about my dad? Does he know?"

"They're trying to contact him".

"He's playing golf with some friends. I'll get him. He shouldn't be driving."

Without another word Rick raced to where his truck was parked. He turned the key in the ignition as he punched a number in his cell phone and listened to it ring as he peeled out of the school parking lot.

By the time Rick and his father arrived at County General, Amber and Rosemary had been rushed into surgery and no one would give them information about their conditions. The best they could get was a nurse who told them Amber and Rosemary had been seriously injured.

Rick guided his father to the surgical waiting room and located seats facing the entrance to the room. He made sure the nurse would let the surgeons know there was family waiting for news about Amber and Rosemary. Then Rick joined his father and slumped forward resting his forearms on his thighs.

"Call your brothers and sister," Quentin said. "Tell Colleen she doesn't need to come."

Rick barked out a laugh. "I don't have a death wish, Dad. Colleen would never forgive me if I told her not to come."

"I guess you're right, son."

COLLEEN WAS IN the middle of a negotiation with Ken concerning the possibility of allowing Alicia a chance to go solo and dismiss Geoff. Consumer surveys had revealed that listeners liked Alicia, but considered Geoff condescending. They were meeting in Ken's office and had been at it for over three hours. Colleen was exhausted, but Ken wanted to make sure they had covered every contingency and that there was a firm plan in place to fade Geoff out over the following month. A tap at Ken's door interrupted their planning. When Ken opened the door and saw Colleen's secretary, he said, "What is it, Heather? Can't it wait a little while longer?"

"I don't think so, Mr. Dickinson," Heather answered. "I have an emergency phone call on hold for Ms. Walters."

Colleen stood and joined him at the door. "Let me take it, Ken. We need a break anyway."

"Well, hurry back, will ya? I'd like to get home at a reasonable hour tonight."

Colleen strode down the long corridor toward her office and waited until Heather punched in the call and handed her the receiver.

"This is Colleen Walters. What can I—" she started.

"Trigger, its Rick. Mom and Amber were in an accident this afternoon. Dad and I are at the hospital now, waiting to hear something from the damn surgeon."

"I'll fly home as soon as possible. Can I speak to Daddy?"

"Hello?" Quentin answered a moment later. To Colleen his voice sounded weak and trembled slightly.

"Daddy. I'll be home soon. Let Rick handle things for you."

"Amber's been badly injured as well and he's worried."

"Are Tom, Charlie, and Matt on their way?"

"Rick called them. I expect them any time now."

"Then let them take care of whatever you and Rick need. Please Daddy. Call Uncle Jack. He'll want to know, too. Love you. Tell Rick I'll be there soon."

"Love you too, sweetheart."

Colleen handed the receiver back to Heather. "Make a plane reservation to Philadelphia. Today if possible. One way. "Her hands were shaking and she held back tears. "Let me know as soon as you can." She turned to go back to Ken's office. "Oh, and please contact Marsha Barrett and ask her to call me in...about an hour."

"Is everything all right, Ms. Walters?" Heather asked.

"My mother and sister-in-law were in an accident. I have to go home and am not sure how long I'll be gone."

"I'm sorry, Ms. Walters," Heather said.

"Thank you. I'll leave you a few things you can handle for me. You can call my cell if you need me."

Colleen rubbed her forehead as she returned to complete her meeting with Ken. Before they were finished, she was irritable and worried about her mother and sister-in-law. True, she'd never gotten along well with her sister-in-law, but had never wished her any ill will. After they wound up their meeting she opened the door to Ken's office and ran into Geoff in the hallway. He dropped his briefcase and glared at Colleen.

"You need to watch where the hell you're going," Geoff snapped. "Get out of my way, dammit!"

"Excuse me?" Colleen said through gritted teeth, her voice low and lethal sounding. Before the conversation went any further, Marsha came around the corner, accompanied by a frazzled looking Alicia. They stopped when they saw Geoff step closer to Colleen and stand virtually nose-to-nose with her.

"You heard me, you stupid bitch."

Blocking his attempt to move around her, Colleen gritted her teeth and snarled, "You are a condescending prick, Geoff. How do you stand yourself?" She looked around him. "Can you be ready to handle your slot alone beginning tomorrow, Alicia?"

Alicia looked at Marsha and sputtered something no one could understand.

"Can you?" Colleen repeated.

Marsha jabbed Alicia in the ribs as if to kick-start her voice. "I can be ready by tomorrow morning, Ms. Walters," Alicia answered.

"Excellent!" Colleen brought her face even closer to Geoff's. "You're fired, asshole! No discussion. Get out and don't let the front door hit you on the ass on the way out. Questions? Good!" Colleen shoved him out of her way.

Marsha briefly congratulated Alicia. Alicia hugged Marsha and danced her way to the front lobby while Marsha followed Colleen back to her office.

Colleen stopped at Heather's desk and took a paper confirmation of her flight home. She opened her office door and held it for Marsha to enter behind her.

"You wanted to talk to me?" Marsha asked. "I was running errands when I got the message. Glad I got here in time to see someone slap Geoff down," she said with a smile. "Remind me to never make you mad."

Colleen turned to face Marsha and her face crumpled. Marsha went to her and took her in her arms. "What's wrong, sweetie?"

Colleen wrapped her arms around Marsha as her body shook. "M-Mom was in an accident today. Rick said it was bad. I'm flying home tonight."

Marsha held her tighter. "God! I'm so sorry, baby. Is there anything I can do to help you? Just name it."

"If...if I call you, will you come to Philadelphia?"

"Absolutely," Marsha whispered, kissing Colleen's neck softly.

Chapter Twenty-two

COLLEEN LOADED HER suitcase into the trunk of her rental car a little before midnight and pulled onto the highway. County General Hospital was located about thirty miles from Philadelphia International Airport. She was exhausted and she feared what she might discover when she reached the hospital. She located an all-night coffee shop a few blocks from the hospital and ordered a large cup of coffee to take to the hospital. She parked near the emergency room and stopped to ask directions to her mother's room.

"Visiting hours ended several hours ago," the nurse at the emergency room desk told her. "According to registration, Rosemary Walters is in the ICU."

"What about my sister-in-law, Amber Walters?"

"Also in the ICU."

"I believe my father and brothers may be with them. I flew in from out of state less than an hour ago."

"If you returned in the morning you might be able to see them."

Colleen set her cup down and slapped the nurse's desk with her fist. "Just tell me how to get to the ICU. Now! I'm not leaving until I see my mother, even if it's through a window. I have to see her, dammit!"

"Trigger?" a man's voice said from behind her.

She whirled around and saw her oldest brother, Tom, standing nearby.

"Tom!" Colleen said as she rushed into her brother's arms. "How are Mom and Amber? Please tell me something."

"Everyone else is upstairs. I'll take you up. Dad's been asking when you'd be here. He won't go home. Maybe he'll listen to you," Tom said, his arm around Colleen.

Colleen grabbed her coffee and followed him onto an elevator that took them to the sixth floor. She saw her father stretched out across several chairs, but quickly hugged Matt and Charlie before wrapping her arms around Rick. His eyes appeared slightly swollen, possibly from crying and his clothes were wrinkled. His whiskers scratched her cheek as he buried his head against her shoulder.

"How is she?" Colleen asked.

"In a coma," he said, sniffing. "We won't know anything for two or three days."

"You should go home, Rick, and get some rest."

He released her and wiped his eyes. "I can't. What if she..." he started.

"She won't, Rick. She needs you to be strong now." She looked at her older brother. "Tom? He shouldn't drive."

Tom stood next to his brother and patted him on the shoulder. "Go with me to pick up some coffee, Studly. Colleen's smells mighty good."

"Ask the nurse if we can get a blanket for Dad, Tom, please." She knelt down next to her father and gently rubbed her hand up and down his back. He gradually opened his eyes and his lips curled into a slight smile. "You made it, baby," Quentin said in a raspy voice.

"Have the doctors told you anything?" she asked when he sat up and she sat next to him with her arm across his shoulders. She had never seen her father look so old.

"Not much." He smiled. "But she squeezed my hand earlier tonight."

"That's a good sign, right?" she said, smiling back at him.

Tears trickled down his cheeks and he took a deep breath. "I love your mother so much, honey. I couldn't bear it if I lost her."

"I know, Daddy," Colleen choked out. "You look whipped. Why don't you let me take you home for a while? We'll come back early in the morning and maybe she'll talk to us then."

Quentin shook his head. "I can't leave her here alone. She'll be expecting to see me when she opens her eyes."

Colleen leaned over and gave him a soft kiss on the cheek. "I'll be back in a minute, Daddy." She handed him her cup of coffee and hoped it was at least lukewarm. She walked toward the nurse's station, but stopped to look into the glass-enclosed intensive care unit. She hoped to catch a glimpse of Rosemary, but curtains surrounding each bed blocked her view. By the time Tom and Rick returned with coffee and pastries, Colleen had made a sleeping area for her father. She sat and brushed her hair back over her head.

"Do the police know what happened?" she asked.

"Just what Amber told them before she blacked out. Some car forced them off the road," Tom answered. "Maybe when she wakes up, she can give them a description of the vehicle."

"You mean *if* she wakes up." Rick rubbed his face with both hands.

"I said what I meant, buddy. Amber's a tougher girl than we've given her credit for." Tom patted his brother's back. "She saved Mom's life."

"When I find out who was responsible for this, I swear I'll kill them with my bare hands," Rick said.

Colleen couldn't bring herself to look at her brother. Rusty had threatened Rosemary when she shoved Colleen down the garage steps a few months earlier. She had threatened them all five years earlier. She cleared her throat and looked across the waiting room as she took a drink of her coffee. "It...it could have been Rusty," she said so softly she wasn't sure Tom or Rick heard her.

Tom pursed his lips. "She did threaten all of us, but she seemed to direct most of her anger toward Mom."

"I knew Mom didn't like Rusty, but I defended her," Colleen admitted.

Rick stood up and glared down at Colleen. "I sure as shit hope she was the best fuck you ever had, Colleen, because she was a world class bitch to the rest of us. I was there when she called Mom a *pathetic cripple*. This is your fault for dragging that viper into our lives in the first place."

Colleen stood quickly, reaching out to shove her brother away. "I didn't know this would happen!" she shouted.

Tom rose and stood between them. "That's enough, both of you. Trying to find someone to blame isn't going to help Mom or Amber right now. So sit down and shut the fuck up!"

They both stared at their oldest brother in shock. Tom was soft-spoken and Colleen had never heard him use profanity...ever.

"I'm sorry, Tom," she mumbled. "I over-reacted. I'm tired."

"We all are," Tom muttered. He looked between his brother and sister, his face red with embarrassment. "I apologize for cursing."

"No problem," Colleen said. She looked around to make sure her father and other brothers were still asleep.

Rick and Tom sat down again and Colleen picked up her purse. "I'll be back in a minute," she said. She left the waiting room and located the door to a stairwell. She sat down on the top step and took her cell from her purse. She pushed a button and hand-combed her hair away from her face. Her eyes misted over and her vision blurred as she waited for someone to answer the call. She covered her eyes with a hand and cried.

"KLEW-FM. You're *In the Midnight Hour* with Desdemona," Boomer's voice answered.

"You don't sound a thing like Desdemona," Colleen sniffed as she wiped her eyes with the back of her hand.

"Hey, Colleen. She's been hoping you'd call. Hang on."

Soft music filled Colleen's ear as she waited. A few minutes later a voice came on the line. "Hi, baby. Why are you still up this late? How's your mother?" Marsha asked.

"I miss you," Colleen answered as her voice quivered.

"I miss you, too, honey."

"You're the only person I know who's up this late. I'm at the hospital. My dad refuses to leave until he can speak to Mom."

"Are your brothers there?"

"Yeah. No one wants to leave Daddy and Rick here alone. They both look so exhausted. They might let us see Mom and Amber in four or five more hours. Dad said Mom squeezed his hand earlier, but she's still unconscious. I don't know if he imagined it or not. It's not good, Marsh." Colleen's voice cracked near the end.

"Do they know what happened?"

"I know what happened. Rusty ran them off the road."

"You don't know that, sweetie," Marsha said.

"Who else would do this? She's threatened my mother twice. Once at her trial and again when she pushed me down the stairs. No one else has a reason to hurt her."

"Do you want me to fly to Philly? I can catch a flight first thing in the morning and be there before lunch tomorrow."

"No. Wait until we know how they respond tomorrow, okay? I need to feel your arms around me, but would rather wait."

"Okay. Do you want me to do anything for you here?"

"I'll contact Ken tomorrow when I know more. Just take care of yourself, baby. I couldn't stand it if anything happened to you."

"Boomer's signaling me to get back on the air. Everything will work out. Love you, baby."

"I'll call when I know something. Love you, too," Colleen said before she disconnected. She stood and returned to the floor, stopping in the restroom to wash her face. She gazed at her reflection in the restroom mirror. She covered her mouth as tears flowed down her cheeks again. Her knees buckled and she fell to the floor sobbing. Rick was right, this was her fault. She brought Rusty into their lives and eventually endangered them all. Why didn't she see the early warning signs of Rusty's instability or her need to control everything around her including Colleen. Especially Colleen.

Chapter Twenty-three

MARSHA MOPED AROUND her house until ten-thirty the next night. She was still upset and hadn't heard from Colleen during the day. She hadn't slept much because she expected a call at any minute. She wanted to beat something, but received no personal satisfaction from pounding the body pillow in her bedroom. No matter what she did, sleep refused to come again. She grabbed her backpack and a snack for the middle of the night before closing and locking her front door. She glanced at her watch and figured her bus should be at her stop in half an hour or less.

Even though it was early, the neighborhood was dark and the weak light at the nearest corner didn't illuminate much. She walked slowly down the cracked sidewalk, careful not to trip, and headed for her stop. There were times she wished she had a vehicle, preferably an old one that she wouldn't have to worry about getting stripped. Then she could leave home a little later and still make it to the station on time. She was absorbed in her thoughts and trying not to think about Colleen when she turned the corner and saw a group of four African-American and Hispanic teenage boys walking toward her. She decided it would be best to ignore them. Probably a group walking home from a movie or something. She kept her eyes on the sidewalk as she passed them and exhaled in relief when they passed her.

A few steps later she glanced over her shoulder in time to see a fist coming toward her. She attempted to duck, but still took a glancing blow to the side of her head. She stumbled, but remained on her feet and turned to face her attackers. The four boys encircled her and one periodically snapped out a jab that struck her in the face, causing her eyes to tear. They laughed when she swung blindly a couple of times, hitting nothing but air. Eventually tiring of the game, two of them grabbed her arms and brought them behind her back painfully. A boy who looked older than the others waited until they held her securely, then stepped closer and delivered a staggering blow to her abdomen. Seconds before his fist struck her, the two holding her released her. She doubled over and fell to the ground, gasping for air. The older boy leaned down over her and seized her jaw between his thumb and forefinger, forcing her to look at him.

"Gotta message for ya," he said, spittle from his mouth striking Marsha's face. When she didn't respond, he shook her head and slapped her on the cheeks, laughing.

"What...message?" she finally gasped, hoping he would stop slapping her.

"That's better, bitch," he said with a grin, his teeth shining in the dark. He spun around and rubbed his forehead. "Now what was that damn message?" He turned back around, his foot striking Marsha's nose and causing it to bleed. When she reached up to cover her nose he knelt down beside her and punched her in the solarplexis sharply with his index and middle finger, again taking her breath away. "Oh, yeah. I remember now," he laughed. He leaned down, bringing his mouth closer to her ear. She could smell his sweat and body odor, which made her gag as she fought to take a deep breath. He jumped up and stared down at her and pointed to one of his companions.

The first boy said, "Stay," and drew his leg back to land a strong kick near her kidneys.

The second boy jumped into the air and drove a fist into her abdomen as he said, "Away."

The third boy kicked the back of her head, saying, "From."

The apparent leader of the thugs landed a solid blow to her face before stomping on her chest and walking away. "Her," he yelled over his shoulder, leading the group of laughing boys away.

Marsha lay on the sidewalk for a moment, struggling to catch her breath. She managed to draw her knees up to her chest, her forehead pressed against the rough cement. Eventually she forced her hands flat on the pavement on either side of her head and pushed up. She could barely see and suspected her left eye was swelling closed. She felt around her eyes and nose. There was blood on her fingertips from her nose and a cut over her left eye. By the time she was able to stand, she wobbled around before finally dropping to one knee at the edge of the grass, or what passed for grass. She lifted her head, in time to see a large black car pull to the curb. She groaned as the back passenger door opened and a foot wearing a shiny black shoe stepped out. As the feet approached her she began curling her body into a ball to protect herself from further assault, even though she was feeling pretty helpless at the moment.

"I don't have anything worth stealing," she managed in a raspy voice and coughed.

Water dribbled on her face, followed by a wet cloth a second man handed to the man who squatted next to her. She reached up and grabbed the man's wrist, forcing the bottle of water down to her lips and taking two or three gulps before releasing it.

"Bus is comin', boss," a man's voice said.

The man next to her stood. "Put her in the car."

Marsha felt strong hands slide under her arms and knees, then lift her effortlessly, and place her into the back seat of the mystery vehicle. The man who'd had the water tossed the wet cloth onto her chest as the car pulled quickly away from the curb.

"Who did you piss off this time?" the man asked, his face hidden in shadow. His voice sounded slightly familiar, but she couldn't place it.

"Nobody," Marsha answered as she folded the cloth and began

wiping the blood from her face. "Who the fuck are you?"

"A mutual friend sent me," the man said calmly.

Marsha intended to laugh, but it came out as a wheeze. She wrapped her arm around her ribcage and tried taking a deep breath.

"Your ribs are probably badly bruised, but not broken," the man said.

"Ya think!" Marsha said loudly. "What are you, a doctor?"

"In a manner of speaking. I fix things."

Marsha grunted as she leaned forward and tapped the driver on the shoulder. "I need to go to KLEW-FM. It's downtown on Marshall." Then she fell back in the seat to force in another breath, which was more like a pant. "Thanks, but I don't need your assistance."

"You're not equipped to handle the person responsible for tonight or the person responsible for Colleen's problems," the man said.

Using all the anger that had been accumulating inside, Marsha lunged at him and grabbed him by the throat. She jerked him far enough forward to see his face and her eyes widened. "Jack?" Her heart rate increased and her ribs ached, but she could breathe in short pants. Something hard jabbed her in the abdomen and she couldn't stop the flinch it caused.

"It's not my intention to harm you any more than necessary. Remove your hand," he said quietly. Marsha heard the distinctive sound of a weapon being cocked. She glared at him as much as her swollen eyes would allow as she spread her fingers apart slowly and released him.

"What are you doing here?" she asked.

"Apparently saving your sorry ass," Jack answered as he readjusted his tie. "My associate and I have been watching you and my niece for a couple of months. I know you're, shall we say, close to her." He held out a photograph. "Have you seen this woman?"

Marsha took the photo and examined it the best she could with her limited eyesight. A woman with deep auburn hair smiled back at her. From what Marsha could see, the woman was fashionably dressed, her arm wrapped snugly around the waist of another woman. There was no doubt the other woman was Colleen who looked at the auburn-haired woman with definite affection.

"Never had the pleasure, but I'm guessing her name is Rusty," she said as she looked at the blurry lights flashing past her window. She blinked hard attempting to clear her eyes.

"You've never seen her then?"

Marsha lifted the picture and studied it. "Once, I think. Ran into her, literally, near the radio station a couple of weeks ago. Almost knocked her down. She's left me a couple of presents." Marsha flipped her wrist and returned the picture.

"Her name is Victoria Manning," Jack said.

"Colleen said her name was Rusty."

"An affectionate nickname," Jack answered with a smile. "Colleen is a lovely girl, but a little naïve. Brought up too nice."

"What do you want me to do?"

"Depends. I know you care for Colleen, but do you love her enough to risk your life?"

"I don't want Colleen or anyone else in her family hurt by this bitch. Colleen thinks she's responsible for what happened to Rosemary. What did she do to you or would you have to kill me after you told me?"

"As ridiculous as it sounds, Victoria did love Colleen very much, more than she expected. When she beat Colleen, she got a little carried away, but my interest in Ms. Manning ended when she went to prison."

"She threatened to kill Colleen and her family when she got out of prison. Doesn't sound like true love to me," Marsha said.

"My people will keep an eye on the Walters family. When Colleen comes home, I would like it if you stayed close to her. Then when Victoria moves in, I will take care of her in my own way. I've watched over Colleen for years and won't allow her to be harmed again." Jack reached out and grabbed Marsha's arm. "Is that clear?"

"Crystal," Marsha answered with a grimace as he squeezed her arm tightly.

Jack grabbed Marsha by the hair and jerked her head back, taking her breath away for a moment. "Are we clear?" he hissed in her ear.

"As a bell," she said as she pulled her head away, sending a stab of pain down her back.

"Good." He tapped the big man in the front seat on the shoulder. "Take her to work," he said and readjusted the sleeves on his suit jacket. "How is she?"

"Who?"

"Colleen."

"You're watching her," Marsha answered.

Jack's hand snapped across the back seat and popped Marsha in the mouth. She covered it with her hand, squeezing her eyes tightly closed to will the sting away. "She's fine. Worried about her mother and sister-in-law."

"I'm sorry I didn't see that coming," Jack said, shaking his head. "Must be gettin' old."

The car pulled to the curb near the radio station and Marsha opened the back door. With one foot on the ground, she picked up her backpack and glanced at Jack. In the light from the station he was an innocuous-looking man in perhaps his late fifties or early sixties. Although his hair was beginning to turn white around the edges, it had been light blond at one time. Steel-rimmed glasses covered his light blue eyes. "Who are you really?" Marsha asked.

Jack turned his head to face her and she noticed his smile was almost identical to Colleen's.

"Just a concerned uncle," he said, not waiting for the door to close before he tapped the driver on the shoulder and pulled away.

"She looks just like you," Marsha mumbled as she watched the vehicle disappear into the night.

MARSHA WALKED CAREFULLY through the lobby of the radio station and stopped at the ladies' restroom to check her appearance. Damn good thing it was radio so she wouldn't have to worry about scaring anyone, she thought. Her ribs ached when she breathed and ugly bruises had blossomed on her abdomen. The area around one of her kidneys was tender. She gingerly touched her still swollen cheek, hoping her split bottom lip and stuffed up nose wouldn't cause a problem when she spoke.

"Whoa!" Boomer said, grimacing when he saw her approaching.

She held a hand up to prevent further comments. "I'm okay."

G-Man's eyes widened when Marsha entered the studio and began her nightly preparation for her show. G-Man continued staring at her as he took the next request. He flipped the switch on the microphone.

"Last time I saw something that ugly was after my dog got himself into a fight over a bitch in heat," he said.

"Did he win?"

"Nah. Had to put him down because the other mutt ripped his balls off," Gary said with a grin.

"I can't tell you how much better that makes me feel," Marsha said sarcastically.

"I bet it made you feel really butch though, didn't it?"

"If I have to look like this to feel butch, I might drop my membership in Lesbians International."

Gary cocked his head to one side. "Can you do that?"

"That would mean I'd have to start going out with guys like you though. Ugh!"

"You could become a nun," Gary said wiggling his eyebrows. "I hear they're a real fun group after dorm hours."

"Does my voice sound all right?" Marsha asked Boomer as she tested her microphone and sound level.

"It's a little raspier than usual, but raspy is sexy," Boomer answered. "I can adjust it a little to give you that sexy, smoky sound that drives the ladies wild."

"Don't tell Colleen about this if she calls tonight. I'll handle it. She has enough on her mind already."

Marsha used the intro music for her show to try to find a comfortable way to sit. She finally decided there was no such position. Her audience might be getting more groans than usual, especially if she had to move quickly.

An hour into the show, during which the minutes were crawling by, Boomer sent through a request.

"This is Desdemona," Marsha said. "Tell me what I can do for you this fine evening."

"Did you get the message?" a voice rasped in Marsha's ear. She cut off the live feed as she glanced at Boomer and moved her index finger in a rolling motion. With the push of a button Boomer rolled the show into a repeat of an earlier one and began taping the caller.

"I get lots of messages. Which one are you talking about?"

"Stay away from her. Otherwise I can't guarantee you won't add to your bump and bruise collection. She doesn't want you."

"She wanted me pretty badly a few nights ago, if we're talking about the same lady," Marsha said more calmly than she felt, but she hoped her caller would say something to let her know where the hell she was. "In fact, the way she touched me was exquisite. Most memorable."

"She's only using you for the sex, as pathetic as it is, nothing more. Catch a clue. She's mine! Always has been, always will be."

"And if I don't stay away?" Marsha asked.

"It would be a poor choice."

"Well, why don't you come on down here and we'll discuss this like a couple of real grown-ups? Then you won't have to worry about paying stupid teenagers to do your dirty work? Is that what you did to her mother, hire someone to hurt her?"

"I have many friends."

"Guess they fucked up then because she's still alive. What was that, another warning?"

"Just keeping a promise and I always keep my promises. I'll see you soon." The woman started laughing before Marsha cut her off.

THE NEXT MORNING Marsha chatted for a few minutes with Boomer about the semi-threatening call she'd received near the beginning of her show. Nothing else unusual had happened the remainder of the night.

"Gonna report it to Dickinson?" Boomer asked.

"I need to think about it for a while first. Most of those calls are cranks with a problem anyway," Marsha said. "Since whoever it was didn't make it live, I might wait and see if she calls back tonight."

They stepped out the front door of the station and Marsha looked up at the sky. Dark clouds blocked the sun and she saw flashes of lightning in the distance.

"Must be that storm front the weather guy was talking about. Want me to give you a ride home so you won't get caught in it when the bottom falls out?"

"Thanks, man."

Marsha followed Boomer into the underground garage. When he

approached what she could only describe as a crotch rocket, she stopped. "You've got to be shittin' me," she mumbled.

"I can outrun the raindrops on this baby," Boomer said with a grin when he saw the look on Marsha's face. He bent over and opened a side pocket of the leather saddlebags and pulled out a leather jacket festooned with multiple silver zippers. He tossed her a matching black helmet. "No wipers, but it'll keep you high and dry. These belong to my old lady, but should fit you."

Marsha wanted to feel brave and cool, but she hated motorcycles and the slickened roads should make for an interesting adventure. She slipped her arms into the jacket and was pleased to find the sleeves long enough to cover her hands. She forced the helmet over her head and flipped the full face visor down She swung her leg over the bike and settled in behind Boomer.

"Wrap your arms around me and hang on," she heard him say. Damn! Her helmet had a built-in communication system. She had to admit that impressed her. She pressed her body close to Boomer's, her arms encircling his thin frame as he backed the two-wheeler up a few feet before smoothly accelerating toward the street. "Now the fun begins. You ready, *chica*?"

"Yeah," she said.

"Hang tight," he said and she felt the surge of speed against her body.

She slammed her good eye shut, not wanting to see what was whizzing past her. "Do you know where I live, man?" she managed to ask.

"Over near Brookside, right?" he said.

"Turn onto Fremont away from Brookside," she answered. "Third house on the left."

"Be there in fifteen. The storm will be behind us, so we should stay dry long enough to get home."

Marsha sent up a few short prayers mixed with an occasional expletive when Boomer took a corner a little faster than he should have and she felt the bike shudder and skid as it regained traction. By the time he pulled to the curb in front of her house and she released him to swing her leg over the bike, every muscle in her body throbbed. Her ribs resisted her attempts to take a deep breath and she felt slightly sick as she pulled her helmet off. She unzipped the heavy leather jacket and peeled it down her arms. "Thanks, man," she uttered.

"Hey you gonna be okay?" Boomer asked. "Maybe you should have a doc check you out."

She shook her head. "A hot shower will help, but I might let Lolita sub for me tonight."

Chapter Twenty-four

AFTER QUENTIN WAS allowed into the ICU to spend a precious fifteen minutes with Rosemary, no one was allowed in again for ninety minutes. Rick was allowed in to see Amber. Tom, Charlie, and Matt had gone home to grab a shower and a change of clothes. Colleen finally persuaded her father to join her and Rick for breakfast.

As they sat at a table with their trays of hospital food, Quentin said, "Rick, can you take me home after breakfast?"

"I can take you, Daddy," Colleen said.

"No, honey. I appreciate it, but your mother asked for you when I was in there. Frankly, I'm whipped." He looked at Rick. "And you need to get at least a few hours of decent sleep too, son. After Colleen sees her mother, she can drive to the house to clean up before we return in the afternoon."

Rick opened his mouth to object, but his father stopped hm. "No arguing, Rick. Amber needs you to be at your best and not ready to fall down from exhaustion."

Colleen watched the two men walk out the main doors of the hospital before stepping onto an elevator alone. She leaned her head against the stainless steel wall and pushed away as the door slid quietly open. She glanced at the clock on the wall inside the ICU. Fifteen more minutes. She couldn't wait to touch her mother and feel the warmth of the hand that had always strengthened her. She had just finished her coffee when a nurse came out of the ICU.

She saw Colleen and asked, "Who are you here for?"

"Rosemary Walters. She's my mother."

"You can stay fifteen minutes, but we'll probably be moving her to a private room this afternoon after the doctor makes his rounds."

"And my sister-in-law, Amber Walters?" Colleen asked.

"I'm afraid she'll be with us a little longer," the nurse said quietly.

Colleen spun around and tried to read what was in the nurse's eyes. "But she'll be okay eventually, won't she?"

"We like to hope all our patients will leave us better than when they came to us." She met Colleen's eyes and a frown formed between her eyes. "I'm not a doctor and I know they're doing everything humanly possible to achieve an optimal outcome."

"Just passing on the party line, huh?" Colleen asked, pulling a head cover over her long hair.

"I'm doing my job. Follow me," the young nurse said.

"I don't know how you do this job, surrounding yourself daily with people fighting for their lives." She touched the young woman's arm. "It takes a special person and I appreciate everything you and the other nurses do."

The nurse reached up and wrapped her hand around the curtain surrounding Rosemary's bed. "Prepare yourself, Ms. Walters. She looks worse than she is."

Colleen closed her eyes and sucked in a deep breath, releasing it slowly through her mouth before nodding to let the nurse know that she was ready. The nurse slid the curtain back as quietly as possible and Colleen stepped to the side of the bed. The outline of her mother's body looked much smaller than Colleen remembered. She reached out and stroked Rosemary's cheek with her fingertips while her other hand wrapped around her arm. Gradually Rosemary's eyes blinked open and a slight grimace passed over her face as she attempted to move.

"I was hoping to see you, sweet girl," Rosemary rasped as her dry tongue tried to wet her lips.

The nurse brought Colleen a small cup of ice chips and a spoon. "This will help for now."

Colleen took the cup. "Thank you." Then she turned her attention back to the frail looking woman on the bed. She bent down and kissed her mother's warm forehead tenderly. "Would you like some ice chips?"

"Very much," Rosemary said.

"Can her bed be raised a little so she doesn't choke on the ice?"

The nurse pressed a button at the bottom of the bed and raised it a few degrees, stopping when Rosemary frowned and groaned. Colleen took a few chips and fed them to her mother. Rosemary sucked greedily on them.

"Delicious, but could use a little more salt," she sighed with what could have passed for a smile. "How is Amber?"

"They won't tell us much yet, but she hasn't regained consciousness," Colleen said as she guided another spoonful of ice chips into her mother's mouth. "Do you know what happened, Mom?"

"Of course I do. Some jackass forced us off the road. Amber tried to keep from going over the edge, but she didn't have a chance. It was deliberate, Colleen. Who would do such a thing?" Rosemary asked, her eyes sparkling as tears formed.

"I don't know," Colleen answered solemnly.

"Amber saved me," Rosemary said. "The car hit a tree, but began sliding into the river. I remember Amber pulling me out of the car."

"The nurse said they might be moving you to a private room this afternoon. That's good news."

Rosemary frowned and managed to raise her arm far enough to touch Colleen's cheek. "It was Rusty, wasn't it?"

Tears filled Colleen's eyes as her mouth moved to form words. "I don't know, Mom, but I'm afraid it was, even though I can't prove it."

"Marsha told me she'd already hurt you. Why didn't you tell me?"

"I didn't want you to worry. I wish she'd just kill me and get it over with without hurting any of you."

"No one blames you, honey."

"Rick does and I don't blame him," Colleen said as tears ran down her face.

"Rick's scared."

"I'll find a place for you all to hide where Rusty can't hurt you again. Eventually she'll get tired and come after me."

"We can't run away, Colleen."

"If anything worse happened to anyone in the family, I couldn't live with the guilt."

"You've always been a strong girl, Colleen. Don't let this incident with Rusty change who you are, no matter what happens."

"Time's up," the nurse said.

"You should go home to Marsha, darlin' girl."

"I will in a day or two. Once I know you and Amber will be okay. I'm leaving now and will bring Daddy back this afternoon." Colleen leaned down and kissed her mother's cheek. "I love you, Mom."

"I'll see you later, sweetie," Rosemary said. Her eyes were growing heavy as she watched Colleen walk away.

SOME TIME AFTER lunch, Rosemary was awakened again, assuming she was being moved to a new room. When she opened her eyes, she looked up at a tall, blond man, who was smiling down at her and holding her hand. His stunning blue eyes met hers and she saw tears hovering along his eyelashes. "You look terrible, Rose," he said, his voice wavering slightly.

Rosemary laughed the best she could and said, "You always were a sweet talker and a liar, Jack."

Jack leaned over and kissed her tenderly on the lips. "But you love me anyway."

"In my own way I suppose I always will."

"I promise you whoever's responsible for this will pay dearly. I could have lost you."

"We were never meant to be, Jack. You've given me the two greatest gifts anyone could ask for. A husband who loves me and a beautiful daughter."

"As long as you're happy, darling."

"I am. Thank you."

"Where is my brother anyway?"

"He went home to rest. Colleen will bring him back later."

"I should get out of here and let you rest now, but I had to see you. I'll be back."

Rosemary nodded and watched Jack slip away quietly.

MARSHA GRABBED SOMETHING to eat and poured a cup of coffee.

She had just settled into a chair on her front porch to watch the rain when her phone rang. She dug her cell from her front pocket and looked at the number before answering. She smiled and pressed the button to speak.

"Hi, baby," she said with a smile.

She watched as a bolt of lightning split the sky, followed a moment later by the crash of rolling thunder.

"What the hell was that?" Colleen asked.

"We're having a bit of weather here," Marsha answered. "How's your mother?"

"Banged up, but they're moving her to a room this afternoon."

"Well, that's good news."

"Amber woke up after lunch today, but will have to stay in the ICU for a few more days."

"How's she doing?"

"Has a pretty serious concussion and a broken arm, but seems to be on the mend except for a splitting headache."

"I bet Rick's relieved. When are you coming home?"

"In a couple of days, I think, unless one of them has a relapse. How are you doing?"

"It's different. I should warn you that I had an incident here a few days ago."

"What kind of incident?" Colleen asked.

"Mostly bruises and a split lip. Nothing broken or anything. Soup is at the top of my food list."

"I thought we weren't going to have any more secrets between us."

"I'm telling you now. You had enough on your plate. A bunch of teenagers mugged me on my way to work." Marsha paused before continuing. "It was a message from Rusty. Pretty sure she paid them to deliver it. Boomer had to adjust for my voice last night, but I'm taking tonight off to recoup."

"I'm sure she was responsible for Mom and Amber, too."

"Well, she can't be too lethal or we'd all be dead. And she seems to prefer doing it all in a flurry, then backing off for a week or two before striking again. What's with that?"

"Where are you now?" Colleen asked.

"Sitting on the porch watching the rain."

"Do me a favor?"

"What?"

"Go inside so you're not just sitting there like a target."

"You worry too much, honey. It's raining so hard that even the ducks have taken up walking."

"Be careful, Marsh. I'll send you the information when I decide to come home and I expect to see you waiting for me."

"Really?"

"Yeah. I remember how your lips feel against mine, but need to feel them again."

"I'll make sure you feel them everywhere," Marsha said seductively.

"That certainly gives me something to look forward to."

Marsha laughed. "We better stop before I make a fool out of myself on the front porch."

"I want you so much, baby," Colleen said. "Do you believe me?"

Marsha paused before answering. "Call me when you know when you'll be back. I'll let you know then."

COLLEEN DISCONNECTED AND stared at her phone. Why had Marsha paused and then not answered her question? She got up and straightened her slacks before opening the door onto the ICU floor. From the corner of her eye she saw a flurry of activity behind the glass walls and stopped to see what was happening. A nurse stepped away for a moment and Colleen saw that they were working on Amber. She went to the window and pressed her hands against it and jumped slightly as everyone stood back. Two bright orange pads were pressed to Amber's bare chest. Her body jolted like she was having a seizure, but only for a second.

Tears ran down Colleen's face when she realized Amber's heart had stopped and doctors and nurses were working to revive her. Colleen leaned her forehead against the glass that separated her from the well-lit room.

In what must have been minutes, but felt like seconds, she watched as a doctor drew a sheet up to cover Amber's face. The doctor left the ICU and walked to the family waiting room. Colleen saw Rick fall to his knees and cover his face with his hands as the doctor spoke to him. Quentin squatted on the floor next to his son and pulled him into a fierce hug. When his father and brothers assisted him to stand again, Quentin continued to hug Rick and stroke a hand through his hair as he sobbed. Rick opened his eyes and glared at Colleen. She knew he blamed her for what had happened and she had a difficult time meeting his eyes. Nevertheless she approached him, taking him into her arms and comforting him as much as she could as tears flowed down her face.

Nearly an hour passed as Quentin told his wife that their daughter-in-law had passed away and arrangements were made for a funeral home to pick up Amber's body. Her body was removed from the ICU and placed in a private room. Rick sat next to her body, holding her hand and rubbing his fingertips over her cheek until someone arrived to take her to the mortuary. Colleen drove to her parent's home, but had to stop halfway there and pull over. She dropped her head onto the steering wheel and cried until she thought she couldn't cry any more. She needed to hear Marsha's voice and pressed a button on her cell phone, waiting for Marsha to pick up on the other end.

"Hello. Colleen? What's wrong?"

"Amber's dead," Colleen said as she sniffed and tried to clear her throat.

"What happened? I thought she was fine," Marsha asked softly.

"A blood clot and there was nothing they could do," Colleen sobbed.

"I can be there in the morning," Marsha offered.

"I'll pick you up," Colleen hiccupped.

"You shouldn't be driving. I'll take a cab."

"I can drive," Colleen said forcefully. "I don't want to argue about it right now."

"Calm down, honey."

Colleen took a deep breath and released it slowly after she blew her nose. "Sorry," she said.

"There's nothing to be sorry for."

"You didn't see the way Rick looked at me, Marsha. Like he hated me."

"He needs to blame someone and you were there. Can you make it to your parent's house okay?"

"Yeah."

"Lie down and rest, okay? I'll text you my arrival time this evening."

"Okay."

Chapter Twenty-five

MARSHA ADJUSTED HER duffle bag on her shoulder as she walked down the long, crowded concourse. She had never faced the death of a friend or loved one other than Paulina, but would do the best she could to comfort Colleen. She shivered as the idea it could have been Rosemary crossed her mind. She didn't want to think about the guilt and grief Colleen would have had to endure then. As she stepped into the main ticket area of the airport, she saw Colleen and walked solemnly toward her. She was glad to see Quentin was accompanying her. He pointed toward Marsha and Colleen ran into her arms, nearly knocking her down. Marsha held her tightly as tears ran down her face, but still managed to extend a hand to greet Quentin.

"How's Rosemary?" she asked.

"Upset, but recovering," Quentin said. "My brother is flying in from Chicago to help us tomorrow. What happened to your face, Marsha?"

"I ran into a fist with my name on it," she answered. "Sorry I look like such a mess."

"Rusty had her mugged," Colleen said as she touched the cut area over Marsha's eye.

Marsha flinched a little. "I don't know that for sure, but it's a good guess. I'll be fine. When is the funeral?"

"In a couple of days and of course Rosemary is adamant about being there," Quentin said.

"I made a reservation at a hotel and after I check in, I'll be glad to go to your house and help, if I can," Marsha said.

"Cancel it," Colleen said. "You can stay at Mom and Dad's house."

"I don't mind being there to help, but I don't want to be in the way."

"I want you to be there with me," Colleen said. Then she frowned. "Why do you have to argue about everything?" she asked as she pushed her hair back over her head.

"I don't, but I don't want to be in the way."

"You won't be," Quentin said. "You can share Colleen's room again."

Colleen wrapped her arm around Marsha as they walked out into the sunlight. That night she just held Colleen in her arms and comforted her as much as possible.

THE NEXT AFTERNOON a black Lincoln Town Car pulled into the driveway of the Walters' home and Jack Walters stepped out. The driver, a large Hispanic man took his suitcase from the trunk and carried it to the front door. Jack rang the doorbell and looked around the neighborhood while he waited.

"Can you get that, Marsha?" Colleen asked as she prepared sandwiches for a couple of her nieces and nephews.

"Sure," Marsha said as she walked quickly to the front of the house. She reached for the doorknob and swung the door open. Her heart jumped into her throat when she saw the man who had come to her rescue in Omaha.

"Uncle Jack!" Colleen said as she greeted the man by throwing her arms around him and hugging him, letting him comfort her.

Jack removed his sunglasses and peered at Marsha over Colleen's shoulder. "How's my favorite girl?" he asked. "You holding up okay? And how is Rosemary?"

Marsha clearly saw his light blue eyes staring at her and spun around to return to the kitchen. Before she took two steps, a hand encircled her arm and pulled her back. "Uncle Jack, you remember my friend, Marsha?"

Marsha flinched when Jack reached out and touched her bruised cheek. "Of course, I do," he said. "What happened to your face?"

"She was mugged, Uncle Jack," Colleen said.

Marsha placed her hand on Colleen's arm and said, "I'll go check to see if anyone needs anything while you chat with your uncle."

Jack nodded almost imperceptively as he smiled at a retreating Marsha.

Marsha entered the kitchen and stopped at the counter, gripping it until her knuckles turned white. She shook her head and wondered how soon she could escape from Philadelphia. A jerk on the back of her shirt caused her to spin around, ready to defend herself if necessary. Her fists uncurled when she gazed down at a big-eyed five-year-old holding an empty glass.

"Can I have more milk, please?" the girl asked.

"Sure, Amy," Marsha answered with a smile of relief as she took the glass.

She handed the glass to the child just as the mountain of a man accompanying Jack entered the room. She placed her hands on the girl's shoulders for a moment, thinking the man wouldn't do anything with the child present. He gave the girl a crooked smile.

"How are you, Amy?" he asked. His gaze met Marsha's and he asked, "Is there any more tea?"

Realizing she looked ridiculous shielding herself behind a small child, Marsha released her. "How many?" she asked, reaching for a glass.

"Two, please."

"Sweet or unsweet?"

"Unsweet." When she turned to pour the tea, he said, "I see your bruises are beginning to change color."

"Yeah. Um...thanks for assisting me that night. Sorry, but I didn't catch your name."

He smiled broadly as he took the glasses from her. "Harold. Harold Gibson." He took a sip of his tea and added, "Jack would like to speak with you in the garden out back in about ten minutes, after he pays his respects to the rest of the family." Without another word he turned and walked back toward the front of the house. Marsha rubbed her sweaty palms up and down the sides of her legs and released the deep breath she'd been holding.

She filled the dishwasher with glasses and tried to make sense of what was happening. She was washing a couple of pots when warm hands slipped around her waist. "You don't have to do that." Colleen whispered.

"I said I'd help," Marsha said. "Not much else I can do."

"Thank you for last night," Colleen said softly before dropping a light kiss on her neck.

"Having you here to just hold me meant more than you'll ever know."

Marsha turned and hugged Colleen. "My pleasure. When is your mother coming home?"

Colleen placed some silverware into the dishwasher. "Daddy said this evening. He and Uncle Jack are planning to pick her up later."

"Your uncle doesn't look much like your father," Marsha commented.

"He and Daddy are half-brothers, but they've always been close. They had different mothers."

"Where does he live?"

"Chicago. He owns an import-export company and travels quite a bit. I used to dream about visiting all the exotic places he does."

"Why didn't you? I'm sure he would have hired you."

Colleen shrugged. "By the time I grew up I wasn't interested in import-export."

The kitchen door opened and Harold returned two empty glasses. "Now," he said softly, then struck up a conversation with Colleen.

"I'll be back in a few minutes," Marsha said and left Colleen chatting with Harold. She walked down the hallway and opened a doorway that led onto the back patio. Jack was sitting comfortably at a round glass patio table, his legs crossed. "Have a seat," he said without bothering to acknowledge Marsha's presence.

She sat in the comfortable, padded deck chair.

"My brother has a beautiful home," Jack sighed. "He has a lovely wife and beautiful children." He turned his head and looked at Marsha. "I trust you won't feel the need to discuss our meeting in Omaha with anyone."

Marsha shook her head slowly, but never took her eyes off Jack's face. "If I did I'd risk adding to my bump and bruise collection, right?"

"Possibly. Colleen cares for you and I would never do anything to hurt her. You have my word."

Marsha squinted into the sun before speaking again. "You're her father, aren't you?"

"My brother is her father and always has been. She loves him as a father. I am merely a protective uncle and nothing more." He stood and put his hands in his pockets, staring down at Marsha. "Victoria Manning was an associate of mine several years ago. She was very beautiful and extremely charming. She's ruthless when it comes to getting what she wants. Unfortunately, when she insinuated herself into Colleen's life, all my niece saw was her beauty and charm. She didn't see her other side until it was too late. No one did."

"Why didn't you stop her before Rosemary was almost killed or after she beat Colleen?"

"The man responsible for Amber's death and Rosemary's injuries has been dealt with and as for what happened to Colleen five years ago, I allowed the law to take care of that. That was a mistake on my part. I won't make another one. When I leave here, Harold will remain to watch over my brother and his family."

"And when Colleen returns to Omaha?"

"She will be protected." He took a deep breath. "But I suggest you end your liaison with my niece. I can't protect you and frankly you are not a member of my family."

"Colleen tells me you're in the import-export business in Chicago," Marsha said.

"There are many importers in Chicago," Jack said.

"You know, I thought you looked familiar the day I met you. Now I remember where I first saw you," Marsha frowned.

"Really? And where was that?" Jack inquired.

"My former girlfriend was a model in Chicago. Paulina Kasmarian. I saw you at one of her shoots."

"It's possible," Jack said with a shrug. "I know many people."

"You import drugs, don't you?"

"You have no proof of that," Jack said defensively.

Marsha stood quickly and said, "Paulina died of an overdose less than six months later! I saw her give you money and you gave her a package." Marsha pointed a finger at Jack. "You and that shit killed her!"

Jack laughed. "From what I remember about poor Paulina, you beat the shit out of her and were cooling your hells in Cook County jail when she died. It forced the authorities to release you! If I'm guilty of what you think, you should thank me."

"I didn't beat her and didn't want her dead!" Marsha said loudly, taking a step closer to Jack.

Strong arms grabbed her from behind and held her. She winced as she struggled to break away.

"Sh-h-h," Jack said softly as he approached her. "Release her, Harold."

Marsha rubbed her arms. Jack stood in front of her and took her chin between his thumb and index finger. "I won't protect you from Rusty, but I want you out of Colleen's life." He pulled a small piece of paper from his shirt pocket and handed it to her. "Contact this number. I've arranged a position for you. Leave after the funeral and be gone by the time Colleen returns to Omaha." Jack patted her on the shoulder as he left the patio. Tears ran down Marsha's face and she wiped them away.

BY THE TIME Marsha re-entered the house, it seemed unnaturally quiet. She walked into the front room and found Harold reading a magazine on the couch. "Where is everyone?" she asked.

"Gone," Harold answered. "Jack told everyone to go home and rest. He and Quentin drove to the hospital to wait for Miz Rosemary to be discharged."

"Did Colleen go with them?"

Harold shook his head. "She went upstairs to clean up and take a nap, I think."

Marsha went upstairs and heard the shower running when she entered Colleen's bedroom. She quietly undressed and made her way into the bathroom. She stepped into the shower behind Colleen and couldn't stop her hands from gliding down Colleen's back. Colleen stepped back into her and tilted her head back.

"Are you all right?" Marsha asked and slid her hands forward and under Colleen's arms until they covered Colleen's supple breasts.

"I am now," Colleen murmured.

This would be her last time with Colleen, Marsha thought as her roaming hands became more aggressive, pinching Colleen's nipples while she kissed the warm, wet skin down her back. She turned Colleen around to face her and kissed her as her hand slipped down Colleen's gently rounded abdomen and through the soft hair at the apex of her legs. When Colleen spread her legs slightly, Marsha's hand cupped Colleen's sex.

"I need you so much, Marsh," Colleen said as she clung to Marsha.

"You'll always have me. Remember that, no matter what happens," Marsha said against Colleen's lips as they parted to greet her eagerly.

When Marsha entered Colleen and felt the muscles tighten around them, she said, "I want you, baby. I never knew how much until now."

As Marsha pumped into her, Colleen bit down on her shoulder to stop a scream of pleasure as her orgasm flooded through her. Their lovemaking continued until Colleen fell asleep from exhaustion, begging Marsha to stop after multiple orgasms. Marsha held her and tried to memorize even the smallest feature of Colleen's face. She never wanted to forget her smile or the hazy look in her eyes when she was overcome with passion. Marsha smiled remembering the elegant look of her neck as she threw it back during her climax or the wild look of her hair flowing across her face as she rode Marsha's fingers. Those memories would be with her until the day she died...and they would have to be enough.

THE NEXT DAY, Marsha held Colleen's hand as the minister completed the graveside service for Amber Walters. Rick's brothers helped him and Amber's parents back to their car while Colleen and Marsha assisted Rosemary, insisting she use a wheelchair. Jack held one hand while Quentin held the other. Harold easily lifted her from the wheelchair into the car. Marsha escorted Colleen to a car behind Quentin and Rosemary's and opened the door for her.

Once they were settled in the back seat, Colleen took her hand and squeezed it.

"I'm flying back to Omaha this evening," Marsha blurted out. "I need to get back to work."

"I'll see if I can change my ticket," Colleen said.

"No. You need to stay here a little longer. Your mom and brother need you. I want you to stay. Please."

"I'll fly back on Friday then. I told them I'd be back then."

"Take longer if you need it, honey. The station will understand."

"After yesterday I don't want you to go, baby." Colleen laughed. "You were like a woman possessed, but I loved it."

"I enjoyed watching you let go."

"You'll see it any time I feel your hands on me. I love you, Marsha, and I hope you believe that."

Marsha smiled and looked down at their hands. "I do."

Colleen insisted on being with Marsha when Jack and Harold drove her to the airport. After Harold pulled to the curb, he popped the trunk of Jack's Town Car. Marsha stepped out and walked to the trunk to grab her duffle and sling it over her shoulder. Jack got out to shake Marsha's hand.

"Got the number I gave you?" he asked quietly.

Marsha patted her back pocket. "In my wallet."

"Take care of yourself. No hard feelings." Jack turned to get back in the car.

"Marsha!" Colleen called out as she got out of the car and ran into Marsha's arms. They kissed and Marsha felt tears building in her eyes when she pulled Colleen's arms away. "I...I have to check in," she said, her voice shaking. She ran the heel of her hand over her eyes and entered the main terminal, leaving Colleen and her last chance at happiness behind.

Chapter Twenty-six

MARSHA SLEPT LATE the next morning and then made arrangements to put her house on the market. Over the next couple of days she sorted through her belongings and packed. As she had many times in the past, she would set out alone with little to call her own. She was planning to be gone before Friday and had already called the number Jack had given her and given her notice at the station, telling them she had been hired by a larger station out west and believed it was time for her to move on. She spent a couple of days prepping Lolita to take her spot as the new hostess of *In the Midnight Hour*. Her last night on the air, she worked alone with Boomer.

"This really your last night, Marsh?" Boomer asked, his voice subdued.

"Yeah. I got a job offer and it was too good to turn down."

"Who's gonna take your slot?"

"Lolita."

"Man, she croaks like a frog."

"She does a good show so give her a break."

"So where you goin'?"

"Out west," Marsha lied.

"So let's burn 'em up tonight and good luck."

Marsha answered the request line smoothly after her intro music faded away. She chose not to announce it would be her last night in Omaha. During a lull between calls, she let her mind stray to the intimate times she had spent with Colleen. She still couldn't understand why the blonde beauty had been interested in her. It broke her heart to think of Colleen's bloodied face in the pictures Rosemary had shown her. She could almost understand if the attacker had been a stranger, but done at the hands of someone you loved struck her as obscene.

She lowered her mouth closer to the microphone and began a slow, romantic instrumental as background music, letting it play a minute before speaking. "This is the music lovers listen to as they cling to one another. Beautiful, isn't it? It's what we all want, that feeling of belonging to someone, the happiness that comes from sharing your life with someone special, the expectation of the touch your body longs for, the look in a lover's eyes that says they want you." After a brief pause she sighed into the mike. "Imagine that touch turning into something unimaginable, causing pain that strikes your core so viciously that it shatters your soul.

"I recently read an interesting report about the abuse women suffer at the hands of the person they're most intimate with. I'm ashamed to admit that I've been injured by a lover. I thought I deserved what happened to me. I made too many demands, I wasn't good enough, wasn't attentive enough. But I have a soul deep truth for you. I finally woke up and realized it wasn't my fault. She didn't love me. She'd never loved me. Nobody talks about it much, but statistics show that abuse within the gay and lesbian community is the same percentage as among hets. An abuser is a sick individual. They hate themselves so much they take it out on someone who loves them.

"When one woman abuses another, it isn't reported very often. You see, we don't want hets to think we're like them. We're better than that. We wouldn't do that to the woman we love. But I'm sad to say we do. We're just people who love a little differently. Within our community are great people, just as there are in the rest of society. And there is unspeakable evil and cruelty. Don't believe an abuser's apology. They always apologize and swear it will never happen again. But it will. Don't forgive them, don't trust them, just walk away as fast as you can and stay away until they get help. Report abuse to the police, press charges. Don't let your memory of intimate moments cause you to stray from that path. Abusers never stop. It's not your fault and you can't make them better by trying to love them more. I'm begging you. Report what happened to you and stop the cycle of abuse before it's too late. There is someone out there who will love you, cherish you, for the incredible person you are. If you haven't been a victim of abuse, hug the lover next to you and thank him or her for respecting you."

For the remainder of her program, Marsha's phone line stayed lit. Most calls didn't request a song, preferring to talk. For the first time she realized how many others like her there were. She hung up on a few and placed their phone numbers on the no-answer list for the remainder of the night.

"You just outed yourself," Boomer said during a short break between calls.

Marsha shrugged. "Management knows," she said.

"How are the callers taking it?"

"About fifty-fifty."

"What about Dickinson? He'll blow a gasket!"

"It was a public service piece," she said with a smile.

"Got another call coming in," Boomer said.

Marsha straightened in her chair and wished she had a large cup of coffee. She pressed the button to open the phone line. "This is Dez. How ya doin' this fine night?"

"I suppose you think that was real ballsy," Rusty's voice said over the line. Marsha shook her head at Boomer when he made the signal to cut the call. She wanted this one to go over the airwaves to anyone who would listen.

"It needed to be said," Marsha said calmly. "A bully is a bully. What do you want?"

"Colleen belongs to me. I'll make you disappear soon enough."

"I can hardly wait." Marsha brought her mouth so close to the microphone that her lips brushed against its cover when she spoke. "You fucked up, Rusty. You lost your chance to feel the softness of her skin, inhale the sweet scent between her thighs when she's aroused, or see the look in her eyes the moment before you take her over the edge. You threw it all away, you stupid bitch. Even if you kill me tomorrow, she'll never be yours again. You're just another psycho stalking someone weaker than you."

The sound of Rusty's throaty laugh was chilling. "You're a gnat. When you least expect it, I'll squash you like the pathetic bug you are. You'll beg to die before I finish with you. Oh, and too bad about your house," she said before disconnecting.

Marsha punched the button that let her speak to Boomer. "Key up the final hour of an earlier show," she said as she stood.

"What about callers?"

"Handle it!" she shouted. She tore off her headphones and tossed them onto the console. She punched a number into her cell and grabbed her backpack before leaving the studio and running down the hallway.

FLAMES LEAPED INTO the night sky as Marsha threw money onto the front seat of a cab and hurried out the rear door. The street in front of her house was blocked by police cars and fire engines. She ran down the street until she saw Jacobi who was comforting Mrs. Funderburk, both in their nightclothes and robes.

"Are you all right? Was anyone hurt?" Marsha asked frantically as she came to a halt near the elderly couple.

"Gertie worried sparks cause her place to burn," Jacobi answered.

"What happened?" Marsha asked even though she was sure she already knew.

"Was explosion. When I get up to check, house already burning like bonfire."

"Did you see anyone around tonight?"

Jacobi shook his head as he patted Gertie on the back. He leaned down. "You see Gertie. The firemen hose your roof so it won't burn."

Gertie laid her thin hand on Marsha's arm. "I'm sorry about your home, dear."

"It's all right as long as no one was hurt," Marsha said, attempting a reassuring smile.

A vehicle came to a fast stop near the blocked intersection and Marsha saw a figure running toward her. Trish wrapped her arms around Marsha when she reached her.

"Are you all right?" Trish asked, trying to catch her breath.

"What are you doing here?" Marsha asked.

"Mattie called me. She's here somewhere, I think."

Trish hugged Marsha. "I'm so sorry, Marsh."

"It's okay, Trish. It was going up for sale tomorrow anyway."

"Why? You loved this old house," Trish asked.

"Tonight was my last night on the air. I'm leaving Omaha tomorrow."

Trish punched her in the arm. "Were you going to tell me or just sneak out of town?"

Marsha rubbed her arm. "I'm not sneaking. Got an offer I couldn't turn down."

"Does Colleen know?"

Marsha shook her head. "She'll find someone else to give her what she wants," she said softly.

"She loves you, you idiot!" Trish said.

Marsha grabbed Trish by the arms. "She'll get over it," she snapped and pushed Trish away. "Leave me alone right now, please," she added through clenched teeth. There was nothing she could do other than watch as the things that had made up a part of her life disappeared with the smoke into the night sky. She looked down when a small, warm hand took hers. Kenyetta stared up at her with tears in her eyes. Marsha knelt down and hugged the girl to her. "Take good care of Miss Gertie and the others for me," she whispered.

Unexpectedly, two shots rang out through the night. Trish grunted and grabbed Marsha's arm as she slumped against her.

"Trish!" Marsha yelled as she caught her friend and lowered her to the ground, watching a red blotch spreading on her chest.

Trish looked up at Marsha and her lips moved. Marsha took her friend into her arms and held her. Trish whispered, "Tell Mattie I love her." Then her head fell lifelessly to the side.

"No!" Marsha screamed. "No, no, no. Talk to me, Trish. This isn't funny." When Trish didn't answer, Marsha pulled her tighter against her and rocked her, letting her tears fall.

A police officer knelt next to Marsha and tried to get her to release Trish and take cover until the shooter was located. Marsha reached out and shoved him away as she continued to cry.

"Trish!" a voice called out

Marsha looked up in time to see a fireman running toward her. "Trish, baby," Mattie called out as she raced to assist Trish. She tore her helmet off and dropped it. Halfway across the street another shot penetrated the chaos and Mattie was knocked off her feet before she could reach Marsha and Trish. Another fireman ran to her assistance, but Mattie didn't move and he shook his head after he felt for a pulse.

"No!" Marsha screamed again. She released Trish and jumped up. "Kill me!" she screamed. "I'm the one you want! They did nothing to you, you bitch!"

She dropped to her knees and sobbed. Then she felt the phone in her pocket vibrate. She ignored it, but it continued to vibrate. She finally took it from her pocket and saw through her tears that she had a message. She pushed a button and looked at the message: *I told you you'd beg me to kill you, bitch. They paid the price for your stupidity! You're next.*

Marsha wobbled as she stood and stared at her phone. She drew her arm back and threw it as far as she could. She ran down the street and turned the corner, continuing to run until she reached the bus stop. She walked around in agitation until the bus stopped in front of her. Her shirt was covered with Trish's blood and streaks of soot from the fire marked her face, leaving lines where she had cried.

"What's going on?" the bus driver asked with a smile. She glared at him and dropped money into the change box before slumping into a seat.

Chapter Twenty-seven

BOOMER WAS BUSY trying to keep up with the phone calls pouring into the request line when Marsha walked purposefully down the hallway toward Studio One. She banged on the door until Boomer opened it.

"Shit, woman, you look like you've been in a battle," he said.

Without speaking, she grabbed her headphones from his head and said, "Get out, Boomer." She pulled her wallet from her back pocket and shoved a twenty into his hand. "Get me a cappuccino and whatever you want. I've got this." Her voice was low and menacing. "I got this. Take your time. No hurry."

"I can't leave you here alone, Marsh."

"Go, goddammit. I won't watch another friend die tonight." She flipped a switch to put her back on the air. "Sorry about that, Omaha. We had a minor emergency in the studio, but it's under control now," she said calmly. "You still out there, Rusty, or have you crawled back into the dark to join the other cockroaches, you fuckin' coward? I guess beating a helpless woman wasn't good enough for you." Her voice cracked and she cleared her throat. "Now you're murdering innocent people who never did anything to you except be my friend. You're pathetic! Striking out at people who never knew your name. I'm here alone now, waiting for you to take your best shot at me, you fuckin' whore! Come and get me, if you have the guts! I'm unarmed and since you seem to prefer your victims without a way to defend themselves, even you should be able to get me."

Marsha queued up several songs and leaned back in her chair. She closed her eyes and took several deep breaths. She might die, but she was certain Jack would protect Colleen until Rusty had been dealt with. Her only regret was that she wouldn't be able to live a life with Colleen beside her. She hoped Colleen would forgive her.

During a song, she moved from the studio to the sound booth, taking the baseball bat Gary kept in the studio, and continued her show. An hour later she heard footsteps in the tiled corridor. Showtime, she thought. She picked up the bat and pressed her body against the wall behind the sound room door. She didn't hear a gunshot, but a bullet shattered the lock on the studio door and it flew open. Marsha reached out and turned the doorknob of the sound room, the bat on her shoulder. She stepped into the corridor quietly, gripping the bat with both hands, prepared to hit a home run as she raised the bat. She watched as the auburn-haired woman moved cautiously into the studio, guided only by a small studio light over the console. The phone on the console rang and Rusty fired a muffled shot. Marsha took a deep breath and funneled all of her anger into her arms as she swung the bat. It wasn't her greatest swing, but was good enough to make Rusty drop her gun. She spun around and Marsha's fist met the face of her enemy. What a shame to mess up such a beautiful face, she thought as Rusty was knocked into the studio, a trickle of blood appearing beneath her nose. When Marsha followed Rusty into the dark studio, prepared to beat her to death with the bat, she was tackled from the side and knocked down. The bat fell from her hand and a fist struck her in her still tender abdomen. Marsha wrapped her arms around the woman's body and held her until she could catch her breath again. While they wrestled on the floor, Rusty managed to break away and, her arm encircled Marsha's throat tightly.

Rusty hissed into Marsha's ear. "I could squeeze the life out of you right now, but you haven't suffered enough yet."

Marsha felt dizzy as she tried to escape Rusty's grip. She threw her head back and head-butted her. As her grip around Marsha's throat lessened slightly, Marsha brought her arm up and drove her elbow into Rusty's ribs. She gasped for breath when Rusty released her, but saw her glance around the studio floor for her weapon. When Rusty moved forward, Marsha saw Trish's face. With a loud scream she grabbed Rusty's leg and crawled to her knees. Rusty kicked out and caught Marsha on the jaw, stunning her. Rusty picked up her gun and turned toward Marsha. She pulled the trigger and Marsha felt the bullet strike her body. Strangely, it didn't hurt. Marsha swung her arm and the back of her hand struck her attacker's face and snapped her head back. The look on Rusty's face was everything Marsha had hoped it would be. Marsha shook her hand. She hadn't expected it to hurt. "How does it feel to have your ass kicked, Rusty?"

Rusty's leg came up and caught Marsha in the lower abdomen and sent her flying against the studio wall. Despite her anger, Marsha was getting tired. Why doesn't she pull the trigger and end this, Marsha thought. She looked up and struggled to stand by pushing against the wall. She watched as Rusty set the gun on the console and pulled a knife from the back pocket of her slacks and flipped it open.

"I'm getting tired of playing with you," Rusty growled as she wiped blood from beneath her nose. "I think your head will look excellent mounted on my office wall," she added as she advanced toward Marsha.

"Then just shoot me!"

"I should have killed that bitch Colleen when I had the chance," Rusty spat. She smiled at Marsha as she prepared to attack. "But, damn, she was a good fuck. I do miss that. Maybe I'll fuck her again as I watch her die. I'll enjoy watching the life fade from her eyes while my fingers are buried inside her."

Marsha felt the rage surge through her at the mention of Colleen. She had to protect her so this bitch would never hurt her again. Marsha pushed away from the wall and launched herself toward Rusty, disregarding the knife in Rusty's hand. She felt the blade enter her body, but adrenaline pulsed through her veins and she struck Rusty on the jaw and knocked her down. Before she could scramble to her feet again, Marsha landed on her and meshed her fingers together to strike her with her doubled fist. With angry tears flowing from her eyes, she ignored her own pain and struck the woman again. "That's for Trish," she gritted out and swung again. "And that's for Mattie." She raised her arms again, fighting past her fatigue, and swung again. "That's for Colleen." As her hands came up again to deliver another blow to the now unconscious woman, she said, "And this is for Amber." Before her hands made contact they were grabbed.

"That's enough," Jack Walters said. "You've got a plane to catch and need to see a doctor. Harold."

A bullet struck Rusty in the forehead. Even though Rusty was unconscious when the bullet entered her brain, Marsha jumped slightly, suddenly feeling sick to her stomach. "What about her?" she managed.

"Harold will make sure she's disposed of. Can you stand?"

Marsha shook her head. "I don't think so. It hurts like a bitch," she said as her face twisted into a grimace.

"Harold," Jack said.

Harold picked Marsha up easily and carried her to a car waiting outside the station, placing her carefully into the back seat. She held her hand over her side, blood oozing between her fingers. As Jack quickly pulled away from the curb she said, "If I die, bury me anywhere. Don't tell Colleen about any of this."

When Marsha woke up she was lying on a bed and felt woozie. A woman sat next to her, reading a book. When she saw that Marsha was awake, she closed the book and took her arm to count her heartbeats.

"Where am I?' Marsha rasped.

"At about thirty thousand feet," the woman answered and gazed out the window. "If I had to guess, I'd say we will be landing in another hour or so."

"Where?"

"New York. It's where you work now. A vehicle will meet us and take you to your new apartment." The woman opened a drawer and took out a messenger bag. "When you get a chance, your papers are inside the bag. You've got two weeks to mend, so memorize it and destroy it."

Chapter Twenty-eight

WHERE DID SHE go?" Colleen asked two days later when Ken called her into his office and told her to cancel the contracts with any new affiliates for Desdemona's show. He read the letter of resignation he'd received in his email after Marsha returned from Philadelphia.

"I don't know where she went," Ken said with a shrug. "Boomer said something about out west, whatever that means. Maybe she's moving to a larger market area."

Colleen returned to her office and paced the floor, trying to think what could have gone wrong. The last time they were together Marsha held nothing back while they made love. She'd been gentle, passionate, almost possessed. She sat behind her desk and picked up her phone to call a few people who might know something, anything. No one answered and Colleen was beginning to feel frustrated.

Heather brought in the mail that had stacked up on her desk, along with the day's newspaper. Colleen glanced at the newspaper and a front-page story about an unexplained fire caught her eye. She read the story and her eyes filled with tears when she learned that Trish and Mattie had both been killed by what was described as random gunfire near what remained of Marsha's home. Colleen crumpled the paper in her fists, certain that Rusty had been responsible. Colleen re-read the story, but there was no mention of Marsha. Perhaps she'd fled to escape Rusty's grasp.

"Come back to me, baby," Colleen mumbled. "I still need you. You're a part of me now."

FOLLOWING TWO WEEKS of recovery and spending time staring at the pigeons that found shelter and comfort by strutting back and forth on the brick windowsill of the apartment she now called home, Elaine Brannigan, once known as Marsha Barrett, looked out the window at the streets below her with tears in her eyes. She would be reporting to her new job and life the following week, but missed everything she'd left behind in Omaha. She was certain Victoria Manning was dead, but somehow doubted her body would ever be found. No one would tell her what happened after Jack whisked her away from the scene. She had missed the funerals for her friends, Trish and Mattie, and hoped one day she would be re-united with the people of her old neighborhood. No memories of her past would be complete without those of Colleen. She ached inside, wishing her hands could caress Colleen's soft skin one more time. Elaine reached up and slapped her own face to drive the memories of Colleen away before they drove her past the brink of insanity. She threw her head back and laughed despite the tears. Running away had always been so easy and she had never looked back. She shook her head and wiped the useless tears away. She would embrace this new life and pray anyone from her past would soon forget they had ever known her. Her old life had been a lie and didn't deserve to be remembered.

"I made a salad if you want some," Karen, the nurse who stayed with her said.

"Thanks," Elaine answered. "I'll be there in a minute."

"Crying again?"

"Does it ever stop?"

"Eventually you will run out of tears," the nurse said as she returned to the kitchen.

When Elaine turned to join Karen for a light lunch, she saw Karen's suitcase sitting in the hallway.

"You leaving?"

"This is my last day, but I left my phone number in case you need it," Karen said.

"Now I have to cook for myself, I suppose."

Karen frowned. "I'm not happy with the weight you've lost and will report it."

"Snitch," Elaine muttered. Then she smiled and looked at Karen as she stuck a grape tomato into her mouth. "I always wanted to be svelte."

"Lose any more and you'll look like a Holocaust survivor and that's not good."

"I'll be okay. I enjoy food too much."

"I'll be checking in on you from time to time."

"Since I'm only doing voice overs, I could be as big as an elephant and it wouldn't matter to anyone." Elaine shrugged.

"Are you getting used to your new name all right?"

"Yeah. Even though I've never used it much, it is my real name. I'm just the little girl Mommy and Daddy Brannigan never wanted."

The next morning Elaine Brannigan stepped into the offices of Stilwell Artists at a large recording studio in Brooklyn. Apparently they made a living by providing artists for voice-overs and as body models. It was different, but Elaine felt certain that her radio experience would prove useful.

IT WAS THE middle of January and the Walters' home was filled with family. Rosemary had recovered from the accident for the most part while Quentin doted on her every minute of the day. It was a weekend that had always been a family event and Colleen had taken a break from her search for Marsha long enough to fly home. Football had been droning from the huge television in the den though the Super Bowl kick-off was hours away. Colleen and her remaining sisters-in-law had spent the morning chatting and preparing a mountain of food the men and children would undoubtedly consume. One of her sisters-in-law had never cared for football and volunteered to entertain the younger children. Colleen glanced at the clock in the kitchen and picked up two huge bowls of popcorn and chips to carry to the den. A couple of trips later there were enough snacks sitting around the den to feed a small army. Tom rolled in a portable cooler and everyone grabbed a drink. Super Bowl Sunday was the one day Rosemary never complained about the mess they all made.

Colleen pulled a beer from the cooler and twisted the cap off. Her father handed her a paper plate filled with snacks and sandwiches before she plopped onto the couch next to her mother and crossed her legs under her. She glanced at her family gathered around the television and smiled slightly. Marsha would love this, she thought. She wiped tears away before they could fall and took a healthy drink of her beer. Rick pulled a piece of paper from his pocket and passed it around. A moment later they all piled money on the den coffee table as they picked numbers for the final score of the game. Colleen leaned back and dug money out of her pocket, adding it to the growing pile in the center of the table. She looked at her brother and smiled. He wasn't over the loss of his wife, but was trying hard to get his life back to as close to normal as he could. Even though Amber had died as a result of her injuries, at least he knew where she was. Colleen, on the other hand, had no idea where Marsha had disappeared to. She only knew she had been left alone and the reality caused her to swallow around a lump in her throat. She excused herself and wandered back into the kitchen. She braced her arms on the counter, trying to get her emotions under control.

A hand gripped the back of her neck and lightly massaged it. Colleen looked over her shoulder and smiled. She brought her hand up and covered the hand on her neck.

"I'm glad you could make it home, honey. Rosemary wanted you to be here," Jack said.

"I'm a little surprised you came back for this, Uncle Jack. You were just here for New Year's."

"Your mother asked me and I couldn't say no. Plus it was another chance to see my favorite niece. Who could pass that up?"

Colleen turned and wrapped her arms around him, letting tears trickle down her cheeks. "I miss her so much, Uncle Jack."

"One day, when you least expect it, someone will come along and make all your dreams come true, baby."

"Why do I always seem to pick the ones who end up breaking my heart?"

"You'll survive this one too," Jack said as he patted her back. "Now we better get back in there while we can still find a seat."

When Colleen resumed her seat next to her mother, Rosemary leaned close to her. "Your eyes are red, dear. By the look on your face I'd guess you've been thinking about Marsha," Rosemary said.

"Sorry," Colleen said, embarrassed she had been caught. "I'll get over her...eventually." She cleared her throat and settled into the soft couch to watch the game.

After the introduction of the starting offensive and defensive line-ups, the teams lined up for the kick-off. That was accompanied by the shouts and cheers of the family. Several plays later a penalty flag was thrown and Rick jumped to his feet. "He was drawn off, ya moron. Show the replay!" he shouted.

Throughout the first half there were a couple of friendly disputes over calls, but as a respite from all the shouting during the game, they quieted down to watch the commercials. Colleen knew they did it mostly for her because the commercials were her favorite part of the game. Large companies paid a ton of money to advertise for thirty-second spots during the Super Bowl. They laughed at a few and usually everyone commented as to whether they had been worth the money. Colleen saw the black-and-white face of a woman fill the screen. As the camera moved back, revealing the rest of her perfect, sexy body, a seductive voice-over introduced the newest line of Calvin Klein perfumes. Water or sweat trickled down the woman's neck and her hand came up and slowly wiped it away. A handsome bare-chested man wearing partially open jeans approached the woman from the side and wrapped a muscular arm around her waist as he appeared to be inhaling the scent along her neck.

"Makes me want to run right out and buy a bottle or two," Charlie's wife said as she poked him playfully in the ribs.

"You don't need expensive perfume to get my attention, honey," Charlie answered, leaning over to give her a kiss.

"That one will make the winner's list tomorrow," Tom laughed. "Right, Colleen?"

Colleen was staring at the television and her mouth was slightly agape. That voice had sounded so familiar. She shivered and closed her eyes, remembering the sound of a similar voice whispering against her ear as they made love. "What?" she finally said, looking at Tom.

"I said that commercial was a good one, wasn't it?"

"Yes. Well worth the money. Very noir." She glanced down at Rosemary. "Excuse me, Mom. I'll be right back. Save my spot."

Colleen unfolded her legs and stepped over a couple of teenage boys who were sprawled out on the floor. She walked through the kitchen and out the back door before releasing a sob and taking several deep breaths. She brought a hand up to cover her mouth and attempted to regain control of herself. She pulled her cell phone from her back pocket and thumbed through the lengthy list of phone numbers stored in her contacts. She needed to remove most of the numbers, but was glad she hadn't now. She found the number she was looking for and waited as it rang on the other end.

Chapter Twenty-nine

COLLEEN STOOD AND smiled as the preppy-looking man sauntered down the carpeted hallway toward her. They had met several years earlier when both attended a broadcasting conference in Atlanta and became close friends. Derrick Fuller stopped in front of her, tilted his head slightly, and hugged her.

"I was surprised to get your call," he said as he released her. "You're looking good, Colleen."

"I don't want to impose on our friendship, Derrick, but when I finally decided I needed a career change, I hoped you would be able to give me a few hints as to where I might start," Colleen said. "How's Mark?"

Derrick shrugged. "As impossible as ever. Now that we've adopted our daughter, he worries about more things than before." He smiled. "But he is thoroughly smitten. We both are."

"Congratulations! When did that happen?"

"A couple of years ago. Life since then has been quite interesting."

Colleen squeezed his arm. "I know it's something you both wanted."

"When I told Mark you were coming to the city, he insisted on bringing her over and joining us for lunch, if you don't mind."

"Of course I don't mind. I love kids. What's her name?"

"Lily. Now let's go to my office and discuss your future. I've been working on a plan that will let you ease in gradually, unless you're ready to jump in with both feet."

"Wait. Here?"

"You don't seriously think I'd turn you over to some other Madison Avenue shark, do you?" Derrick asked, looking somewhat offended.

"You do remember my background is mostly in radio, right," Colleen said as they walked down the hall toward his office.

"Of course I do and I have the perfect campaign for you," he said as he opened the door to his office. Fuller and Associates Media was a relatively new, but growing advertising agency that began representing mid-level clients and gradually expanded to higher stake areas such as fashion houses.

Derrick walked across a thickly carpeted office and dropped into a plush-looking leather chair behind a large antique oak desk. He punched a button on the desk, summoning his secretary. A well-dressed woman who appeared to be in her forties entered the office a moment later. Derrick smiled and said, "What are the chances of getting a couple of coffees, Tori?"

"About the same as usual," Tori said.

"Black okay?" he asked Colleen.

"Cream and sugar, if it's not too much trouble," she replied.

"Wimp," Derrick snorted.

"Not a problem," Tori said with a smile at Colleen before leaving the office. Colleen's gaze followed Tori.

"She's available, if you're interested," Derrick said smugly when Colleen leaned back in her chair and took a deep breath.

"I'm not," she said. "So tell me about this new campaign."

Derrick wrote on a pad and shoved it across his desk toward Colleen. "First things first," he said. "That's what I can offer you, increasing incrementally with seniority. I already know how good your work ethic is unless you've suddenly changed dramatically."

Colleen picked up the paper and her eyes widened. She cleared her throat and said, "This is extremely generous, Derrick."

"If this campaign does what I think it will it can be worth millions to us as well as the client."

"But if I screw it up–"

"You won't," he insisted. "I have confidence in you, Colleen."

"I can't start for a couple of weeks," she said with a frown. "I have to find a place to live, resign my current position, pack, move, and a million other things."

Tori returned and handed Derrick a large mug and another to Colleen. Colleen took a tentative sip and nodded. "Thank you, Tori. It's perfect."

"Tori can help you with a few things here. Tori, this is Colleen Walters, our new account executive. She'll be handling the Corcoran account beginning in a couple of weeks."

Tori's eyebrows shot up and she looked at Colleen. "Welcome aboard and I hope he's paying you plenty to take over that account."

Colleen choked on her coffee and stared at Derrick. He looked back at her sheepishly.

Colleen set her mug down and crossed her arms across her chest. "Spill it, Derrick."

"Bring in the Corcoran file, Tori."

He leaned back in his chair and steepled his fingers. "The account is Kylie Corcoran. She started a new fashion house last year and is willing to spend a chunk of change to make her line a household name. You will be the fourth account executive who's tried to impress her. We have already invested a small fortune producing mock campaigns for her and she's rejected them all."

"Why?"

Derrick shrugged. "She said none of them really identified her, set her apart from her competition. Our thinking so far hasn't been edgy enough for her. I don't think she trusts us to free think her campaign. I don't want to lose her account to one of the bigger agencies, but we could unless we find someone who can work with her."

"So you're willing to hire me as a sacrificial account executive."

"That's a little harsh."

"I don't think so. If I can't carry this off, I risk being seen as just another failure. That won't improve my resume."

"But if you're successful, you'll be a legend and sought after."

"I'll take the file and think about it," Colleen said. "I'll let you know my decision before I fly back to Omaha."

"Fair enough." Derrick glanced at his wristwatch and smiled. "Shall we leave to meet Mark and Lily? I can show you where your office will be on the way out."

"I haven't accepted your offer yet."

Derrick laughed as he walked around his desk. "I know you can't turn down a challenge."

AFTER LUNCH AND getting acquainted with the new woman in Derrick and Mark's life, Colleen returned to her hotel room and went through the Corcoran file, jotting down ideas. She was excited to finally have something tangible to concentrate on, something that took her mind off her fruitless search for Marsha. As the account campaign consumed her, she spent most of the night sketching ideas for the printed media. But first she had to find out what made Kylie Corcoran's fashions different from the big couture houses.

The following day Colleen left her hotel and took a cab to the address listed in the file as the home of Kylie Corcoran Fashions. She stepped out of the cab and stood on the sidewalk in front of a non-descript storefront. Large, thin black letters spelled out "Kylie Corcoran" in a wave over the entrance. Gold paint, outlined in black, announced what was apparently a statement regarding the fashions located inside. "Not your mother's style, but do you really want to be your mother?"

Colleen smiled to herself and pushed the door open. She took in a breath and vanilla mingled with something she couldn't identify filled her nostrils and seemed to draw her deeper inside. She moved past what appeared to be a receptionist's desk and stepped into a second room. Bright colors blended with muted shades filled her eyes and she felt compelled to reach out and touch the fabrics, which were unbelievably soft. As her fingers let the fabrics fall over them, she couldn't help but wonder how they would feel against her body.

"Is there anything you'd care to try on?" a short woman asked as she entered the showroom carrying two or three dresses on hangers.

"These feel amazing," Colleen said.

"Thanks. They're designed to caress you like a lover's caress," the woman said. Her eyes traveled the length of Colleen's body and the corners of her mouth curved into a grin. "They are created for someone who appreciates not only the fabric, but the styling."

"What would you suggest?"

"Perhaps we could discuss it over dinner," the woman answered with a wink. "Any of these would look fabulous on you."

"Is that your standard approach to potential customers?" Colleen asked, her body stiffening slightly.

"No need to get uptight about it. I simply appreciate beauty when I see it. It's who I am. You shouldn't be upset by a compliment." The woman extended her hand. "I'm Kylie Corcoran. Let me know if you find something you're interested in. Someone on my staff will assist you. I have work to finish." She turned and walked away after motioning to an older woman to help Colleen.

Kylie Corcoran was an attractive woman, slender with an engaging smile and an open face. Her eyes seemed to take in everything around her. Not a people person, but strangely alluring in her own way. Colleen chose two dresses that appealed to her and accompanied the woman into a fitting room. She was happy with her eventual choice. After she changed into her clothes, she paused before going to the register. She knocked lightly on the door to the room Kylie had entered earlier.

"Come in!" a voice called out loudly.

Colleen opened the door and stuck her head in. Kylie stood next to a tall, bored-looking model, pins protruding from her lips as she gathered material along the model's waist to fit it correctly.

"What time?"

"What?" Kylie managed around the pins in her mouth.

"Dinner. What time?"

"Seven."

"I'm at the Plaza. I'll meet you in the lobby."

A LITTLE BEFORE seven that evening, Colleen was seated in the main lobby of the Plaza Hotel, wondering whether this had been a good idea. She smoothed the skirt of the dress she'd purchased that afternoon. The fabric hugged her body and felt luxuriant against her skin.

"Good choice," Kylie's voice whispered over Colleen's shoulder. "It puts your body on display for everyone to appreciate. I know I do."

"Are you always so brazen?"

"Pretty much," Kylie said with a shrug and a smile. "Nothing ventured, nothing gained. Shall we?"

Kylie opened the back door of the cab waiting at the curb and slid onto the seat after Colleen. "DeMedici's in Little Italy," she told the driver. "Take the long route, please."

"The long route?" Colleen smiled.

"It will give us a chance to get acquainted. I don't even know your frickin' name. You could be a serial killer for all I know," Kylie laughed. Then her face turned serious. "You're not, are you?"

Colleen shook her head. "You're safe with me, Kylie."

"Well, that's a little disappointing. You're very attractive and I probably wouldn't fight too hard if you took a notion to attack me," Kylie said waggling her eyebrows suggestively.

Colleen leaned away and stared at Kylie. "Does this usually work for you?"

"God no! But it never hurts to see how far I can get before being shut down. Actually, I'm pretty harmless. So tell me your name and whether you're currently attached?"

"Colleen Walters and not at the moment."

"Nice name and a positive sign for me. I like you. You've taken everything I've thrown at you and are still here."

Colleen smiled. "Considering I'm in a moving vehicle on a freeway, I'm not likely to jump out. So you're stuck with me, at least for now."

"I can handle that," Kylie smiled back.

They spent the time over dinner and the taxi ride back to the Plaza discussing Kylie's business and her hopes for its growth. She was adamant about what she wanted and Colleen successfully deflected any discussion about her job. Kylie was an appealing woman and one Colleen was sure she could work with. Kylie walked her into the hotel lobby and said good night at the elevator rather than hinting at following Colleen to her room.

TWO WEEKS LATER Colleen walked to her office at Fuller and Associates. When she opened the door to the large office with an attached work area, everything was in disarray. She spent the remainder of the day arranging furniture and unpacking boxes. Derrick dropped by to inform her that Tori had arranged several secretarial interviews for the next few days. He had also scheduled a meeting with Kylie Corcoran for the end of the week. Colleen hadn't divulged her previous meeting with Kylie yet. She had already prepared her presentation for Kylie's business and prayed Kylie wouldn't feel ambushed. She did like Kylie and it had been more than nine months since Marsha had evaporated from her life. However, she wasn't sure she was ready to move on. She had cried so many nights, wondering what had gone wrong. What had driven Marsha away? No matter what, Colleen couldn't forget the last night she'd spent with Marsha. No one could ever love her with more passion. The memory of that night still took her breath away. Had Marsha known then she was going away and it had been her way of saying goodbye?

By Friday morning, Colleen was ready to meet with Kylie Corcoran. She spent more time than normal getting dressed and making sure her make-up was perfect. She chose to wear the dress she had purchased at Kylie's showroom. It was her way to show Kylie she was vested in promoting her clothing line. She felt comfortable in the dress as she approached her new secretary's desk. She had hired a young woman named Melanie Grossman, who was confidant in her ability to multi-task and eager to learn more about the advertising business. They had spent most of the day Thursday displaying the aggressive print and broadcast campaign Colleen had designed. In her opinion, it demonstrated not only the clothes themselves, but also the brash personality of the designer

A knock at her door a little after two that afternoon announced that Kylie had arrived for their meeting. Colleen glanced around her office quickly to determine that everything was as it should be. Derrick opened the door before she could get to it and stepped in, followed by Kylie.

"This better be good, Derrick," Kylie said. "I left an important production meeting for..." Kylie stopped when she entered and saw Colleen standing in front of her. "Colleen?" she questioned.   .

"Kylie, this is the new account executive who's taking over your account, Colleen Walters," Derrick announced brightly. "Colleen, this is Kylie Corcoran."

Colleen stepped forward and extended her hand. "We've already met. It's good to see you again, Kylie."

Kylie didn't take the offered hand. "What is this, Fuller? A joke? Because I'm not laughing." She turned to leave and the look on Derrick's face was one of panic.

"Kylie! Wait! Please!" Colleen said. She quickly moved forward and took Kylie's arm.

Kylie jerked her arm away and continued toward the elevators, Colleen following close behind. "Kylie—"

"That was pretty slick, Colleen. It's been a while since I've let a beautiful woman use me like that."

"I didn't use you. In order for me to sell you I needed to know more about you and why your clothing was different. I went to your showroom for that. Meeting you was a bonus because it allowed me to see the real you. I'm selling you as well as your designs."

"At least I know why you agreed to have dinner with me."

"That wasn't the only reason."

Kylie folded her arms over her chest and leaned back against the wall. "I'm going to regret this later," she mumbled.

"If you hate what I've prepared, you can still walk away."

Kylie pushed away from the wall and strode purposefully back to Colleen's office, hesitating a moment to take a deep breath before entering. She began at the nearest grouping of sketches and layouts and moved slowly around the workspace without speaking or stopping to examine the materials in front of her.

Colleen refrained from adding verbal explanations and waited with Derrick near her secretary's desk. Half an hour later Kylie joined them. She nodded at Colleen without smiling and said, "I'm impressed.

Excellent work. Have the contracts couriered to my showroom this afternoon." She returned to the elevators and left.

Colleen looked at Derrick. "What just happened?" she asked.

"You closed the deal," Derrick answered with a smile.

"That's it? I worked my ass off for this presentation and all I get is courier the contracts to my showroom!"

"She said it was excellent work. What else were you expecting, Colleen? Our clients expect you to work hard on their behalf."

"I hoped to discuss strategy with her," Colleen huffed.

"Strategy isn't our client's business. It's ours. Welcome to the big time, kiddo."

Chapter Thirty

SEVERAL WEEKS LATER, just as the first chilling breezes of fall found their way down the city streets, Colleen pushed through the front door of Fuller and Associates. She stopped long enough to pull calfskin gloves onto her hands before walking to the curb to flag down a cab. Derrick had called earlier to invite her to dinner at a new bistro he'd heard about in the Village. Not inclined to spend the evening cooking for one, she accepted his invitation.

When she arrived at the bistro a waiter escorted her to Derrick's table. She wove her way through tables, pulling her gloves off along the way. When she glanced up, she stopped. Derrick wasn't alone at the table. A woman with curly brown hair sat across from him, her back to Colleen. They seemed to be involved in an intense conversation. Derrick looked relieved when he noticed Colleen approaching and stood. The woman with him turned her head to see what had gotten Derrick's attention. When Colleen saw the woman's face, she stopped and felt all the breath in her lungs sucked away. She was light-headed and barely able to force her legs forward.

Derrick reached out and took Colleen's arm to steady her. "Are you all right, Colleen?"

After two or three attempts to utter a sound, she finally managed to breathe in enough air to speak. "I'm fine, Derrick. Thank you," she said as the waiter held a chair for her. As she sat, she asked the waiter, "Could I have a glass of water, please?" When the waiter hurried away, she looked across the table with a tight smile. The woman she had been searching for now sat less than three feet from her and looked as startled as she was. The waiter set a goblet of water in front of Colleen. She picked it up and gulped down half the liquid.

"Colleen, this is Elaine Brannigan. She's the most sought after voice-over artist in town and I think she would be the perfect voice for the Corcoran account."

Colleen simply stared at Derrick, knowing she should say something, anything. A thousand questions ran through her mind, but this wasn't the right time. "Possibly," she finally said.

"I think we should set up a recording for next week to determine whether Kylie thinks the voice is right, don't you Colleen?" Derrick asked.

Colleen couldn't force her eyes to look at Elaine Brannigan. "Of course," she mumbled. "I'll schedule it tomorrow."

Elaine cleared her throat. "I should go," she said. "I'm supposed to meet some friends later."

"No," Derrick protested. "Eat dinner first. I hear the food here is excellent."

Before she even realized she'd spoken, Colleen blurted out, "Please stay."

Colleen found it difficult to chew and swallow throughout their meal. She spent most of her time shoving food around on her plate. A glance at Elaine's plate indicated she was having a similar problem. After their waiter cleared the table and prepared to serve the dessert Derrick had ordered, Colleen jumped when the cell phone in his coat pocket trilled. He pulled the phone out and glanced at it quickly, then stood.

"If you'll excuse me, ladies, I have to take this," he said before weaving his way out the front door.

Colleen looked across the table and her eyes met Elaine's. She wiped her mouth with her napkin. "You didn't even have the decency to say goodbye," she said, tearing her eyes away.

"I wasn't given the chance," Elaine mumbled.

"And you've never heard of a telephone? Do you have any idea how many nights I cried myself to sleep wondering what I'd done wrong that drove you away? Did you even care?"

"Of course I cared!" Elaine said loudly. She looked at the tables surrounding them and lowered her voice. "I cried the same number of nights."

"Then why didn't you contact me?"

"I couldn't," Elaine insisted, clenching her hand into a tight fist on the table.

"After all that bullshit about trust. I trusted you! I gave you everything I had. Was it all a lie?" Tears gathered in Colleen's eyes as she leaned over the table and she wiped them away angrily. "Well say something for God's sake!" she demanded.

"What do you want me to say, Colleen? Leaving you wasn't my decision."

"Who the hell is Elaine Brannigan?"

"I am. Marsha Barrett never existed. At least for no more than a few months. I found her name in a cemetery after I got out of jail and created everything else. It gave me a new start. What are you doing here?"

"I obviously work here. You're not the only one who needed to start over," Colleen snapped. She reached across the table to cover Elaine's fist with her hand, but Elaine pulled her hand away before they touched.

Elaine pushed away from the table and stood. "When Mr. Fuller returns, tell him I said thanks for dinner. I have to leave," she said. "Goodbye, Colleen." Without another word she turned and walked out of the bistro. Colleen stood and considered going after her. She had so many questions and wanted answers.

ELAINE BRANNIGAN ENTERED her apartment, leaned against the door, and closed her eyes. How could this have happened? She opened her eyes and sucked in a deep breath as she ran her hands through her curls. Her hands were shaking and she clenched them into fists. What could she possibly say to Colleen to explain the reason for her sudden disappearance from Omaha? This wasn't what was supposed to happen. She leaned her head back and continued taking deep breaths to clear her mind. But the only thing that came to her like a series of photographs was the look on Colleen's face, thrown back and sweaty the last time she made love to her. A moment later, tears formed as she looked down to see the light fade from Trish's face. Then the panicked look on Mattie's face as she ran to be at her lover's side. The last face that swam through her mind was the surprised look on Rusty's face as Jack's bullet ended her life. Then suddenly the young face of Paulina stormed her senses and her knees buckled, dropping her to the floor. Every woman she had ever cared about was gone. Now the only survivor had found her. Jack had been right. It wasn't safe for Colleen to be around her. All the others died because they had associated with her in one way or another.

Elaine stood up and made her way to the phone. She punched in a pre-programmed number and sat down on her couch. She didn't know what she would say. She couldn't handle her current situation alone and couldn't bear to hurt Colleen any further.

When she heard a familiar voice, she said, "She's here and she hates me. We have to talk."

EARLY MONDAY MORNING Colleen sat at her desk going over a stack of paperwork and pretending to concentrate on the words before her. This is ridiculous she thought. I can solve this problem right now and move on. I don't need her and she obviously doesn't want me. She pinched the bridge of her nose to stave off the pain that was building behind her eyes. The buzzer on her intercom interrupted her thoughts.

"What is it, Melissa?" she asked, desperately trying to maintain control of her voice.

"Ms. Brannigan is here to sign her contract," Melissa answered.

"Give me a moment, please."

Despite Colleen's arguments with Derrick over the voice-over artist, she had lost and in a minute or two she would be facing her worst nightmare. She had decided to move on and leave her past as far behind her as possible. Now that past was walking back into her life and she was powerless to stop it.

A tap on Colleen's office door made her jump. Melissa stuck her head inside. "Are you ready for Ms. Brannigan now?"

"Might as well get it over with," Colleen mumbled. "Send her in, Melissa. Leave the door open, please."

Her secretary pushed the door wide open and motioned Elaine Brannigan inside. Colleen walked behind her desk and picked up the contract that would link Elaine's voice to Kylie's fashion business. Colleen set the contract at the front of her desk and uncapped a pen. It was all Colleen could do to force herself to look at the woman who had shattered her heart, leaving her to pick up the pieces. Elaine stepped forward and picked up the contract, sitting on the edge of the closest wingback chair. She flipped through the pages to read a section.

"It's a standard contract for your services. Sign the last page and initial at the bottom of the others," Colleen said. "Questions?"

"Why did you pick me? There are thousands of voice-over artists available."

"I didn't. You were selected by Mr. Fuller, with approval of our client, Kylie Corcoran. Apparently they, like others before them, were mesmerized by your voice."

"Is this the last time I'll have to see you?"

The question surprised Colleen and she cleared her throat. "Yes. Any further contact will be through Mr. Fuller, if necessary."

Elaine signed and initialed the contract and placed it back on Colleen's desk. She stood and turned to leave the office. The sound of Colleen's voice stopped her.

"You didn't even bother to attend Trish and Mattie's funerals," Colleen sniped.

Elaine spun around, tears in her eyes. Her voice shook when she replied. "I watched them die. They paid the price for my loving you." Elaine balled her hands into fists. "What did you expect from me?"

"I expected an explanation! I need to know what I did wrong!" Colleen demanded.

"Nothing. I'm sorry. That's the best I can do."

Colleen's voice hitched. "It's not good enough." She leaned forward on her desk. "I loved you so much, Marsha. I didn't know it was possible to love anyone the way I loved you."

Elaine stiffened and stood straighter. "My name is Elaine and you'll eventually get over it. I...I have."

"I don't believe that."

Elaine opened her mouth to reply, but knew anything she said would be useless. She spun around and left as quickly as possible.

COLLEEN LEANED BACK in her seat and watched the fields covered by a blanket of fresh snow flash by. The constant clickety-clack of the Amtrak wheels over the tracks was oddly soothing. She couldn't get her last conversation with Elaine Brannigan out of her mind. She needed answers to her questions and didn't know where to get them. On a whim she decided to take the train to Philadelphia to visit her parents. She needed to talk to her mother. If she could only talk it through, she might find the answer she was searching for. She hoped.

It was already dark when Colleen stepped off the train at the Philadelphia Amtrak station. She pulled her rolling bag through the station and hailed a cab for the thirty mile trip to her parents' home. She hadn't called to let them know of her arrival. Although she spoke to her mother weekly, this was her first trip home since moving to New York in late January, and she hadn't told Rosemary about finding the woman they knew as Marsha. The trip would give her a chance to catch up with the news about her brothers' families and hopefully distract her from thinking about Marsha constantly.

When her cab pulled to the curb in front of the familiar house, Colleen couldn't stop the smile that tugged at her lips. She made her way up the sidewalk and climbed the front stairs. When the door opened, she fell into her father's arms and wasn't able to stop the tears that had blurred her vision. Quentin wrapped his arms around her and she absorbed his strength.

"Rosemary!" Quentin called out. "Our girl is home!"

Colleen heard the sound of her mother's crutches approaching and stepped farther inside to greet her. She smiled when she saw Rosemary accompanied by Jack. Tears ran down Colleen's cheeks as her mother hugged her.

"You have to stop this sneaking up on us, baby," Rosemary said against Colleen. "Did you come alone?"

"Yes," Colleen answered softly. "We need to talk," she whispered.

"Jack, take Colleen's suitcase to her room, please."

"Not until I get my hug," Jack answered with his usual charming smile.

Colleen threw her arms around her uncle's neck and squeezed him tight. When she released him, Rosemary threaded her arm through Colleen's and pulled her into the den. Although Rosemary had recovered from the accident, Colleen could feel her mother clinging to her for support.

"How is life in New York?" Rosemary asked as she settled in her favorite chair.

Colleen laced her fingers together and leaned forward. "I found Marsha," she murmured. "She's in New York."

"Did she say why she left Omaha so unexpectedly?"

"No. She said it wasn't her decision, whatever that means." Colleen shrugged and leaned back, shoving her hands through her hair.

"You're still in love with her, aren't you?"

"I've tried, but I can't stop loving her like it never meant anything to me. She was everything to me, Mom."

"Did you tell her that?"

Colleen nodded. "Yes, but she told me to move on. I said some things I regret."

"What are you going to do now?"

"I don't know. If I knew what drove her away maybe I could still fix it, but I don't. She's afraid of something." She shrugged. "Maybe it's me. I dragged Rusty into her life and her best friends died...because of me."

"That wasn't your fault," Jack said as he walked into the den, his hands in his pockets. "Rusty was responsible for their deaths."

"But she wouldn't have even known about them if I hadn't fallen in love with Marsha. Rusty threatened to take away everyone I loved. Marsha was the last one besides my family. I could have lost Mom as well."

"Rusty can't hurt you anymore now," Jack said solemnly. "She'll never hurt you again."

"I know," Colleen said quietly.

"Maybe you should move on, Colleen," Jack suggested.

"Could you walk away from the person you loved so easily? As if she meant nothing to you?"

Jack glanced briefly at Rosemary. "If I thought it was the right thing to do. No matter how hard it was," he said.

"But I'm in love with her. I can't give up!" Colleen pushed her hands through her hair and tears filled her eyes. "I need her," she managed. "I need to feel her touch, her warmth. I refuse to believe she doesn't still care about me. Why can't you understand that?"

"So what are you going to do?" Rosemary asked.

"Even if she doesn't love me anymore, I have to know why she ran."

"I'm sure she loves you, Colleen," Jack said. "But you may not like what else she tells you," he added as he crossed his legs.

"Why does life have to be so complicated?" Colleen groaned.

"It's only as complicated as we make it," Rosemary said with a smile.

Chapter Thirty-one

COLLEEN SAT NERVOUSLY in her vehicle watching the front of the apartment building through the rearview mirror. Her heart jumped every time someone approached the entrance. A phone call to the company Elaine Brannigan worked for confirmed that she was in the studio recording voice-overs for a few commercials that day. If Colleen wanted to contract her for a voice-over there was a waiting list because Elaine's voice was currently in demand by several large advertising agencies.

Colleen had gotten Elaine Brannigan's address from her file at Fuller and Associates. She had kept the information on her desk for over a week without attempting to contact Elaine or Marsha or whoever the hell she was that day. Did she really want to see her? Could she forgive the woman who'd torn her heart apart without an explanation? Could she forget the feel of Marsha's hands and lips on her body? Did she want to forget?

Her eyes on the rearview mirror were beginning to water from the strain of staring into the glass. It was getting late and the sun was dropping in the winter sky when she saw a woman dressed in jeans turn the corner. Colleen couldn't see much else because the woman's shoulders were hunched against the cold wind and her head was covered. The woman stopped for a moment and fished something out of her pocket before trotting up the steps and pushing the door open.

Colleen took a breath and noticed her hands were shaking and it had nothing to do with the flakes falling from the gray clouds overhead. She pulled her coat tighter around her and leaned against the car a minute. This was the moment she'd been waiting for. If the woman who'd just entered the apartment building was Marsha, then she might get some answers to her questions.

Colleen pushed away from her car and walked purposefully to the building's entrance. She entered the lobby area and looked around. It was an older building, but appeared well-maintained.

"Can I help you, miss?" an older gentleman behind the main desk asked pleasantly.

"I'm here to see Elaine Brannigan," Colleen answered.

"She's on the fourth floor. Would you like me to announce you?"

"No," Colleen answered. "She's expecting me."

The man returned to shuffling the papers in his hand as Colleen approached the elevators and stepped inside. She pushed the button for the fourth floor and looked at her reflection on the elevator doors. By the time the doors slid quietly open, she had smoothed her hair down and unzipped her coat. She followed the signs in the hallway until she stood in front of the apartment where Elaine Brannigan lived. She pulled her gloves off and stuffed them into her coat pocket, then raised her arm to rap on the door. She stuffed her hands back into the coat pockets and waited. It may have only been only a few seconds before the door opened, but it seemed like an eternity. When the door finally opened, the face she saw didn't belong to Marsha.

"Yes?" the woman asked.

"I'm sorry. I must have the wrong apartment. I was looking for Elaine Brannigan," Colleen managed.

"This is her apartment. She's in the bedroom changing. Is she expecting you?"

"No," Colleen admitted. "I brought a contract for her to sign."

"Come on in. She'll be out in a minute. Can I offer you something to drink before I leave?"

"No, I'm fine."

The woman opened a closet near the door, pulled out a jacket, and slipped it on. "I'm leaving, babe," she called out. "You have a visitor." She stepped to the window, shook her head, and grunted. "Snowing again, I see. I'd better hurry before it dumps a ton. Have a seat," the woman said as she backed out the apartment door.

Colleen didn't know what to do and continued to stand where she'd stopped after she entered the apartment. It was nicely furnished and heated enough to make it feel cozy. She finally moved to look out the window in the front room and smiled at the pigeons huddled against the heated glass for warmth. The door to the bedroom opened and Colleen turned around.

"Sorry to keep you waiting, Rhonda, but..." Elaine started. She jerked to a stop when she saw Colleen. She cleared her throat and stuffed her hands into the pockets of her jeans as she wandered into the small kitchen that opened into the front room.

"What do you want now? I told you to leave me alone," Elaine growled.

"Who was that woman who answered the door?" Colleen asked.

"My roommate," Elaine answered flatly. "She works nights and I work days, so it works out."

"I've never had a roommate who called me 'babe'."

Elaine smiled briefly. "She calls everyone that, including her fiancée."

"Are you ever going to tell me the truth about why you left Omaha?"

Elaine poured a cup of coffee and leaned back against the counter, her brow furrowing as she sipped her drink. She set her mug down and stood taller. "I had to leave, Colleen, and you couldn't be involved."

"I could have helped—" Colleen started.

"You couldn't have done shit!" Elaine shouted. "Jack was right!"

"What's my uncle got to do with any of this?"

Elaine's eyes met Colleen's for a moment. "Jack killed Rusty to save my life. I know a few things about him that he wouldn't want his favorite niece to know. Bad things. Let's just say he made me an offer I couldn't refuse," Elaine said humorlessly. "He set me up here, but told me to stay out of your life."

Elaine paused, gathering her thoughts and trying to decide how much to tell Colleen. Finally, she continued. "After Trish and Mattie's deaths, I dared Rusty to kill me. I wanted her to pay for what she did." Elaine shook her head and took a deep breath. "She managed to shoot me and planned to gut me. No matter how much I wanted to kill her, I knew I was going to die. I would have if Jack hadn't stepped in. Leaving was my only alternative. Honestly, I wasn't sure he wasn't going to kill me, too."

"Why would he?"

"I recognized him the moment I saw him at your parents' house. He's a big-time dealer in Chicago and supplied the drugs that killed Paulina." Elaine shrugged. "It doesn't really matter where she got the drugs. If it hadn't been from him, she would have gotten them from someone else, I suppose. I can't blame him for her decisions and don't have any proof."

"Jack won't hurt you," Colleen said.

"You can't know that!"

"He'll leave you alone or risk losing his daughter. I think that frightens him more than anything in the world."

"You know?" Elaine asked.

"I'm not an idiot, Marsh. I've known a long time how he made a living. That's why I don't work for him. And I know he's my biological father."

"Does he know you know?"

"I've never told him, so I don't know what he knows. I know he'd never hurt anyone I cared about," Colleen said. She took two hesitant steps toward Elaine. "I still care about you...deeply. You're ruining my sleep because I can't get over the way you...the way you touched me."

Elaine crossed the room quickly and took Colleen in her arms, hugging her desperately. Tears filled her eyes when she felt Colleen's hand caress the back of her head. She buried her face against Colleen's neck and breathed in the essence of her as her hands traveled over the familiar landscape of Colleen's body until they gently caressed her breasts.

"After what I did, why would you still want to be with me?" Elaine asked.

"Because I love you," Colleen sighed as her hands traced the features of Elaine's face softly. "Because I can't forget the way you touched my body like it was precious to you." She wrapped her arms around Elaine's neck and let her fingers play in the curly hair. She dipped her head and trailed kisses along Elaine's neck and jaw, ending at her ear. "Don't make me beg any more, baby," Colleen whispered. "Please."

"God, you're so damn beautiful," Elaine breathed.

"More beautiful than Blondie?"

"More beautiful than any dream."

Colleen pressed against Elaine, her mouth open and inviting. "Show me," she said.

Elaine turned her head and smiled, her lips millimeters from Colleen's. She teased Colleen's lips before drawing her into a devastating, hungry kiss.

When the kiss ended, Elaine took Colleen's hand and backed toward the bedroom. "One thing though," she said.

"Anything, sweetheart."

"When you scream out my name later, please call me Marsha."

More Brenda Adcock titles:

Game of Denial

Joan Carmichael, a successful New York businesswoman, lost the love of her life ten years earlier. Alone, she raised their four children, always cherishing her deep love for her wife. Her memories of their life together come back even stronger as one of their daughters prepares to marry. Joan and her four adult kids fly to Virginia to meet the groom's family and attend the ceremony at the small horse farm owned by the mother of the fiancé.

Evelyn "Evey" Chase, also a widow, has secrets in her past, and her memories of her dead husband aren't pleasant. She's concerned about meeting her future daughter-in-law's family, certain that she and her three kids will have little in common with the wealthy New Yorkers. Besides, the thought of two women in a relationship bringing up a family together makes her uncomfortable, even though her daughter-in-law assures her that lesbianism is not hereditary or catching.

When the two women meet they are drawn to one another in a way neither anticipated, and the game of denial begins. Evey fights her attraction and doesn't realize the effect she has on Joan. Joan tries to shake off her feelings, seeing them as a betrayal to the memory of her wife. Besides, isn't Evey Chase straight? After Evey and Joan share an intimate moment at the wedding reception, they are both emotionally terrified and Joan flees. Will Joan overcome the feeling of betraying her former mate and stop denying her desire to be happy again? Can Evey finally face her past in order to accept the love of another woman and the desire to live the life she had once dreamed of?

ISBN: 978-1-61929-130-0
eISBN: 978-1-61929-131-7

The Sea Hawk

Dr. Julia Blanchard, a marine archaeologist, and her team of divers have spent almost eighteen months excavating the remains of a ship found a few miles off the coast of Georgia. Although they learn quite a bit about the nineteenth century sailing vessel, they have found nothing that would reveal the identity of the ship they have nicknamed "The Georgia Peach."

Her rescue at sea leads her on an unexpected journey into the true identity of the Peach and the captain and crew who called it their home. Her travels take her to the island of Martinique, the eastern Caribbean islands, the Louisiana German Coast and New Orleans at the close of the War of 1812.

How had the Peach come to rest in the waters off the Georgia coast? What had become of her alluring and enigmatic captain, Simone Moreau? Can love conquer everything, even time?

ISBN 978-1-935053-10-1

Available in print and eBook formats

Pipeline

What do you do when the mistakes you made in the past come back to slap you in the face with a vengeance? Joanna Carlisle, a fifty-seven year old photojournalist, has only begun to adjust to retirement on her small ranch outside Kerrville, Texas, when she finds herself unwillingly sucked into an investigation of illegal aliens being smuggled into the United States to fill the ranks of cheap labor needed to increase corporate profits.

An unexpected visit by her former lover, Cate Hammond, and the attempted murder of their son, forces Jo to finally face what she had given up. Although she hasn't seen Cate or their son for fifteen years, she finds that the feelings she had for Cate had only been dormant, but had never died. No matter how much she fights her attraction to Cate, Jo cannot help but wonder whether she had made the right decision when she chose career and independence over love.

ISBN 978-1-932300-64-2

Available in print and eBook formats

Reiko's Garden

Hatred...like love...knows no boundaries.

How much impact can one person have on a life?

When sixty-five-year old Callie Owen returns to her rural childhood home in Eastern Tennessee to attend the funeral of a woman she hasn't seen in twenty years, she's forced to face the fears, heartache, and turbulent events that scarred both her body and her mind. Drawing strength from Jean, her partner of thirty years, and from their two grown children, Callie stays in the valley longer than she had anticipated and relives the years that changed her life forever.

In 1949, Japanese war bride Reiko Sanders came to Frost Valley, Tennessee with her soldier husband and infant son. Callie Owen was an inquisitive ten-year-old whose curiosity about the stranger drove her to disobey her father for just one peek at the woman who had become the subject of so much speculation. Despite Callie's fears, she soon finds that the exotic-looking woman is kind and caring, and the two forge a tentative, but secret friendship.

When Callie and her five brothers and sisters were left orphaned, Reiko provided emotional support to Callie. The bond between them continued to grow stronger until Callie left Frost Valley as a teenager, emotionally and physically scarred, vowing never to return and never to forgive.

It's not until Callie goes "home" that she allows herself to remember how Reiko influenced her life. Once and for all, can she face the terrible events of her past? Or will they come back to destroy all that she loves?

ISBN 978-1-932300-77-2

Available in print and eBook formats

Redress of Grievances

Harriett Markham is a defense attorney in Austin, Texas, who lost everything eleven years earlier. She had been an associate with a Dallas firm and involved in an affair with a senior partner, Alexis Dunne. Harriett represented a rape/murder client named Jared Wilkes and got the charges dismissed on a technicality. When Wilkes committed a rape and murder after his release, Harriett was devastated. She resigned and moved to Austin, leaving everything behind, including her lover.

Despite lingering feelings for Alexis, Harriet becomes involved with a sex-offense investigator, Jessie Rains, a woman struggling with secrets of her own. Harriet thinks she might finally be happy, but then Alexis re-enters her life. She refers a case of multiple homicide allegedly committed by Sharon Taggart, a woman with no motive for the crimes. Harriett is creeped out by the brutal murders, but reluctantly agrees to handle the defense.

As Harriett's team prepares for trial, disturbing information comes to light. Sharon denies any involvement in the crimes, but the evidence against her seems overwhelming. Harriett is plunged into a case rife with twisty psychological motives, questionable sanity, and a client with a complex and disturbing life. Is she guilty or not? And will Harriet's legal defense bring about justice—or another Wilkes case?

Recipient of a 2008 award from the Golden Crown Literary Society, the premiere organization for the support and nourishment of quality lesbian literature. *Redress of Grievances* won in the category of Lesbian Mystery.

ISBN 978-1-932300-86-4

Available in print and eBook formats

Tunnel Vision

Royce Brodie, a 50-year-old homicide detective in the quiet town of Cedar Springs, a bedroom community 30 miles from Austin, Texas, has spent the last seven years coming to grips with the incident that took the life of her partner and narrowly missed taking her own. The peace and quiet she had been enjoying is shattered by two seemingly unrelated murders in the same week: the first, a John Doe, and the second, a janitor at the local university.

As Brodie and her partner, Curtis Nicholls, begin their investigation, the assignment of a new trainee disrupts Brodie's life. Not only is Maggie Weston Brodie's former lover, but her father had been Brodie's commander at the Austin Police Department and nearly destroyed her career.

As the three detectives try to piece together the scattered evidence to solve the two murders, they become convinced the two murders are related. The discovery of a similar murder committed five years earlier at a small university in upstate New York creates a sense of urgency as they realize they are chasing a serial killer.

The already difficult case becomes even more so when a third victim is found. But the case becomes personal for Brodie when Maggie becomes the killer's next target. Unless Brodie finds a way to save Maggie, she could face losing everything a second time.

ISBN 978-1-935053-19-4-

Available in print and eBook formats

Soiled Dove

In 1872, sixteen-year-old Loretta Digby fled her home in Indiana to escape an abusive step-father. Rescued from the streets of St. Joseph, Missouri by brothel owner Jack Coulter, she turns to the only work available. By twenty she became a much sought after prostitute catering to St. Jo's most influential men and dreaming of the day she can leave her past behind and start her life anew. Working with teacher, Hettie Tobias, who is traveling west for a teaching position in Trinidad, Colorado, Loretta and Amelia leave their former lives behind.

In the foothills of the Sangre de Cristo Mountains outside Trinidad, Clare McIlhenney has been struggling for years to make her father's dream of owning a cattle ranch in the west come true. Working with a few ranch hands and her foreman, Ino Valdez, Clare has slowly built the ranch over the last twenty years while overcoming everything that should have stopped her.

In the spring of 1876 Loretta and her friends arrive in the dusty Colorado town. Her first meeting with Clare McIlhenney is less than inspiring. When Clare is injured, over her strenuous objections, Ino hires Loretta as a temporary cook and housekeeper for the ranch. Over the next few months, Clare struggles with her unwanted attraction to the much younger woman, unable to forget the events of her past that led to the deaths of everyone she had been close to. Determined to never lose anyone else, Clare closed off her emotions and became a distant and disliked stranger to everyone around her.

Will Loretta be able to keep her past a secret and find a new life? Will Clare open herself up to loss yet again and put her own prejudices behind her? In a story of the struggles in a harsh and unforgiving time will the two women find peace at last?

Recipient of a 2011 award from the Golden Crown Literary Society, the premiere organization for the support and nourishment of quality lesbian literature. *Soiled Dove* won in the category of Historical Romance.

ISBN 978-1-935053-35-4

Available in print and eBook formats

The Other Mrs. Champion

Sarah Champion, 55, of Massachusetts, was leading the perfect life with Kelley, her partner and wife of twenty-five years. That is, until Kelley was struck down by an unexpected stroke away from home. But Sarah discovers she hadn't known her partner and lover as well as she thought.

Accompanied by Kelley's long-time friend and attorney, Sarah and her children rush to Vancouver, British Columbia to say their goodbyes, only to discover another woman, Pauline, keeping a vigil over Kelley in the hospital. Confronted by the fact that her wife also has a Canadian wife, Sarah struggles to find answers to resolve her emotional and personal turmoil.

Alone and lonely, Sarah turns to the only other person who knew Kelley as well as she did — Pauline Champion. Will the two women be able to forge a friendship despite their simmering animosity? Will their growing attraction eventually become Kelley's final gift to the women she loved?

ISBN 978-1-935053-46-0
eISBN: 978-1-61929-032-7

The Chameleon

Six years ago Detective Christine Shaw left her happy life and a good job in Texas to follow her libido to New York City. She's still a cop, but her stewardess girlfriend has flown the coop and Chris hasn't been able to fill the void. Everything in her life begins to change when she and her partner are assigned to a high profile case.

The murder of Broadway star Elaine Barrie propels Chris into a whole new world. A fan of the murdered actress since she was a teenager, Chris isn't prepared for the secrets she uncovers during their investigation, including her attraction to the daughter of her number one suspect.

Was the victim any of the personalities witnesses describe, or was the real person a chameleon, satisfying the expectations of each person she met?

ISBN 978-1-61929-102-7
eISBN: 978-1-61929-103-4

Picking Up the Pieces

Athon Dailey hasn't had many breaks in her life other than the ones she made for herself by living up to her reputation as a tough girl until she meets Lauren Shelton, a new girl at school in Duvalle, Texas. Tamed by Lauren's affection, Athon begins to believe there could be a brighter future. When Lauren's parents discover the growing relationship they send her away, making sure the two girls never have contact, leaving Athon alone and abandoned.

Twenty years later the two women meet again. Athon has established a successful military career as a helicopter pilot while Lauren has returned to Duvalle to teach. It doesn't take long for them to rekindle their feelings for one another and they finally get the chance to rebuild their teenage dreams. Permanent happiness is within their grasp when Athon's unit is deployed.

Athon comes home in a coma, diagnosed with a traumatic brain injury. She awakens to find Lauren by her side to welcome her home. When Athon chooses to retire and return to Texas, neither realizes the twists and turns the journey home will take. The Athon Dailey who returned to Lauren is not the woman she remembers. In order for their relationship to survive, Lauren begins her search for the woman she loves. Will Athon finally find her way back to Lauren and the dream they both once had? Does Lauren have the courage to live with a woman who is now a stranger?

ISBN 978-1-61929-120-1
eISBN: 978-1-61929-121-8

Other Yellow Rose Titles You Might Enjoy:

Christmas Crush
by Kate McLachlan

Jazzy's Fresh Christmas Trees is Jasmine Oliver's last ditch attempt to rescue the family finances and send her little sister to college. She did some research, selected a prime location, and bought the very best Christmas trees available. What she didn't do, though, was check out the competition.

SleepSafe Youth is Darcy Gabriel's baby, her way of paying back the help she received as a homeless teen. The charity she established gives homeless kids a safe place to sleep, and *SleepSafe's* annual Christmas tree sale is the organization's biggest fund-raising event of the year.

When Jasmine learns that *SleepSafe's* Christmas tree lot is only a block away from her own, she turns her dismay and anger into determination and vows to give *SleepSafe* a run for its money. Sparks fly between Jasmine and Darcy as they compete for the Christmas tree business. Before long, sparks of a different sort fly, and they find themselves experiencing a Christmas they'll never forget.

ISBN 978-1-61929-196-6
eISBN 978-1-61929-195-9

Mountain Rescue: On The Edge
by Sky Croft

Dr. Sydney Greenwood and expert climber Kelly Saber are back in this sequel to *Mountain Rescue: The Ascent.*

Having settled into their relationship, life is sweet for the devoted couple, and a brief trip away allows Saber to meet Sydney's family.

Upon their return, rock slides, torrential rain, and surging rivers cause no end of problems for the Mountain Rescue team, while on the home front, Sydney needs her partner's support more than ever when faced with a family tragedy.

Together, the two women have to navigate between personal trials, and the trials of the mountain. This is...On the Edge.

ISBN 978-1-61929-206-2
eBook ISBN 978-1-61929-205-5

A Majestic Affair
by Sharon G. Clark

A decade ago, Tiara Summers was forced to leave her home with her alcoholic mother, and contact was lost with her father and friends. Tiara built a profitable construction business in Colorado Springs and, if not exactly happy, is comfortable with her life. Then she receives a letter from her father asking for help with a horse, which means returning to Silver Waters, Colorado with all the old memories of kisses and running away...and Jayce.

Jayce Mansfield trains horses for a living. Her focus is specializing the equines for stunts in the movies. Then Tiara returns, though her father is AWOL, and Jayce sees promise in a second chance. Hopes for the happily-ever-after she'd envisioned for them are reanimated, until Jayce realizes the sweet, caring teenager that left ten years ago has turned into a bitter woman.

Can Jayce get Tiara to realize she belongs in Silver Waters, that they belong together?

ISBN 978-1-61929-178-2
eISBN 978-1-61929-177-5

April's Fool
by Vicki Stevenson

In 1886 Arizona, April Reynolds, sophisticated and city bred, unexpectedly falls in love with rugged frontier woman Mandy Wells. Together they face the difficult challenges of a brutal physical environment, as well as harsh treatment with potentially devastating consequences from an intolerant society.

Their quest for a peaceful life free of violence and harassment leads to a treacherous journey from the infamous Lost Dutchman Mine to the fledgling tourist village of Palm Springs and then the new and growing community of Los Angeles. Along the way, they encounter a startling array of criminal activity, much of it placing them directly in harm's way.

Driven by a deepening love for each other and a continuing wish for a life of tranquillity, April and Mandy reluctantly embrace a perilous series of challenges as they pursue their elusive goal.

ISBN 978-1-61929-192-8
eISBN 978-1-61929-191-1

OTHER YELLOW ROSE PUBLICATIONS

About the Author

Originally from the Appalachian region of Eastern Tennessee, Brenda now lives in Central Texas, near Austin. She began writing in junior high school where she wrote an admittedly hokey western serial to entertain her friends. Completing her graduate studies in Eastern European history in 1971, she worked as a graphic artist, a public relations specialist for the military and a display advertising specialist until she finally had to admit that her mother might have been right and earned her teaching certification. Amazingly, she retired from teaching world history and political science in December of 2013 after thirty years. Brenda and her partner of nineteen years, Cheryl, are the parents of four occasionally grown children, as well as five grandchildren, soon to be six. Rounding out their home is a laid back blonde cat named Tudie and a three-year old Puggle named Peanut, who snores like a freight train. She may be contacted at adcockb10@yahoo.com and welcomes all comments.

VISIT US ONLINE AT
www.regalcrest.biz

At the Regal Crest Website You'll Find

- The latest news about forthcoming titles and new releases

- Our complete backlist of romance, mystery, thriller and adventure titles

- Information about your favorite authors

- Current bestsellers

- Media tearsheets to print and take with you when you shop

- Which books are also available as eBooks.

Regal Crest print titles are available from all progressive booksellers including numerous sources online. Our distributors are Bella Distribution and Ingram.